the lady dragons of brookville

the lady dragons of brookville

a
lady dragons
of brookville
mystery

karen fritz

LEVEL
BEST BOOKS

Author Photo Credit: Rebecca Fritz

First edition

ISBN: 978-1-68512-495-3

Cover art by Level Best Designs

This book was professionally typeset on Reedsy.
Find out more at reedsy.com

To my family for their constant encouragement and support.

Praise for The Lady Dragons of Brookville

"Three strangers—women of a certain age—happen upon a murder victim. The accidental discovery launches a delightful cozy mystery, featuring an unlikely sisterhood of sleuths. Author Karen Fritz delivers a compelling plot with generous sides of laughter and romance. *The Lady Dragons of Brookville* reveals how life's later chapters can kindle a new zest for life."—Linda Lovely, author of the HOA Mystery Series

"Mix a condo community, murder, three middle-aged ladies determined to find themselves anew, as well as the killer of a young woman, and you have mystery, murder, and a touch of mayhem. Karen Fritz's *The Lady Dragons of Brookville* is a delightful and engaging read populated by an interesting cast of characters who you'll be sorry to see go when you reach the book's last page."—Award-winning author Debra H. Goldstein

"Karen Fritz delivers a fast paced read that will keep readers turning the pages. It was fun watching Trixie, Martha and Kathleen join forces to become the Lady Dragons of Brookville after they discover a body on the grounds of their condo development. Their varied backgrounds made them an interesting crew with a variety of skills as they set out to find the killer. It is a satisfying book with characters you can root for and a plot that makes the book impossible to put down."—Betty Hechtman, national bestselling author of *Killer Hooks*

"How do I love thee? Let me count the ways…

1. Strong female friendships—check.
2. Middle-aged, relatable female protagonists—check.
3. Loads of thrills—check.
4. Lots of laughs—check.
5. A twisty mystery, suspenseful enough to keep me guessing, not creepy enough to keep me from sleeping—check.
6. Empowered women constructing new lives atop the wreckage of divorce, widowhood, and missed opportunities—check.

"Three unlikely friends-to-be cross paths over a dead body in the woods and follow up the tragedy with the sort of female bonding that only too many mimosas and whisky-laced morning coffees can induce. The empowered gal pals share a history of shattered dreams, but they're determined to protect their future happiness, their threatened small town, and each other from a brutal murderer. The Lady Dragons of Brookville are breathing fire and on a quest to slay a killer. Loved it!"—Gabrielle St. George, award-winning author of the Ex-Whisperer Files series

"When a timid Southern belle, a forensics-obsessed bossy librarian, and a woman bent on hiding her past all stumble upon a dead body, they throw caution and common sense to the wind and join forces to find the killer. However, it soon becomes clear that their seemingly idyllic small town hides many secrets, and as their investigation digs deeper, the body count rises in this cozy Southern Gothic mystery."—Lois Winston, author of the bestselling Anastasia Pollack Crafting Mysteries

Chapter One

Trixie Tanner ran to calm the chatter in her mind and the deadly self-doubt. Running was all the therapy she needed. She wasn't second-guessing the divorce, nor did she view moving to Brookville as a mistake. Lord knows, she needed out of Charlotte and away from her third husband, Alex. The constant harassment and salacious details of her marriage and divorce plastered on social media was bad enough, but the sympathetic looks from friends made her feel pathetic. And the nosey neighbors, well, they just pissed her off. She needed a place to breathe, and Brookville was that place.

Trixie finished her warm-up and jogged away from the Brookville condominiums toward the wooded trails. If she ran all three, she'd get in a solid four and half miles.

Once on the trail, the beautiful spring morning and the exertion did their job. The tension eased from her shoulders, and slowly, her mind cleared. Early morning was her favorite time of day. She loved how the sun seemed different, softer, more inviting, and how the first morning rays filtered through the tree branches and kissed the dew with that special morning sparkle. Everything was fresh, and the day full of possibilities.

Trixie found her rhythm and was at full stride.

Starting over wasn't so bad. It wasn't like she hadn't done it before. Besides, no one in Brookville knew her or her past.

She raced up the incline. As she crested the top, Trixie glanced at the sports watch on her wrist and increased her speed. Long legs pumping, her auburn ponytail swung like a metronome. She felt good—like she was flying.

Another glance at the watch—if she kept the current pace, she would beat her best time.

In her mid-forties, exercise wasn't as easy as it had been in her twenties, but damned if she'd be a willing victim to the march of time. She would fight it, and if that meant early morning runs, weight training at the gym, and expensive face creams, then so be it. Besides, wasn't forty the new thirty?

A mile left—she pumped her arms harder, forcing herself to go faster. Her quadriceps and calves burned. Through her earbuds, the driving lyrics of Guns N' Roses urged her on. Hard rock wasn't her favorite, but something about the beat helped her fly.

A scream, sharp with fear, penetrated the pounding drums and electric guitars, shattering the tranquility of the early morning. Trixie yanked the buds from her ears. She strained to hear over her labored breathing and pounding heart. Her eyes moved to the shadows of the forest. Had she heard the snap of a twig, a rustle in the brush? Movement to her left. She tamped down the primal instinct to turn and run.

Sunlight punched holes through the dense tree canopy, leaving small pools of light along the trail. Moments earlier, what had been an idyllic setting was now unsettling. Uncertainty crept in. Maybe she imagined the scream. The music was loud; maybe it was her overly fertile imagination? A breeze rustled the tree leaves. Trixie spun to look behind her. She was acutely aware of the deafening silence—no birds or chattering squirrels, even the insects, had hidden themselves away. Self-preservation urged her to go back the way she'd come. But maybe someone was hurt and needed help.

Her eyes moved quickly to the thick, dark undergrowth. Was someone hiding in the tangle of greenery and shadows? A tremor of apprehension shimmied up her spine. Sean, her first husband, had always cautioned her about her curiosity and frequently reminded her what curiosity did to the cat. He was also quick to remind her to be aware of her environment. She chastised herself on both counts. There was no one out here, right? After all, this was Brookville. But what if there was? Trixie rubbed her sweat-slicked hands on the sides of her black leggings and wished for the small revolver tucked safely in her bureau drawer.

She stuffed the earbuds into the pocket of her jacket, tightened the elastic band holding back her thick hair, and resumed her run. Only now she was keenly aware of her surroundings.

As Trixie rounded a bend in the trail, a woman's scream shattered the silence and her doubt. She stumbled, regained her footing, and, despite the fear that gnawed inside her gut, sprinted toward the scream.

A petite blonde dressed in a coral sweater and jeans stood at the trail's edge near a cluster of spindly pines. She looked to be in her early fifties. Her knuckle was crammed into her mouth, and her eyes wide and focused on an area beyond Trixie's view. The woman swayed unsteadily, and for a moment, Trixie thought the blonde might faint, and then she screamed again. As Trixie moved closer, a lone blue sandal came into view. Lifeless bare legs protruded from the undergrowth. The mate to the sandal clung to the body's left foot. Blood thundered in Trixie's ears, and her stomach did an unsteady flip. Not her first dead body, but it was a sight she never got used to seeing.

She rushed to the hysterical woman and grabbed her by the shoulders. "Are you okay, are you hurt?" Trixie gave the blonde a quick once over. Streaked mascara and trembling body aside, there didn't seem to be any noticeable signs of injury. "What's your name?"

"Kathleen Avery," she whispered. Kathleen squeezed her eyes shut. "Is she…is she dead?"

Trixie wrapped her arm around Kathleen. "Let's find a place for you to sit down." She glanced back at the body. *What happened to her?* Blood covered the ground. The victim stared skyward. Kathleen whimpered. Trixie swallowed hard and said, "Kathleen, my name's Trixie. Come with me." She gently maneuvered the woman toward a large oak and sat her down against the tree. "Stay here."

Kathleen reached for her. "Wait. Where are you going? Don't leave me."

Trixie gave Kathleen's trembling hand a gentle squeeze and hoped she wouldn't feel the tremor in her own. "I need to call 911. I'll be back." Returning to the grisly site, she pulled her cell from her armband, sucked in a deep breath, and punched in the numbers. Trixie turned away from the body.

"911, what's your emergency?" Trixie provided the dispatcher with the pertinent information and disconnected.

"Hey Kathleen, you okay?" Kathleen turned her pallid, tear-stained face toward Trixie and nodded. She didn't look okay.

Trixie knelt beside the dead woman. Flies buzzed around her as she carefully pushed aside the vegetation. Cloudy eyes in an ashen face stared upward at the beautiful blue sky. Had she noticed the sky as she drew in her last breath? The woman's pale lips were slightly parted as if to speak. A fly crawled from inside her mouth and across her lip. It lifted and relocated to the woman's open eye. Trixie watched the fly walk across the cornea, its tongue constantly flicking out, and in then it buzzed around Trixie's head. She gagged and turned away, uncertain her breakfast would stay down. Gulping several deep breaths, her stomach settled. Boy, was she out of practice.

The victim was young, maybe mid to late twenties. Chestnut hair tangled with leaves, twigs, and blood crowned her head. The young woman lay on her back—arms outstretched. Congealed blood pooled beneath her head. Claw marks in the soil bore witness to her struggle—mud streaked her bare legs. Beneath her bunched the skirt of her floral print dress.

Trixie noticed an identification badge clipped to a blood-encrusted lanyard encircling the woman's neck. She picked up a small stick and lifted the badge. The picture was of an attractive, smiling woman on a better day. Camille Jackson had been an employee of Brookville Corporation. She didn't look familiar.

She pushed the dress collar to the side. A deep gash ran from ear to ear. Trixie's eyes traveled to the woman's hands; her fingernails were encrusted with dirt and dried blood. Cocking her head, she said, "What happened to you? And here of all places." Brookville was a small, friendly community; people didn't get murdered here. Her gaze moved to the motto printed at the bottom of the badge. "Brookville, your vacation destination for everyday living." *Not for Camille.*

She glanced back at Kathleen; her face was buried in her hands, muffling

4

her sobs.

Rapid movement in the undergrowth caused Trixie to jump to her feet; her eyes darted to the shadows in the dense foliage. Every nerve in her body hummed. Was the killer here, watching them now? Why hadn't she stayed on the phone with the 911 operator? From beneath the impenetrable vegetation, a squirrel darted out, and then another hot on his tail. They scrambled up a nearby tree. It was just a couple of squirrels, right? Hair bristled at the base of her neck. Behind her, a twig snapped, and she felt the pressure of a hand on her shoulder.

Chapter Two

Trixie spun and slapped the hand away. She lifted her fists in a defensive move, then halted. A plump middle-aged woman dressed in navy sweatpants and a white sweatshirt peered at her through large, dark-rimmed glasses. Her gray hair was twisted into a long braid that hung over her right shoulder. A black fanny pack encircled her waist. Trixie dropped her fist but kept a distance. "Who are you, and where did you come from?"

"Sorry. Didn't mean to startle you. Martha Kline is the name. I was up the trail and heard the screams. Who are you?" Martha craned her neck to the side for a better look.

Trixie blocked her view. The last thing she needed was a civilian tramping over the crime scene. "Trixie Tanner, and you didn't answer my questions." *What did it matter? This wasn't her crime scene. Why was she being so protective? Old habits?*

"Incorrect. You asked two questions. I answered both." Martha pushed past her and knelt beside the body. "Why are you here? Do you have forensic training? By the way, that was an exceptionally smooth move. Which martial art do you study?"

Trixie's lips compressed into a tight line. "Like you, I heard the screams?" For all she knew, Martha was the murderer returning to tidy up the scene of the crime. Were she and Kathleen loose ends? For the second time that morning Trixie wished for the revolver.

Martha unzipped the fanny pack and withdrew a pair of blue nitrile gloves. She pushed up the sleeves of her sweatshirt and drew them on.

"What are you doing? Hey, don't touch anything. I called the cops. They'll be here any minute, and they aren't going to like you contaminating the crime scene."

Martha moved the collar of the woman's dress to the side and looked closer at the gash on her neck. "Did you notice the bruising on her cheek?"

"Don't touch the body." Trixie knelt beside her. "And no, I didn't. Do you have an extra pair of gloves?"

Martha pulled gloves from the pack and handed them to her. "Judging from the available evidence, it appears she put up a fight. Unfortunately, she exsanguinated."

"You seem to know quite a bit about forensics. Are you in the field?"

"Not exactly." Martha looked up. "However, I have been taking night classes for quite some time." She leaned in for a better look. "Yes. She definitely bled out." Martha pointed to Camille's neck. "Notice how deep the cut is on the left side and how it trails off and is shallower on the right? I would submit this woman's assailant was right-handed. With the amount of blood around the body, the carotid artery was severed. Obviously, the medical examiner will have to confirm my findings. I imagine the victim died in less than a minute."

Martha was right, but the thought of someone's life ending so quickly was more than a little disturbing. "Did you notice her fingernails? There's dried blood beneath them."

Flies buzzed furiously around the body. One landed on the victim's hand. Trixie brushed it away. "I hate these things."

"Blowflies? Don't hate them. They are the start of nature's cleanup crew. They really are amazing little creatures." Martha's brown eyes twinkled. "And beetles, they come next. I've always had a fascination with entomology."

"Bugs?"

"The study of insects. Fascinating." Martha laid the back of her hand on the woman's cheek. "She's cool to the touch, and her skin is rigid. It was chilly last night, which would have slowed decomposition."

Trixie sat back on her heels and scanned the trees again. "Did you notice her Brookville badge?"

"Did you touch it?"

Trixie rolled her eyes. "Of course not."

Martha turned back to the woman. "I think I've seen our victim around the Brookville properties."

Our victim? Trixie shifted her attention from the wooded area back to Camille. She was a firm believer that nothing happened without there being a purpose and that people were brought together at specific times and places to serve a greater good. Maybe, the three of them converged at this spot and time to find this woman's murderer. Maybe she was *their* victim, and they were supposed to be her voice.

Martha snapped her fingers in front of Trixie's face. "Pay attention."

Trixie turned to look in the direction Martha was pointing. Deep grooves scarred the soft dirt. Evidence of a fight. Trixie moved to the edge of the brush. "Did you see this partial footprint?"

Martha moved beside her. "I wish I had my casting kit. I could've made an impression. I hate a missed opportunity."

Trixie frowned. "Ah, I don't think that would've been such a great idea. Wait, you know how to do that?"

"Of course I do. I'm not an amateur."

Trixie held up her hands. "Just asking, not judging." She stared down at Camille. "Hell of a way to go."

"There's a good way?"

Behind Trixie, the crunch of footsteps on gravel caught her attention. Kathleen moved toward them. Her blue eyes were wide with fear and fixed on the body. She pressed her shaking hands together.

Trixie said, "Maybe you shouldn't come any closer."

"I'm fine."

"You do not look fine," said Martha. "You look like crap."

Trixie shot Martha a warning look. "Martha, this is Kathleen. She found the body."

Kathleen took a step closer. "Martha, how do you know so much about this crime scene stuff? Are you with law enforcement or the medical field?"

"Librarian, Brookville Library, twenty-one years."

"You really do have varied interests," said Trixie.

"My hobby is forensics, and as I mentioned earlier. I am taking night classes."

"We should move away from this area," said Trixie. "The cops aren't going to be happy that we've trampled their crime scene."

"Give me a minute." Martha removed two small brown paper bags from her pouch and carefully placed them over the woman's hands.

"Now, what are you doing?" asked Kathleen.

"Preserving the evidence. There is trace evidence under her nails. I want to ensure we protect it."

"Do you always carry that stuff with you?" asked Trixie.

Martha patted her fanny pack. "One must always be prepared. You never know when it might be needed. Today is a perfect example."

Trixie shook her head. *We are in so much trouble.*

As Trixie herded the women away from the body, Kathleen said, "What was her name?"

Trixie said, "Camille Jackson. Did you know her?"

Kathleen shook her head. "I've seen her around. She's the new condo manager." She hesitated. "I guess I should say, was. Who would want to hurt her?"

Trixie glanced back at Camille. "I don't know, but I may need to rethink my early morning runs."

Chapter Three

The *whoop, whoop* of fast-approaching sirens sounded. A moment later, in a hail of flashing red and blue lights, EMS and law enforcement skidded to a stop at the edge of the service road. Trixie directed the deputies to the body. First responders exited vehicles and hurried toward the victim. A few cops strung crime scene tape around the area.

After the initial flurry of activity, one of the deputies made his way to where the women stood. Tall with the beginnings of a middle-aged paunch, he still held on to some of his youthful looks—a firm square jawline and a face void of wrinkles. A gold name badge with Nelson engraved into the metal was positioned slightly above the left breast pocket of his beige uniform shirt.

Nelson called to another deputy, "Hey, Roger, got an ETA on the ME?"

"Dispatch said he was at another crime scene and would be here in ten." Roger looked at his watch. "Should be here any time."

Nelson turned toward the women. He pulled a small notepad and pen from his breast pocket. "Ladies, I'm Deputy Jack Nelson." A toothpick bobbed between his lips. "I understand you found the deceased."

Martha stepped toward him, her expression grim.

She tore off a blue nitrile glove and extended her hand. "Deputy Nelson, Martha Kline. I've secured the area. The victim's throat was cut. Based on my examination, I have reason to believe the killer was right-handed."

Trixie looked from the Deputy to Martha and back to the Deputy. His face shifted from surprise and disbelief to annoyance and anger. The toothpick bobbed rapidly between his lips.

Nelson slowly removed the toothpick from his mouth and pointed it at Martha. "Ms. Kline, are you admitting to tampering with the crime scene?"

Martha's chin jutted out defiantly. "Tampering? No. You are mistaken. I preserved the evidence following standard protocol. I'm confused by your...accusation. Perhaps, being from a small town, you aren't familiar with the standard protocol for preserving a crime scene. I'd be happy to offer my assistance if that's the case."

Color rose in Nelson's cheeks and ears. "Ma'am, you are not authorized to touch a crime scene. And we do not need your assistance. Do you realize you are meddling where you don't belong?"

Trixie interrupted, "Excuse me, Deputy, meddling is such a strong word. Perhaps a better word choice would be assisting."

Through gritted teeth, Nelson said, "She contaminated the crime scene. Anything else you want to contribute?"

"I'll admit, there might have been minimal contamination, but we really didn't have a choice. Had Camille been alive, we would've been obligated to help her. And we wouldn't have known that unless we examined her, right?"

Nelson glared at Trixie. "Did you know the victim? What's your full name?"

"No. I did not. Beatrice Tanner, but my friends call me Trixie."

Nelson made a note. "I'm sure they do. Which one of you found the body?"

Kathleen took a small step forward. She looked like a delicate porcelain doll next to Nelson's tall, bulky frame. "It was horrible. I've never found a body before."

His face softened. "What's your name, ma'am?"

"Kathleen Avery."

"Ma'am, I'm sorry you had to go through this experience." He gave her a little smile. "Did you touch anything?"

Kathleen shuddered. "Goodness, no. I would rather die than touch that poor dead woman."

Nelson made another note. "Ladies, I realize the scene here is upsetting. Why don't we finish this interview at the station? It will be a more comfortable environment."

"Surely, you don't think we had anything to do with Camille's death," said Trixie. "Taking us in to be interrogated seems a bit extreme, don't you think?"

Nelson leveled his gaze at her. "You've trampled all over my crime scene and tampered with evidence. In my position, what would you think?"

Trixie opened her mouth, then snapped it shut. No point digging the proverbial hole any deeper. She looked at Kathleen and Martha. There was no way they looked like a band of murderers.

Nelson called to a ginger-haired deputy assisting the forensic tech. "I'm taking these women to the station. You're in charge." Nelson moved the women toward the cruiser. His hand froze over the car's rear door handle as a large black SUV pulled to a stop. A cloud of dust swirled around the vehicle, obscuring the driver. "Dammit," mumbled Nelson.

Trixie's eyes shifted from the deputy to the SUV. "Who's that?"

"The ME." Nelson looked at the women and shook his head. "Nobody, and I mean nobody, touches the body at a crime scene until Doc Stone arrives. He's not going to be happy." Nelson glared at Martha. "Especially with you."

Doc Stone stepped out of the vehicle. Tall, broad-shouldered, and narrow-hipped, he wore faded jeans and a white dress shirt, sleeves rolled mid-way up brown sinewy forearms.

As he made his way to the victim, forensic techs and law enforcement cleared a path much like Moses' parting of the Red Sea. The chatter from moments earlier stopped. Doc placed his hands on his hips, walked around the body, then crooked an index finger at a young forensic tech. The tech tentatively moved beside him. Doc stepped closer—his face animated and angry. The tech vigorously shook his head and pointed at the women.

"Stool pigeon," muttered Trixie. Nelson shot her a side glance.

Doc looked over his shoulder in their direction. His deep, irritated voice filled the forest. Thankfully, due to distance, most of what he said was unintelligible. However, a few salty phrases coupled with his gesticulations made it clear he was not happy. Doc spun on his heel and marched toward them. His facial expression was fierce, like a raging storm. Trixie braced herself for the assault and took an involuntary step back. He was an imposing figure. His shoulder-length black hair was gathered at the base of his neck with a large silver clip. As he closed in on them, she noticed strands of silver peppered the black, and his thick black brows were furrowed over dark, hooded eyes. He stopped inches from her.

"What in the hell were you thinking?"

His dark eyes bore into hers. He was so close she smelled his woodsy cologne and the scent of peppermint on his breath. His commanding voice and swarthy looks reminded her of a renegade pirate demanding the surrender of a ship.

Doc continued, "Of course, you weren't thinking, or you wouldn't have touched the body."

Trixie squared her shoulders and lifted her chin. She wasn't going to continue listening to his tirade. She jabbed a well-manicured pink-tipped index finger into his chest. "Back off." She glared up at him. "We didn't do anything wrong. In fact, we did exactly what we were supposed to do."

Stone took a step closer. "I don't recall bagging a victim's hands as being what the public is supposed to do. Why didn't you call 911 like any other normal citizen and then leave the scene alone instead of pretending to be a couple of Nancy Drews."

"I did call, otherwise, you wouldn't be here." Trixie took a step closer. Inches apart, she looked up into his stormy face. "We checked the victim to see if we could offer medical assistance."

"You contaminated my crime scene, compromised my investigation, and tampered with the body. I won't be able to ensure my findings are accurate. Hell, for all I know, you three killed that woman." He turned toward Nelson. "Are you taking them in for questioning?"

Before Nelson answered, Martha tapped Stone on the shoulder. "Doctor Stone, Martha Kline. I am the one responsible for securing the area."

Slowly, he turned and glared at her.

Trixie squeezed her eyes shut. *Oh, dear God, no. She couldn't believe it. The woman had no sense of self-preservation.*

"I can assure you, we acted appropriately. You will find I have preserved the crime scene following standard protocol. The body's position wasn't altered. I'm not an amateur." Martha straightened her shoulders and stood a little taller. "After all, I have had forensic training."

Doc loomed over Martha by a good six inches. "And where did this supposed training occur?"

Martha pushed her glasses up on her nose. "I am taking night classes at the community college."

He stared at her in disbelief. "Sweet mother of God." Stone turned and stormed back toward the body. Over his shoulder, he yelled, "Nelson, get those women away from me and my crime scene."

"Ladies, it is in your best interest to get in the cruiser."

Martha opened the front passenger door. Nelson shook his head. "Criminals ride in the back."

Chapter Four

Twenty minutes later, the women were seated in an interview room at the Brookville sheriff's office. Trixie looked around the stark room; black scuff marks marred the white walls. A square gray metal table was positioned in the middle of the small rectangular space. The women sat in brown folding chairs placed around it. Lukewarm coffee served in Styrofoam cups sat in front of them. Trixie had seen worse. She sipped the tepid coffee and grimaced. "The coffee stinks."

Kathleen wrung her hands. "What's taking so long? Is he going to arrest us? This is terrible. My children can't find out I've been taken in for questioning, let alone about a murder. They'll have me committed. They already think I've gone a little…nuts."

Trixie slid down in the chair. "He's probably checking to see if we have any priors." She grumbled, "All I wanted to do this morning was take a leisurely run and enjoy this glorious spring day. Instead, I'm sitting in the Sheriff's interview room like a common criminal."

"You seem well-versed in police procedures," said Martha.

"I read a lot of true crime."

"Priors? What's that?" asked Kathleen.

"Convictions," said Martha. "I'm assuming neither of you have a RAP sheet."

"RAP sheet?" squeaked Kathleen.

Trixie shifted in the hard metal chair. "Kathleen, relax."

The door opened, and Deputy Nelson entered. "Ladies, I trust you're comfortable."

Martha sat up in her chair. "Actually, do you have—"

"Martha, stop. He doesn't care if we're comfortable," said Trixie.

Deputy Nelson looked at Martha for a long moment, then placed a legal pad on the table. He pulled an extra folding chair into the room and settled into it. The chair groaned under his bulk. Nelson removed a pen from his shirt pocket and said, "So, let's start at the beginning. Who found the body?"

Kathleen raised her hand as if in a classroom. "I did. I was out for my morning walk and then…" She took a deep, unsteady breath, "and then I saw her laying in the underbrush."

"What time was that?"

"Sometime between seven-thirty and eight."

"You see anyone else or hear anything?" Kathleen shook her head. Her bottom lip quivered. Nelson patted her shoulder. "You okay, ma'am? You still look a little peaked."

"I'm fine, thank you. I just want this over with."

He smiled, then turned toward Martha and Trixie—the smile vanished. "What about you two." His gaze moved to Trixie. "What were you doing in the area?"

"Running. Kathleen's scream led me to her and the body."

"Yeah, me too," said Martha. "Well, not the running part."

Deputy Nelson tapped the end of the pen on the table. "Ms. Kline, exactly what *were* you doing in the woods at that hour?"

"Bird watching." She pulled collapsible binoculars and the Field Guide to North American Birds from her fanny pack and held them up.

"Did you know the victim?" asked Nelson.

"No. I never had the pleasure of meeting her."

Nelson leveled his gaze in Trixie's direction. "What about you?"

"Don't look at me like that. I never met the woman."

"She was the new condo manager," said Kathleen. "But I never actually met her."

Nelson made a note on the pad. "Any idea how long she's been on the job?"

"Not long," said Kathleen. "Although, I overheard her telling another resident she'd been with the corporation for several years."

"You should check with her employer," said Martha.

Nelson pinched the bridge of his nose with his thumb and forefinger. "Yes, ma'am. I think I got that figured out, but thanks for your help. Did any of you see or hear anything? Maybe someone running through the woods, anything?"

Trixie shook her head. "There was nothing after Kathleen screamed. The forest was silent—like creepy silent."

"I didn't hear or see anything either," said Martha. "Given the coolness of the victim's skin, whoever killed her was long gone by the time we got there."

Nelson studied Martha for a moment. "Is there anything *you* want to tell me?"

"Only if you need assistance, I would be happy to offer my services." Martha gave Nelson a broad smile.

"Thank you, but we've got the situation covered." He made several more notes on his pad, flipped the page, and then slid it in front of Trixie. "I want each of you to write down your name and contact information."

Trixie scribbled her phone number on the pad and passed it to Martha. "Why? To harass us later. Are we suspects? Are you holding us?"

Martha picked up the pen. "Everyone is a suspect." She looked up at Nelson. "If you need something, call me. This is all very exciting."

Nelson frowned at Martha. "Right. I'll keep that in mind."

When the women had given Deputy Nelson their contact information, he picked up the pad and stood. "Since footprints are all over the crime scene, we'll need to get impressions of your shoes before you leave."

Kathleen closed her eyes and pressed her hand to her chest. "Thank God."

Martha blinked and pushed her glasses up on her nose. "You're not arresting us?"

Nelson glared at her. "Should I?"

Kathleen's eyes widened. "Well, of course not. We were only trying to help. It was quite a shock seeing a dead body in the middle of such a beautiful place."

"I'm sure it was." Nelson reached into the breast pocket of his shirt and pulled out business cards. "If additional details come to you later, give me a call." He handed Trixie and Martha a card. He wrote on the back of the third card and handed it to Kathleen. "Ms. Avery, that's my cell. Call me if you think of something or just need to talk. Finding a murder victim can be traumatizing."

A technician entered the room and took prints of the women's shoes. Nelson said, "You are free to go. I'll be in touch, and the DA may be contacting you as well."

Kathleen's head jerked up, her eyes wide. "The DA? Why would the DA want to contact us?"

"He'll be reviewing the case, and it's possible there could be charges pending," said Nelson.

"For what?" asked Trixie.

Nelson turned toward Trixie. "Tampering with a crime scene."

Kathleen's bottom lip began to tremble. "Can we leave?"

"Yes, ma'am, and don't you worry about the DA, I'll put in a good word for you. If you don't mind, maybe I could drop by—you know, to check on you."

Kathleen blushed. "That would be very kind of you."

"Ladies, you may leave. Ms. Tanner, may I have a word?"

Trixie said, "I'll meet you outside." She turned to Nelson. "What can I do for you, Deputy?"

"Ms. Tanner, I received an interesting call after I ran you through the NCIC."

"I imagine you did. It's good to have friends."

"Apparently. You're retired?"

"Looks that way."

"Your driver's license doesn't denote a CCW." He cocked his head and studied her for a moment. "Do you have a weapon? Are you carrying?"

"Weapon, yes; carrying no. If there's nothing else, I'm going to join my friends. And, Deputy, I'd prefer my past to stay there."

Chapter Five

Trixie, Martha, and Kathleen stood outside the sheriff's office. "How are we getting back to the condos?" asked Martha.

Trixie said, "I'll call an Uber."

"What did Deputy Nelson want?" asked Kathleen.

"Nothing important." Trixie checked her watch. "It's only eleven thirty, but I could use a drink. We could get mimosas at the café. It's just a few blocks from here. What do you think?"

"That's the best idea I've heard all day," said Kathleen.

Martha frowned. "I'm unfamiliar with mimosas. What are they?"

Trixie draped her arm over Martha's shoulders. "Let us introduce you. I think you'll find them very tasty."

A short while later, the women sat in a brightly upholstered booth at the back of Emile's Café. Emile's was a small restaurant located in the center of town where Chef Emile prepared a select menu. The charming café with eclectic furnishings and art hosted small jazz bands Friday nights in the summer. Emile was a bit of a mystery. No one knew why the Le Cordon Bleu chef decided to set up shop in a town like Brookville, but Trixie was glad he had.

Kathleen settled back into the booth seat. "I can't believe that poor woman was murdered—literally in our own backyards. And no one heard or saw anything."

"It's unsettling," said Trixie.

Emile returned with fresh mimosas. "You ladies appear to have enjoyed your brunch."

Martha beamed up at him. "That was the best Egg McMuffin I've ever had. What was that delicious sauce?"

Emile lifted his chin indignantly and sniffed. "That, madam, was *not* an Egg McMuffin. If you'll excuse me." He straightened his shoulders, gave Martha a disdainful look and marched back to the kitchen, slamming the door behind him.

"I can't believe you called Emile's fabulous Eggs Benedict an Egg McMuffin?" Trixie shook her head and frowned at Martha. Where had this woman been living? Under a rock?

"I am confused. I said it was delicious." Martha wiped up the last of the hollandaise sauce with her index finger and stuck it into her mouth.

Kathleen looked down at her empty plate. "After all we've been through this morning, I wasn't sure I'd be able to eat. But once Emile sat the plate in front of me, I realized I was famished."

"Maybe all that flirting with a certain deputy worked up an appetite," said Trixie.

Color rose in Kathleen's cheeks. "Flirting? Who? Oh, stop. I did no such thing. Deputy Nelson was just being nice."

"To you, maybe, not so much to Martha and me."

Martha leaned back in the booth with the glass of mimosa firmly grasped in both hands. "This is the most delicious drink I've ever tasted. Wonder why I've never heard of it before?" She cocked her head toward Trixie. "And you say there's alcohol in it? Amazing. I don't feel a thing." She took another long pull from the glass.

Kathleen moved her plate to the side and leaned forward. "I don't know about you two, but my sense of security has been destroyed. Someone murdered that woman on Brookville property less than a mile from our condos. I'm not sure I feel safe living there anymore."

Martha leaned forward, wobbled slightly to the right, and whispered, "Maybe Camille was murdered by a serial killer." Martha gave a loud belch, then placed her fingers over her mouth and giggled.

Kathleen's eyes shifted to nearby tables filled with customers. "For heaven's sake, stop saying things like that. You're scaring the people next to us and me. And if that were true, it would be horrible and very alarming. Trixie, take her glass; she's had enough to drink." Kathleen shifted worried eyes toward Trixie. "You don't think Martha's right, do you? You know, about the serial killer."

Trixie shook her head. "Doubtful. I know murder so close to our condos is unsettling, but I love my new home, and I'm happy. I'm rid of that dinosaur of a house and all the crap in it, including my third husband."

Kathleen raised a perfectly penciled brow. *"Third* husband?"

Martha propped both elbows on the table, her hands cupped each side of her face. "Was the breakup painful?"

Trixie faced Kathleen. "Yes, third husband." Then she turned to Martha. "Hell, no, the breakup wasn't painful. The house was cluttered with expensive art and sculptures by up-and-coming artists that Alex couldn't live without. Only problem was, he also collected the artists; female or male made no difference to him. I'm not sure what was worse, the insult to my confidence or that I just wasn't enough. So, one day, I'd had all I could take of his assortment of the animate and inanimate collectibles. I kicked him out, sold the house, and moved to Brookville." Trixie rubbed her hands together. "Good riddance to bad rubbish." She picked up her mimosa and took a sip. "My condo is exactly as I want it, and for the first time since I married my first husband, Sean, I feel like I'm in the right place. I'm not moving, murder or no murder."

"How long were you married to your first husband?" asked Kathleen.

"Fourteen years. It's been nine years since his death."

Kathleen reached across the table and gave Trixie's hand a light squeeze. "I'm sorry. I didn't realize you were a widow. Who knew being a widow and stumbling on a murdered woman would give us so much in common?" Kathleen gave a nervous laugh. Do you think we need to worry?"

Martha slid down in the booth seat and clutched her glass. "Well, I'm not worrying, and I'm not moving. I would have to go back to my mother's house. I refuse to go back there and live with her verbal abuse and demands." She shook her head. "Nope. Not doing it. I scrimped and saved my entire adult life to have my own place—I've sunk every penny I have into that condo. I'm finally free and happy." She hiccuped. "Frankly, they could be knocking people off like little ducks in a pond, and I would still stay." She stuck the straw in her mouth and slurped up the last of the mimosa.

Trixie turned to Kathleen. "What's your story? What brought you to Brookville?"

Kathleen carefully folded her napkin and tucked it under her plate. "I was married for thirty-three years to the most wonderful man in the world. He treated me like a queen and did everything for me." She looked up from the napkin. "And then, when Mac died, I realized I didn't know how to take care of myself. I didn't even know how to pump my own gas. I never had to balance the checkbook or renew the tags for my car. Mac did it all." She brushed crumbs from the table. "Mac and I had an agreement. I would retire early from teaching, and we'd travel the world. Only Mac didn't keep his part of the agreement." She looked away and swiped at a tear.

Trixie knew the pain. "How long have you been widowed?"

"Almost a year."

"You've made some really big life changes in a short amount of time."

Kathleen gave a humorless laugh. "Yeah, my two adult children have been very vocal and critical about my life-altering changes."

"They don't approve?" asked Trixie.

"My son and daughter think I'm too old to have desires beyond being there for them. They wanted me to stay in the home they grew up in. They think I've betrayed the memory of their father. I believe they think I've gone off the deep end."

Trixie said, "But it's not about that, is it?"

"No. I had to get away from the memories. I felt like I was suffocating. If I stayed in that house, I wasn't sure I'd be able to move on with my life. Nothing would've changed. Fifty-three is not old, but my kids were making me feel like my life was over—that it was my obligation to their father to keep things the same, to never change. I liked being married, and I don't want to be alone the rest of my life. I hope I'm fortunate enough to find love again, but that wouldn't happen if I stayed there. I had to get out of that house—I had to move."

Kathleen picked up her napkin and dabbed at the tears that ran down her cheeks. She leveled her shoulders and continued, "So, one day, I took off my wedding rings, put them in the safe deposit box, and bought the condo. If I can't make it here, I'll never hear the end of it." She looked up at Trixie, surprise in her blue eyes. "I guess I'd rather take my chances here than admit defeat and go back to my old life."

"Good for you. You're doing the right thing." Trixie leaned back into the booth seat and looked from Kathleen to Martha. "We've all made big changes in our lives." Martha's gaze was fixed to a spot on the wall. "Martha, you still with us?"

"I am great." She looked at Trixie and gave her a lopsided smile. "You think they could make another one of these teeny weenie drinks?" She waggled her empty glass.

Trixie motioned to the waitress. "I think we should order coffee."

Trixie scooted to the edge of the booth seat and propped her elbows on the table. "None of us are going to move. We love our new homes and lives. We don't have to become a victim of circumstances. Instead of hiding and worrying, we need to be proactive."

"What exactly are you thinking?" asked Kathleen.

"I'm not sure. But once word gets out that there was a murder on Brookville properties, residents are going to be worried."

Martha sat her mimosa glass on the table with a loud thud and leaned forward, "Self-defense classes. That's what we need." She pointed her index finger at Trixie. "And you could teach them 'cause you got moves. Yes, siree. And we would be the three musketeers." She straightened her glasses and wobbled forward. "No. We're more than musketeers; we're brave and fierce. We're like dragons." Martha lifted both hands, forming claws, and made a growling sound. "We're the Lady Dragons of Brookville."

Trixie laughed. "Yeah, you've definitely had enough alcohol, but you have a good idea. In fact, it's a great idea."

Chapter Six

The next morning, Trixie threw back the comforter and tentatively sat on the edge of the bed. Fitful sleep had aggravated her back, and the familiar ache ran from her lower back down into her right leg. She rubbed her back and felt the small scar. For a moment, the ache turned into a searing pain, and then gradually, it eased. "Damn bullet."

Trixie pulled on a peach silk robe and followed the scent of freshly brewed coffee into the kitchen. In her opinion, whoever invented the programmable coffee maker was a genius. There was nothing better than getting up in the morning, and the coffee was ready. And it was cheaper than a fourth husband.

She filled a large blue mug with the steaming brew and walked out onto the twelve-by-twelve screened-in back porch. Sitting at the round glass-topped table, Trixie drank coffee and watched the day begin as streaks of pink and purple colored the sky.

Sleep had been elusive and fitful, and her dreams were filled with scenes from the previous day. Camille's vacant eyes followed her no matter which direction she moved; her mouth gaped open and closed as if trying to speak, and her hands contorted into hooked claws that reached for her. Trixie shivered at the recollection and pulled her robe tighter. She went back inside the house and returned with a bottle of whiskey—poured a liberal amount into the cup and took another sip.

"Mind sharing with a friend?" Kathleen stood at her back door wrapped in a pink chenille robe.

Trixie sucked in a quick breath. "Crap. You scared the life out of me." She unlocked the door. "I'll get you a mug." She turned back to Kathleen. "You want coffee in it, too?"

"Please. I don't want the neighbors to know I'm drinking before breakfast."

Trixie returned with a mug of steaming coffee. She pushed the whiskey bottle across the table. "I don't know about you, but I had a miserable night's sleep."

Kathleen stirred whiskey into the mug. "That would make two of us. I don't think I got an hour of continuous sleep. My dreams looped all night with me finding Camille's body." She shivered and took a long pull from the mug.

The women sat silently at the table, sipped coffee, and listened to the morning sounds. Kathleen was pleasant company, and Trixie appreciated the fact she didn't need to fill the silence with idle chatter.

The porch door flew open, and Martha burst onto the porch wearing a white blouse tucked into black cargo pants and high-top black Converse sneakers. The black fanny pack completed her ensemble. "Hey. What's going on?"

Trixie and Kathleen jumped. "I've got to get a bell or something so people can't keep sneaking up on me. Have a seat and join us, Martha. You want coffee?"

"Yes, please. You should have told me we were having an early morning coffee klatch."

Martha sat at the table and picked up the bottle of whiskey. "Are you two drinking at this hour?"

Remembering the mimosas, Trixie took the bottle. "No, I must've forgotten to put it away. She went into the kitchen and returned with another mug and the coffee pot. "I hope you slept better than we did."

"Like a log."

Kathleen lifted her mug and stopped midway. "Really?"

Martha nodded. Her long hair spilled over her shoulder like liquid silver. "Sure." She sipped the coffee. "Didn't you?"

"Yesterday's events didn't bother you?" asked Trixie.

Martha pushed her glasses up on her nose. "Not really." She lifted the mug." Good coffee. You know what would go great with it?"

"No idea," said Trixie.

"Cinnamon rolls from the bakery. It's just around the corner. I'll get some."

"Sure. That'd be great," said Kathleen.

Martha jumped up. "We investigators must keep up our strength. Back in a jiff."

They watched her hurry down the sidewalk and around the corner. Kathleen turned to Trixie. "Investigators? Us? Where did you go with that bottle?"

"I'm on it." Trixie went back into the kitchen and returned with the whiskey. She added an additional splash to the mugs and topped them off with fresh coffee. "Martha is certainly excited about the murder investigation."

Kathleen absently stirred her coffee. "Yes, she is."

"What's on your mind?"

Kathleen laid the spoon on the table. "Why Camille? Why would someone want to take her life?"

"I don't know. Maybe someone had a bone to pick with her. Maybe it was a crime of passion—a lover's quarrel that got out of hand."

"It could be random. Perhaps Camille was in the wrong place at the wrong time."

A chill settled over Trixie. She hugged her body. "I wonder if Camille was dating someone."

"Maybe she met someone online, and they turned out to be a serial killer."

"Kathleen, you're sounding like Martha. And don't you think that's a little extreme? However, I almost wish it were premeditated or a crime of passion. The thought of a stranger committing a random act of violence is more disturbing."

The screen door slammed as Martha entered the porch. "What stranger?"

"Wow, that was fast," said Kathleen.

Martha held up a white paper bag. "Seriously, the bakery *is* just around the corner. You people need to pay more attention to your surroundings."

Trixie stood. "I'll get plates."

Martha pulled a large cinnamon roll from the bag and took a bite. "What were you two talking about?"

Trixie set paper plates on the table. "We wondered if Camille was murdered by someone she knew or a stranger."

Martha brushed crumbs from the front of her white blouse. "Probably someone she knew. In an analysis of over two thousand murders, it was estimated that eighty percent of the victims knew their killer. I guess that would mean the remaining twenty percent could be attributed to serial killings, murders for hire, and random killing sprees." She took another bite of the pastry and looked up. "Why are you two staring at me?"

"Seriously, who are you?" asked Kathleen. "Are you sure this crime stuff is just a hobby?"

Martha's face brightened, and her brown eyes twinkled. "As I mentioned earlier, crime fascinates me. I wanted to go into some branch of law enforcement or forensics, but at the time, my mother told me it was not lady-like. She was certain if I went into the field, I'd never find a husband. So, I became a librarian. I guess we can see how well that worked out." She drank her coffee, and the twinkle disappeared. "Anyway, I don't want you to think I'm insensitive to what happened yesterday, but stuff like that generally doesn't bother me."

Kathleen nibbled the cinnamon roll. "I wish we could do something. I feel responsible. We found her, and it feels like it's our duty to help find Camille's killer."

Martha placed her mug on the table and scooted to the edge of her chair. "Maybe we can."

"Can what?" asked Trixie.

"Help. Maybe we can help." Martha looked excitedly at Kathleen and Trixie. "Let's go back to the crime scene. I'm well-versed in forensics. Maybe we'll find something that can help move the case along. The quicker the murder is solved, the sooner we can return to our normal lives." She took a large bite of the bun and chewed. "So, what do you think?"

Kathleen sat erect in her chair. "I think that's a brilliant idea."

Trixie gave both women a dubious look. "Kathleen, I think you've had *too* much coffee. Returning to the scene of the crime is a bad idea. Have you forgotten the DA may charge us with tampering? And now you want to go back to the scene." Trixie shook her head. "I don't think Deputy Nelson needs our help doing his job. And I'm not very anxious to end up in jail for meddling in things that don't concern me."

Martha sighed and flopped back in her seat. "I suppose you're right."

Kathleen adjusted her robe. "Yeah, I'm sure you are. However, it would have been exciting if we found something. You know, it does happen. Occasionally, some random person will find an important piece of evidence that law enforcement overlooked. Isn't that right, Martha?"

Martha nodded vigorously. "Absolutely. I can't see how doing a little investigating, *especially* since the forensic team has finished with the scene, could hurt anything. And you must admit, it would put everyone's mind at ease if this case was wrapped up sooner than later."

Martha's expectant expression reminded Trixie of a puppy waiting for a treat. Trixie stood and paced the length of the porch several times. The idea had merit; she couldn't argue that. Sean was right; her unbridled curiosity was going to get her in trouble one day. She stopped and turned toward Martha and Kathleen. "I guess I can't argue with your logic. However, I want the record to state I don't think this is a good idea. And, if Nelson or that insufferable medical examiner is on the scene or shows up, we're leaving. Are we clear?"

Martha jabbed a fist in the air. "This is great."

"Well, if I'm going to stomp around in the woods, I need to change clothes," said Trixie.

Kathleen looked down at her robe. "Oh, me too."

Trixie glanced at her watch. "Let's meet back here in thirty minutes."

Chapter Seven

Trixie stepped out of her condo dressed in jeans, a white tee shirt, and running shoes. Kathleen and Martha waited for her on the front lawn. Martha paced back and forth, hands clasped behind her back much like a drill sergeant preparing for maneuvers. A camo ball cap sat on her head; the bill pulled low over her eyes. Her camo tee shirt was tucked into black cargo pants, which were tucked into highly polished black boots. The black fanny pack was cinched firmly around her waist. Martha grimaced at Kathleen. Dressed in flowered capris, pale blue tee shirt, and white canvas sneakers, she looked like she was going anywhere but a crime scene.

"Are you ready?" called Kathleen.

Trixie shouldered a small red nylon knapsack. "I am."

Kathleen pointed to the bag. "What's in there?"

"Cell phone and a few odds-and-ends that might come in handy. And I'm bringing a little something extra—just in case." Trixie lifted her pant leg, revealing an ankle holster with a small pearl-handled revolver nestled inside.

Kathleen's eyes widened. "Trixie, where on earth did you get that? Do you even know how to use it?"

"Of course, I know how to use it. I'm actually a pretty good shot. Sean bought it for me." She held up the weapon and grinned. "He used to say there was nothing sexier than a woman packing a little heat. It was a present."

"Present? That's not the kind of present my husband used to give me," said Kathleen. "He'd leave me little gifts around the house. You know, small

29

things, earrings, a book, sometimes a card. But never a gun."

Martha stepped closer to Trixie. "What are you talking about? A gun is a spectacular gift. So, how did he give it to you? Was it a Christmas present, birthday present?"

Trixie smiled. "We'd spent the day on this beautiful, secluded beach in the Keys. The sands were so white they were blinding in the sun. The water was a gorgeous turquoise. The day was perfect. I was lying on a large blanket soaking up the sun when Sean pulled a beautifully wrapped package with an enormous pink bow from his backpack. I was so surprised. And when I opened the package and saw the small revolver, well, it was perfect." Trixie drew in a steadying breath. "He said he loved me and wanted to ensure if he wasn't around to be my protector that, I could take care of myself."

Trixie's mind drifted back to that warm summer afternoon. Sean had cupped her face in his hands and slowly kissed her. She lingered in the memory. His kisses were slow and sensual and always took her breath away. She missed them.

Kathleen touched Trixie's arm. "You, okay?"

"Sure." She felt the sting of unshed tears. Anyway, if this little gun could talk, the stories it could tell." She gave the weapon a wistful look, slid it back into the holster, and pulled down her pant leg. "So, let's get started."

Kathleen shook her head. "I've never met anyone quite like you."

Trixie laughed. "I'm fairly certain when the good Lord made me, that mold was thrown away."

Martha sighed. "I want a gun."

"Oh, for heaven's sake, let's go," said Kathleen.

The women walked toward the access point for the trails that wound through the Brookville property. There were three different trails. Hummingbird veered to the left. It was a quick half-mile walk. Mockingbird went to the right and was a mile. The women took the third, Raven Trail, which was a hilly two and a half miles of densely wooded trail that wound around a small lake.

A mile into the walk, Kathleen said, "If we weren't on our way to investigate a murder scene, this would be a wonderful morning for a walk. I've never been down this trail. It's so beautiful and secluded. It feels like we're out in the middle of nowhere."

"Perfect place for a murder," said Martha. "And this isn't exactly nowhere. Until the land was sold to the Brookville Corporation, it was part of a large plantation owned by several generations of the Jeffries family. During the early to mid-1800s, the Jeffries family grew cotton. Then, after the Civil War, they transitioned to growing tobacco. At some point in the late Seventies early Eighties, the plantation was no longer a producing property. Then in the Ninety's, the home burned to the ground."

"How do you know that?" asked Trixie.

"I don't just re-shelve books. Research *is* part of what I do."

"Okay," said Trixie. "But this isn't just general research. That information is incredibly detailed."

"Before I decided to buy the condo, I spent time digging into the history of the area. I wanted to know where I was investing my money."

"You get most of that information during the closing process," said Trixie.

"Some of the information is presented during closing. However, I desired to know more than if the land flooded, and I was interested in the history. When I am spending my life savings, it's important that I know exactly what I am spending it on. I didn't want to make my home on land with a sorted past. Sometimes, that can come back and bite you. Did you know there were several Civil War battles fought in this area? I found that fascinating. And, because I have an inquisitive nature, I was curious about the people who owned the land. That type of stuff."

Trixie studied Martha for a beat. "You don't strike me as a superstitious type. You're always so pragmatic."

"Where did you get the idea I'm superstitious? I do not believe in supernatural beings."

"Oh. Well, never mind," said Trixie.

"So, what caused the Jeffries' home to burn down?" asked Kathleen.

"The house was abandoned. Initially, officials thought the fire was started by kids, but then they found human remains. Unfortunately, the remains were that of Richard Jeffries, the property owner."

"That's terrible," said Kathleen, her eyes widening to the size of small saucers. "Was the fire...accidental?"

Martha gave a little shrug. "Initially, there was some debate as to how the fire started. Ultimately, arson investigators determined an accelerant was used. Mr. Jeffries' body was so severely burned the only way they were able to identify him was through dental records."

"Was anyone arrested?" asked Trixie.

Martha shook her head. "Based on the investigator's report, it was assumed Mr. Jeffries may have started the fire."

"Why would he do that?" said Kathleen.

"According to Inez, my co-worker, there was speculation he may have committed suicide. Another vein of conjecture was he did it for the insurance money. However, I was unable to find any proof to support that claim."

Kathleen shuddered. "What a horrible way to die."

"Who else would have benefitted from the insurance money?" asked Trixie.

"According to the newspaper, he had a daughter, but officials were unable to locate her. I'm uncertain if she was the beneficiary."

"If the house was abandoned," said Trixie, "Where was Mr. Jeffries living?"

"He was a resident of a local nursing home. Apparently, he left the home without anyone's knowledge. Eventually, his death was ruled an accident. After that, the whole incident just disappeared. Very strange."

"Where was the house located?" asked Kathleen.

"Actually, we're walking near the area where the home place once stood." Martha stopped and pointed to an area a hundred yards to the right and just before the tree line. "Do you see the cylindrical stone structure?" Both women nodded. "That's what is left of the family's well. Back in the day, that well provided water to the main house and several other outbuildings. It's slightly larger than the typical well of that era. But it had to be to provide enough water for multiple structures. At the time, the aquifer that fed the well was quite robust. If you look further to the right, you'll notice the brick rubble. That was the fireplace and all that is left of the main house."

"I've lived in Brookville my entire life and never knew any of the history," said Kathleen. "The Brookville properties are so beautiful and idyllic. It seems unfathomable to think about the battles and suffering that occurred on this land." She shivered. "And poor Mr. Jeffries burned to death in that old house. So sad." Kathleen stopped walking. "You don't think this land is cursed or, worse, haunted, do you?"

Trixie rolled her eyes. "Kathleen, don't be silly. I imagine if we went back far enough in the history of any land, we'd find tragedy."

Kathleen shook her head. "And here we are, snooping around and digging into someone else's tragedy. It isn't normal for three middle-aged women to be trotting down to the local crime scene to snoop around. I'm concerned about us. If my children saw me, they'd seriously wonder about my sanity. And my son, oh good Lord, I can hear him now. He'd have lots to say about my lack of judgment and inability to be on my own."

Trixie spun around and grabbed Kathleen's shoulders. "May I remind you, you agreed to this crazy idea? And quit letting your children or anyone else determine who you are and what you do. You are an intelligent woman. I'll concede this may not be typical behavior for middle-aged women, and some might question our reasoning, but it is not crazy. Our logic is sound—more or less."

"I think you're splitting hairs," said Kathleen.

Trixie linked her arm with Kathleen's. "Maybe, but that's my story." She gave Kathleen's arm a little squeeze. "Now, let's get this over with before I change my mind."

As they approached the crime scene, remnants of yellow police tape tied to a few of the trees fluttered in the late morning breeze. Tree leaves rustled, and dapples of sunlight danced on the trail.

The women stood silently, looking at the spot where they'd found Camille's body 24 hours earlier. The soil was churned up with a multitude of footprints. Small amounts of plaster crusted around a few of them. Dried blood spotted the leaves of the nearby undergrowth. Kathleen vigorously rubbed at the gooseflesh that appeared on her arms. She kicked at a clump of weeds with the toe of her sneaker. "Sitting on your porch this morning with coffee and a cinnamon roll, this seemed like a good idea. But now…."

Her eyes darted from the dried blood spatter to the shadow-filled woods. "Now, I'm not so sure. It feels creepy and unsafe." She glared at Martha. "You shouldn't have told us about poor Mr. Jeffries' burned remains. Now, I'm even more freaked out."

"You are overreacting. It's not like it happened last week. That was sixteen years ago."

"Yeah, but I've watched those ghost shows on television where bad things happen on the land, and it holds on to all that evil and sadness. Then, when the next tenants arrive, they're haunted by some malevolent spirit, and it follows them forever." Kathleen shook her head. "I don't want anything to do with that. We shouldn't be here."

Trixie and Martha stared at her. "Ghosts do not exist," said Martha. "I didn't realize you were prone to hysteria and superstition."

Kathleen straightened her shoulders. "I'm not superstitious, nor am I hysterical. But I will admit to being concerned."

Trixie lifted her pant leg. "We're fine. I've brought protection."

"I don't think a gun is going to do much to stop a ghost," said Kathleen.

Trixie struggled to control the eye roll. "We're here now, so let's get on with it. Martha, you're the expert. How should we proceed?"

Martha examined the area for a moment and then moved into the brush. "This is a good place to look for some undetected piece of evidence. I'll start here.

"Watch out for snakes," said Kathleen.

Martha lifted her booted foot in the air. "I came prepared." She looked at Kathleen's and Trixie's sneaker-clad feet. "You two are the ones who should watch out for snakes."

Kathleen's eyes darted to the underbrush. "Oh, I don't know about this. I hate snakes. Really, we should go back. What if the murderer returns?"

Martha pushed the brush to the side. "It is highly unlikely the murderer will come back this soon. He or she would've been more interested in watching the police and forensic teams doing their investigation yesterday. I doubt we need to be concerned—at least, not yet."

Kathleen squeaked, "Not yet? What does that mean?"

Trixie gave Kathleen a reassuring smile. "We're fine."

"Kathleen, why don't you check out the trails and surrounding area leading to the crime scene." Martha turned to Trixie. "And you should search the area where the body was found. Sift through the soil and check the underbrush. It's possible forensics missed something. If you find anything of interest, don't touch it." Martha patted her fanny pack. "I've got a fresh supply of gloves. We must preserve the evidence."

The women split up, each moving into their designated search area. Trixie walked slowly around the site where Camille's body was found. She studied the disrupted soil and then knelt on the soft earth. Pulling the knapsack from her shoulders, she retrieved a small trowel and sifter. Starting at the edge of the trail, Trixie excavated and sifted the soil. She made her way toward the tangle of underbrush. It was slow, tedious work, and she wondered about the futility of the effort.

After an hour of sifting, Trixie sat back on her heels and stretched. Pain shot through her lower back and down into her right leg. She stood, stretched again, and the pain eased. She'd managed to sift through the bulk of the area and had found nothing. Sweat rolled down her face and dripped off the end of her nose. Trixie brushed it away, streaking dirt across her cheek.

In the distance, she heard approaching footsteps. They were coming fast. Someone was running in their direction. She scanned the wooded area but saw no one. Trixie pulled the revolver from the ankle holster and held it at her side. "We've got company."

Chapter Eight

Trixie pointed to the bend in the trail where a tall, twenty-something athletic woman rounded the curve. Her blond hair was pulled into a ponytail, and she was dressed in a bright pink form-fitting tank top, black spandex capris, and matching pink and black running shoes. Trixie relaxed and slid the revolver into the back of her waistband. Martha and Kathleen moved beside her.

The blonde slowed to a stop and glanced at the remnants of yellow crime scene tape, then turned her attention to the women. "Oh, my gosh, is this where Camille's body was found? Are you with the forensics team?"

"No. Who are you?" asked Trixie.

"Brittney Fields. This property is for Brookville residents only. So, who *are* you?"

"Brookville residents, just like you."

"Right," said Brittney.

"It's so sad what happened to Camille. Did you know her?" asked Trixie.

"Yeah, she was an employee of the Corporation. We worked together, occasionally."

"I'm sorry for your loss. Were you close?"

"Ah, no, we weren't friends." Brittney shifted her weight. "If this is a crime scene and you obviously aren't with forensics, what *are* you doing here? And who exactly are you?"

"You said your last name was Fields? Are you related to Dan Fields? Isn't he one of the co-owners of Brookville?" asked Trixie.

"Yes, he's my husband." Brittney's eyes narrowed suspiciously. "Do you know him?"

Interesting. Not a woman who trusted her man. Trixie shook her head. "I haven't met him, just know the name from the condominium's marketing."

Brittney looked down at her perfectly manicured fingernails. "He's had a lot to contend with lately, and Camille's death has added to his worries. It's been overwhelming, to say the least." Her lips curved into a smile that didn't quite reach her eyes.

"Do you live at the Brookville Condos?" asked Trixie.

Brittney smoothed back her hair. "No way, we live in the Brookville Country Club estates."

"I feel like I've seen you before," said Kathleen.

"You probably have. I'm always doing things around the condos to help Dan. I give tours around the property, show potential buyers the condominium model, and work with groups to put on events. I'm here all the time."

"Oh," said Kathleen, her expression pensive.

"And, if you're a frequent user of the trails, you may have seen me running."

Trixie said, "Funny, I run the trails just about every day, and I've never seen you. Maybe we could run together—especially now with the murder."

"Unless you're training for a triathlon, I don't think so. I doubt you could keep up."

"Wow, a triathlon. That must be exciting and a lot of work," said Trixie. "Have you participated in one before?"

"This will be my fourth. After winning the Ms. Fitness America title, I needed something new to challenge me."

Trixie's eyes widened. "Really? Ms. Fitness America. Nice. You're quite the athlete."

Brittney smiled, showing perfect white teeth. "If I want to keep my man happy, I have to stay in shape." The smile faded. "So, why *are* you women digging around at a crime scene?"

Brittney was like a dog with a bone. She wasn't going to let it go. Trixiewas searching her mind for a reasonable explanation when Martha stepped forward.

"I have great friends who indulge my attraction to forensics and all things crime-related. They came with me so I would not be poking around the crime scene alone." Martha gave Brittney a concerned look. "You know, until law enforcement finds Camille's killer, you should be careful." She slowly shook her head. "A young woman running all by herself in the woods— probably not a good idea." Martha's eyes darted around the area. "There are ample places for a person to conceal themselves." She lowered her voice. "Besides, no one knows if the murderer will return—sometimes they do."

Brittney's eyes shifted to the shadows. "Yeah, I guess you're right. Anyway, I'm cooling down too much; I've got to get back to my run." She gave Martha a curious look and then took off down the trail at a slow jog.

Martha waved. "It was nice meeting you."

Trixie turned to Kathleen. "What's bothering you about Ms. Perky?"

"Nothing specifically, but Dan Fields is closer to my age. What's he doing with someone that young?"

"Kathleen, don't look so shocked, it happens. An older man seeking out a younger companion is not that unusual. And, if he's got money, a young girl can overlook a big belly and wrinkles. I guess you could say it's a win-win."

"You sound like a woman who might have some experience in that area."

"That would be husband number two. I was looking for a distraction after Sean died. He was a nice man but too old for me. The marriage didn't last long." She watched Brittney disappear down the trail. "I hope Dan Fields is working out because that woman could seriously hurt him."

Martha blew out a loud, exasperated breath. "Could you people focus for just one moment?"

"Yes, and thanks for stepping up to deflect Brittney's questions," said Trixie. "That was brilliant."

Martha pursed her lips. "Not trying to deflect. I wanted to get rid of her. Now, focus, please. I'm uncertain if this is relevant, but I found a spool of fishing line."

"Where?" asked Trixie.

Martha pointed in the direction of the two large oak trees. "It was lying on the ground beside one of those trees." The women walked over to the oaks. Laying at the base of the tree was a spool of fishing line. Several feet of line had been unwound from the spool.

"It looks new," said Kathleen. "Maybe someone was going fishing and dropped it."

"Doubtful," said Martha. "The lake is not near this end of the trail."

"Maybe we should call Deputy Nelson. It might be nothing, but at least he could check it for fingerprints," said Trixie.

"That seems a logical course of action." Martha looked at Kathleen.

Trixie draped her arm over Kathleen's shoulders. "You're making the call."

"Me? Why me?"

Martha grinned. "Deputy Nelson likes you. Me and Trixie, not so much."

Chapter Nine

Kathleen pulled her cell and a white business card from her pocket and stared at it. Martha looked down at the card. "You brought Deputy Nelson's number with you?"

"I wanted to be prepared in case we needed help. Why can't one of you call him?"

"We've already been over this," said Trixie. "The deputy likes you better than us. So, dial the number and put it on speaker."

Kathleen pulled her cell from her pocket. She glared at Trixie and Martha, then punched in the numbers and put the phone on speaker. "It's rung four times. I'm hanging up."

Deputy Nelson's deep voice came over the phone. Kathleen froze. Trixie motioned for her to talk. "Ah, yes, um, Deputy, this is Kathleen Avery. You know, the one who found the body."

"Yes, ma'am. I recall." His voice shifted from professional to a more genial tone. "This is a pleasant surprise. Is everything okay?"

"It is, but I, well, we, have something to show you. It's possible what we found could be relevant to the case. Could you meet us at the crime scene?" There was a long pause. "Deputy, are you there?"

He exhaled. "I'm here." Gone was the genial tone. "I'm assuming you ladies are there now?"

Kathleen gave a nervous laugh. "We were out walking and just happened to go by the crime scene. And that's where we found it." Silence again. "Deputy?"

"What did you find?" Nelson's voice was tinged with irritation.

"A spool of fishing line. We think you should come and get it."

"Fishing line. That's what you found? Ms. Avery, you realize I'm a busy man. I don't have time to chase down every would-be clue."

"Deputy Nelson, this could be important." Kathleen made a face at Trixie and Martha.

"Fine. I'll be there shortly." He disconnected.

Kathleen looked at her phone. "That was rude. He didn't even say goodbye. You don't think he'll arrest us for tampering with a crime scene, do you?"

"He and the forensic team have finished processing the scene," said Martha. "Besides, he should thank his lucky stars we came along and found potential evidence."

A short while later, they heard the crunch of tires on the gravel service road. Nelson and a compact, broad-shouldered female deputy carrying a black case got out of the car and walked toward them. "So where exactly is this spool of fishing line?"

Trixie ignored the question and held out her hand to the female deputy. "I'm Trixie Tanner, and these are my friends, Martha Kline and Kathleen Avery."

The deputy shook hands. Her dark hair was pulled into a tight knot at the nape of her neck. Williams was imprinted on the metal plate pinned to her left uniform shirt pocket. "Yes, ma'am. I've heard quite a bit about you ladies."

Trixie looked at Nelson. "I'm sure you have."

"If you're done with the social graces, can we get on with the business part of this event?" asked Nelson.

"Are you always so grumpy?" asked Kathleen.

"No, ma'am. I'm generally a very pleasant man." He glanced at Trixie. "Sometimes people just irritate me. So, where's this fishing line?"

Martha led the deputies to the large oak trees. She pointed to the spool of fishing line lying on the ground. "There, beside the tree. If you'll notice, it appears someone has unwound several feet." She paused and looked from the oak tree to the one directly across the trail. "Interesting."

"What's interesting?" asked Nelson.

"Do you suppose the intent was to string the line across the trail to clothesline someone?" asked Martha.

"You've been reading too much true crime," said Nelson. "Williams, take some photos and then dust the spool for prints."

Deputy Williams pulled a camera from the black box and took several photos of the spool of fishing line, then removed a brush and black fingerprint powder from the box and dusted the spool. She frowned.

"What's wrong?" asked Nelson.

"No prints. I would expect an item such as this to have multiple prints, but it's been wiped clean."

Nelson rubbed his chin and looked at the spool. "Huh. That's odd."

Kathleen looked from Nelson to Williams and then to Trixie. "What does that mean?"

"It means a thank you is in order," said Trixie.

Nelson glared at Trixie for a moment and then said, "Right. Thanks. Williams, bag it, and let's go."

Kathleen watched the deputies get into the sheriff's sedan and drive away. "That has to be the rudest man I've ever met. Just goes to show, good looks don't mean a good person."

"So, you do think he's attractive," said Trixie.

"I didn't say that. I'm hungry. Let's get lunch."

Trixie looked at her watch. "I'll drive, but I need to stop at the mail center and check my mailbox first."

A short while later, Trixie pulled her red Mercedes into the parking lot of the Brookville condominium mail center. It was a small building with cream siding and green trim. A flagpole stood in the center of a small patch of freshly mowed lawn at the front of the building. A crowd gathered around it. The looks on their faces were worried and fearful.

Trixie unbuckled her seat belt. "I wonder what's going on. Stay here." She got out of the car and walked toward the crowd.

As she approached, a tall, lanky man said, "I heard she was found on one of the trails."

Another man wearing a blue ball cap said, "My neighbor works for EMS;

he said her throat was cut."

"What is law enforcement doing to find her killer?" asked a gray-haired woman. "I don't feel safe here."

"My brother-in-law works for the construction company that's building the new Brookville condos. He told us a skeleton was uncovered at the construction site the same day the woman was found. The sheriff's office ordered the workers to leave and to shut down the site until their investigation was finished."

Skeletal remains? Trixie hadn't heard about that discovery. Why hadn't there been anything on the news? The morning they'd found Camille, Trixie recalled hearing one of the deputies telling Nelson that Doctor Stone was at another crime scene. Had he been called to the construction site?

A woman in her mid-forties wearing jeans and a red blouse said, "This is very concerning, and I'm worried. What's the condominium association doing about providing extra security? I was assured this was a safe area, but now, I'm not so sure."

The seed Martha planted days earlier sprouted and took root. "Excuse me, I don't mean to eavesdrop. While all of this is concerning, we can't wait for the condominium association or the Sheriff to do something. We need to be proactive." The crowd gathered around Trixie.

The gray-haired woman said, "What did you have in mind?"

"Self-defense classes. My friends and I can arrange for a trainer to teach classes on-site. They would provide us with basic self-defense skills."

"What do you know about self-defense?" asked the tall, lanky man.

Trixie turned toward him. "Probably more than you. But as I said, if there's enough interest, we'd hire an instructor. I'm hoping to enlist someone from the Sheriff's office." Trixie turned back to the crowd. "Are you interested? Would you support the classes?"

Everyone talked at once. "Where will they be? Is there a charge?"

The gray-haired woman shouted over the voices, "Where do we sign up? How many classes a week?"

Trixie waved them into silence. "I'm working on smoothing out the details. Once that's done, I'll post fliers with more information. By the way, my name is Trixie Tanner."

The lanky man squinted at her. "Hey, didn't you find the dead woman?"

"Yes, my friends and I found her." Before anyone could ask more questions, Trixie said, "It was quite horrific. I'd prefer not to talk about it. I'll post fliers here in the mail center once we've firmed up the details for the class. Sorry I can't talk longer, but I've got to go." Trixie hurried into the mail center and retrieved her mail. When she returned to her car, the crowd had dispersed.

"What was that about?" asked Kathleen.

"I followed Martha's suggestion; I've just started a self-defense class. Now, all I need is for the condo association to buy into the plan, an instructor, and a location. No problem, right?"

"So, where do you plan on holding classes?" asked Kathleen.

"She could use the clubhouse," said Martha. "No one uses it, and it is large enough to allow people to spread out."

Trixie turned to Kathleen. "See, problem solved."

"Not yet, it isn't. You still need to get Brookville Corporation to agree. And what about an instructor?"

Trixie looked out the car window and watched the last of the crowd meander away. "I'll take care of that first thing tomorrow. Besides, I've been looking for a reason to speak with Ms. Perky's husband, Dan Fields. I'd like to pick his brain." Trixie turned in her seat to face Kathleen and Martha. "Did you know they uncovered a skeleton at the construction site the same day we found Camille?"

Kathleen's hand flew to her mouth. "I told you. I told you the land was cursed."

"Kathleen, get a grip. I'm sure there is a logical explanation," said Martha. "As I mentioned earlier, Civil War battles were fought here. The remains could be quite old." Martha's eyes had the beginnings of a twinkle. "And if that is not the situation, we have another case to investigate."

Chapter Ten

The next afternoon, dressed in a navy suit and turquoise blouse, Trixie walked into the Brookville Corporate offices. Getting time with Dan Fields, co-owner of Brookville Corporation, had taken a bit more effort than she'd expected. But once she'd explained the extreme dissatisfaction and concern of Brookville's residents, she was given a ten-minute appointment.

The last time she'd been in the corporate office was when she purchased her condo. She had been impressed with the opulent lobby then, and now, several months later, her opinion hadn't changed. Trixie took a moment to admire the exquisite taste of the decorator. Everything about the space was sophisticated, stylish and spoke of success and money.

The walls were painted a soothing neutral color, and large oriental rugs covered the highly polished hardwood floors. Plush cream leather chairs and a large sofa wrapped in colorful fabric with a geometric design invited visitors to sit and linger. But the focal point of the lobby was a gorgeous hand-blown glass chandelier that hung from the vaulted ceiling. She was admiring the beautiful creation when the receptionist called to her.

"Can I help you?"

Trixie pointed to the chandelier. "I never tire of looking at it. The entire reception area is quite lovely. Who was the decorator?"

"Ms. Fields."

"Brittney?"

The receptionist gave a tight smile. "No. The other Ms. Fields, Sandi."

"She certainly has exceptional taste. My name is Trixie Tanner. I have an appointment with Dan Fields."

The young woman consulted the computer, then stood. "Please follow me." She led Trixie down the hall to a large corner office. Two of the walls held expansive windows overlooking the Brookville golf course. Trixie saw Sandi Field's hand in the elegant décor of the office.

Dan Fields stood. "Ms. Tanner, a pleasure to meet you." They shook hands. His nails were perfectly manicured, and his grip wasn't quite firm. An indicator of character? Dan Fields was a well-maintained tall, handsome man with a trim athletic build. He was probably in his early fifties but could easily have passed for late thirties or early forties.

"Please call me Trixie. Thanks for seeing me on such short notice." Trixie walked to one of the windows overlooking a lush green golf course. "This view is fabulous."

Dan smiled, his overly white teeth a stark contrast to his tanned complexion. "It is a great view; however, there are days it's very distracting. Sometimes, I'd rather be golfing. But you aren't here to talk about my work habits. Please, have a seat." Fields settled into a brown leather upholstered chair. "I understand you and your friends found Camille's body. I'm sorry you had to experience that. Are you okay?"

"It's something we hope to never experience again, which is why I'm here. I'm sure by now, you've received calls and emails from the residents. They're afraid and want to know that the Corporation has their best interests at heart and are willing to put precautions in place to protect them."

Dan leaned back in his chair. "We've hired a private security company, and the Sheriff's office is monitoring our community as well. Other than that, I'm not sure what else I can do."

"That's good to hear, but I think people want to be able to protect themselves. Based on conversations with some of the residents, we'd like to start a self-defense class here on the property. There appears to be a good bit of interest. By doing so it would send a message that the Corporation is being proactive, cares about their residents, and is doing everything possible to protect them. A side effect of that kind of support could be good PR for the Corporation. With a murder on Brookville's property and finding the human remains at the construction site, I'd think a little positive PR would be welcomed."

"You know about the skeleton?" Dan stood and moved to the window. "Of course, you do. Brookville is a small community, and the gossip runs rampant. I'll admit, lately, things have been stressful. When I received the call from the foreman that they'd unearthed bones at the site, I never dreamed they would be human, let alone that the site would be treated as a crime scene."

"Does law enforcement have any idea as to the identity of the remains?"

"According to the M.E., the body was wrapped in some sort of shroud, and the bones appeared to have been there for quite some time."

"That doesn't necessarily mean murder."

Dan turned to face her. "The head was missing." He returned to his chair.

"Oh," was all Trixie could muster. Several thoughts rushed through her mind. Had the victim been a casualty of a long-ago war? Or, was Kathleen right? Was there a murderer in their quiet community hunting Brookville residents?

"I hadn't had time to digest that news when I received the call that there was a murder on one of the Brookville trails." He sucked in a sharp breath. "I never dreamed it would be someone I knew, let alone Camille." Fields rubbed his temples. He looked weary. "I would appreciate you not contributing to the rumor mill regarding the skeleton. I shouldn't have shared that information."

"Of course. Does the Sheriff have any leads on who might have killed Camille?

He shook his head and picked up an oval glass paperweight from his desk—rolled it between his hands.

"Were you and Camille close?"

Fields' facial features softened. "She was my dearest and closest friend. We've known each other for many years. She was the one person on this earth I trusted. I'm going to miss her desperately."

Interesting. Wonder how Brittney felt about that? "Dan, was Camille involved with anyone?"

He stopped rolling the paperweight between his hands and looked up at Trixie. "Not that I know of."

"Did she have any enemies?"

"No. Trixie, you seem to have an intense interest in Camille. Why is that?"

"We found her body. Nobody should be left to die alone like that, and my friends and I are invested in helping to find her murderer." Trixie studied Dan's face, looking for guilt or remorse, something. All she saw was sorrow and loss. "What about the skeletal remains? Are there any leads?"

"Unfortunately, without the head, it's more of a challenge to identify the victim. Anyway, you're right. Brookville Corporation could use some positive PR. You've presented a good plan." Fields sat the paperweight to the side. "Do you have an instructor in mind, and where would the class be held?"

"I have a lead on an instructor at the Sheriff's office. Having someone from law enforcement will provide credibility to the quality of the instruction." There was no instructor, but she was confident one could be found. "The clubhouse would be an ideal location."

"Would you expect the corporation to take care of the advertising?"

"No, I will handle that, but I'll need a small stipend to cover ancillary expenses such as paying the instructor and the cost of printing fliers. I've created a rudimentary budget." She pulled a folded sheet of paper from her handbag and handed it to him.

Dan skimmed the paper. "You've really thought this out." He punched in several numbers on his calculator. "The budget is reasonable, and it's a small amount to pay for the residents to feel safer. Brookville Corporation would be happy to support the class. See my secretary on the way out. She'll make sure a check is sent to you. Once everything is settled, send me a financial accounting of how the money was spent. Let me know if you need anything else."

Trixie stood. "Dan, thank you for being so responsive and generous." She gave the room a final look. "Your ex-wife has quite the eye."

Dan looked around the room. "Yes. She really is exceptionally talented."

"Is she still in the area? I've been thinking about having my kitchen remodeled."

"Yes. Sandi lives on site." He reached into his desk drawer and retrieved a card. He handed it to Trixie. "This has her contact information. I'm sure she'd be happy to discuss any remodeling you might have in mind. As much as I'd like to continue chatting, I need to get back to my day."

"Of course. Thanks again for your time and help. I'll be back in touch with the details."

As Trixie walked to her car, she wondered about the relationship between Dan and Camille. And, for that matter, what was his relationship with his ex, Sandi? And how did Brittney feel about Sandi living so close? And what were the odds of finding a murdered woman and unidentified human remains on the same property and on the same day? Astronomical.

Chapter Eleven

On a whim, Trixie called Deputy Michelle Williams and asked her to instruct the Brookville self-defense classes. Deputy Williams had agreed and as it turned out, she taught self-defense in the evenings at the local community college and was eager to help.

Trixie poured a fresh cup of coffee and re-read the poster. Classes would start on Saturday of the following week. Per Kopy Kats' online instructions, she uploaded the document to their site. A few minutes later, she received an email letting her know copies of the flier would be ready later that afternoon.

Trixie finished her coffee, rinsed, and dried the cup, and returned it to the cabinet. She checked her watch. There was time for a run before going to the print shop. She wasn't ready to go back to the Brookville trails just yet, however, there was a park not far from the condos. It wasn't as challenging, but she wasn't looking for that today. When she finished her run, she'd drop by Kopy Kats and pick up the fliers.

Fifteen minutes later, Trixie pulled into the small parking lot of the Jeffries Memorial Park. She'd never given the name of the park much thought until now. After Martha's local history lesson, she realized in addition to the park, there were several buildings in Brookville with the Jeffries family name on them. Obviously, a prominent family and a generous benefactor to the community.

She got out of the car, walked over to a grassy area, and began her warm up. Trixie stretched slowly, giving the muscles in her back time to loosen. Earbuds in place, she started off at a slow jog. Before long, between the music and the delight of running, she was at full speed, focused on nothing but the trail and flying.

In the middle of her peace, she became aware of movement to her left. Sean's words floated to the front of her mind, "Always be aware of your surroundings." Was it another runner? She edged over, giving space for the runner to pass, but they didn't. The euphoria from moments earlier dissipated when Trixie glanced at the figure running beside her. The man was tall and muscular. His long black hair flowed freely behind him, his face hard and determined. Trixie jerked the earbuds from her ears. "What are you doing?"

Doc looked at her from the corner of his eye. "Running."

"Do you have to do it here?"

"As a matter of fact, I do. I live in this area."

Trixie increased her speed. Doc matched it. "I'm surprised you aren't running the Brookville trails."

"What exactly is that supposed to mean?"

"I didn't think a murder would keep someone like you, with your background, from the trails. Which leads me to surmise you are either possessed with common sense or a large dose of self-preservation—I'm not sure which."

Trixie stopped mid-stride, jammed her hands on her hips, and spun toward Doc. "What has that damn Nelson been telling you?"

"You're an interesting woman with an interesting past."

"Yeah, I get that a lot. What do you want?"

"What makes you think I want anything? I'm just making conversation and commenting on your good judgment."

"Let me make myself clear. I don't give a rat's ass what you think about my past or my good judgment. However, you've imposed yourself into my space, which gives me the right to tell you what I think."

The corners of his mouth tipped into a smirk. "Which is?"

Trixie hated smirking. Everything about him, body language, and his attitude annoyed her.

She took a step closer. "Without a doubt, you are the most vexing, rude, condescending man I have ever had the misfortune to meet. There's really nothing else we need to discuss." She turned and walked in the direction of her car.

Doc called, "Ms. Tanner."

She stopped. Gave him her back.

"I look forward to seeing you again."

Trixie lifted her right hand and gave him the finger. Not an overly mature action, but deeply satisfying. She took off running. She could've sworn she heard him laugh. It would be a cold day in hell before she gave him any more of her time.

* * *

Trixie parked in front of Kopy Kats and went inside. There was a small line of customers waiting. She took her place in line behind two middle-aged men. One had a navy ball cap perched on the back of his head. The bill of the cap faced her, the image of a large fish emblazoned across the front. Bass Pro-shop was embroidered beneath the fish. The other man wore a red tee shirt with a large-mouthed fish printed on the back. That, too, must have been a large-mouthed bass.

The man in the navy ball cap turned to his friend. "What's the Sheriff doing about this mess? We got a nice quiet town, and now in one day, there's a murder, and they say them bones they found is human. And," he lowered his voice, "they say the head is missing. What's that about?"

Trixie had been going over her to-do list for the self-defense class, but now her full attention was focused on the conversation in front of her. She took a small step closer.

"Don't know," said Red Shirt. "Maybe a dog dragged it off."

Ball Cap shook his head. "I was told them bones was wrapped in a sheet." He scratched his forehead, and the cap wobbled. "Naw, there's something going on. My informant also said the medical examiner was bringing in some doctor from the university to look at them bones."

"Hell, what's that gonna tell 'em?"

Ball Cap shrugged. "They think them bones is old. Mabel, from down at the Piggly Wiggly, said they think they might have somethin' to do with a cold case."

"How old do bones gotta be before they a cold case?"

Ball Cap rolled his eyes. "You dummy, don't you watch Forensic Files? It's a cold case 'cause the cops ain't found the murderer."

Red Shirt rubbed the stubble on his chin. "You remember that girl that disappeared? We was maybe thirteen, fourteen years old when it happened?"

Ball Cap nodded. "She was a couple years older than us. I think she might've been in my sister's high school." Trixie took another step closer.

Red Shirt shrugged. "Maybe. Funny, don't know what made me think of her. I guess all the commotion in town reminded me of when she disappeared. I remember the Sheriff gathered a search party to look for the girl; my daddy joined them, and momma wouldn't let us kids outta her sight. The men spent days searching the woods, abandoned houses and even dredged the lake, but they never found her."

"Some of the kids in the neighborhood heard she might have run off with a boy from another town, and others said she was murdered by a vagrant." The clerk called the men, and the conversation ended.

Trixie was still thinking about the missing girl when she returned to her car. She thought about Kathleen worrying that the land was cursed. "Ridiculous. Superstitious crap," said Trixie, jamming the key into the ignition. And then Martha's words floated into her mind. She'd told them that Brookville Corporation bought the land from the Jeffries family. Had someone long ago buried a secret there? How long had the remains been hidden on that land? Was it possible it was the missing girl? And if so, why was she murdered? Curiosity tickled the edges of Trixie's mind. The library would have archives of old news articles. Maybe she could find more information there. Excitement fluttered in her stomach, and she could almost hear Sean saying, *Careful, Trix.*

Chapter Twelve

Trixie pulled into a space of the recently built parking deck of the Brookville City Library. The newly renovated library boasted freshly painted walls in bright, inviting colors. Drab carpet had been replaced with gray vinyl planking, and new lighting fixtures gave the space a light, airy feel. The library had gone from looking like a dark medieval dungeon to an upbeat, enticing place to spend time browsing through the wide array of books.

Kathleen took in the scenery as they walked through the library entrance. "Gosh, I haven't been here since they renovated. It's lovely. And exactly why are we here?"

Trixie hooked her arm with Kathleen's. "Let's find Martha, then I'll tell you both."

Kathleen leaned in closer to Trixie. "Does this have anything to do with murder?"

Trixie turned innocent green eyes toward Kathleen. Was she that transparent? Obviously, she needed to work on her powers of deception and persuasion. "Camille's murder? No, of course not."

"If not that, then what?" The words had barely left Kathleen's lips when her eyes widened with realization, and she shook her head. "No. I'm not doing it. I absolutely refuse. We are not investigating those old bones. That's a job for law enforcement."

"Not doing what?" asked Martha.

"Jesus, Mary, and Joseph," said Trixie. "Must you always sneak up on us? You're too quiet."

"Hate to state the obvious, but we are in a library," said Martha. "I'd like to remind *you* to be quiet. And why are you here? Has something happened?" Her eyes twinkled with anticipation. She whispered, "Has there been another murder?"

"No. Is there somewhere we can talk privately?" asked Trixie.

"Sure. We can use the break room."

Once settled around the small coffee-stained table, Martha said, "So what's so important you had to interrupt my workday?"

"I'd like to know that as well," said Kathleen. "After all, I was practically kidnapped."

Trixie looked at Kathleen. "Must you be so dramatic?" She leaned forward in her chair. "I needed to tell you what I learned today when I was at Kopy Kats." She looked over her shoulder and then proceeded to tell Martha and Kathleen about the conversation she'd overheard. "Which brings me to the reason we're here. We should search through the archives for information on the missing girl." She looked expectantly at both women. "So, what do you think?"

Kathleen shook her head. Martha said, "Why would we want to do that?"

"Aren't you the least bit curious? You must admit two murders on the same property is more than coincidental. Don't you want to know what happened?"

Kathleen folded her arms over her chest. "No, I don't. Besides, we don't know if that poor soul was murdered. Those remains could have been from an old family cemetery, and for that matter, those bones could date back to Civil War times. Maybe it was a soldier who died on the battlefield. You know, the Jeffries' land was an old plantation. Isn't that right, Martha?"

Martha said, "That's correct." She looked at Trixie. "Why would your mind make a leap to murder?"

"Because, when they found the skeleton, it had been wrapped in a sheet."

"And?" said Kathleen.

"And the head was missing."

"You should've led off with that," said Martha. "We could've saved valuable time. How did you come by this information?"

55

"Dan Fields mentioned it when we met, and there were two men in Kopy Kats who were also talking about it. Besides, if Mabel down at the Piggly Wiggly knows about it, it's got to be true." Kathleen and Martha stared at her.

"Who?" asked Kathleen.

"That was a joke. I guess you had to be there."

"Perhaps the head was dragged off by wild animals," said Kathleen.

"I don't think so. According to Dan, the shroud was intact. It was fortunate the construction workers were using shovels instead of the backhoe at the time. So, the burial site was basically undisturbed, which again leads me to think foul play." Trixie turned to Martha. "Now, will you take us to the archives?"

"Fine. Follow me, but I cannot help you. I have a job to do, and the expectation is that I will perform my duties to get paid."

"That's fine, and I appreciate your help. Come on, Kathleen. We've got work to do."

Martha led the women to the lower level of the library. It was dark and smelled damp and musty. Kathleen wrinkled her nose. "Obviously, the money ran out before they could refurbish this area. Do you know if there's black mold down here?"

Martha stopped abruptly. Trixie slammed into her back. Martha turned and glared at Kathleen. "Either you want the information, or you don't. I have no control over the décor or the environment."

"Okay. Don't be so touchy. It was more an observational comment than criticism."

Martha gave a curt nod. "However, to allay your fears, the mold was eradicated from this area."

"Good to know." Trixie pointed to an enormous archaic machine. "What is that?" She walked over to it. Sharp teeth-like blades encircled large cylinders, and a conveyor belt ran beneath them. "This looks extremely dangerous. What does it do?"

"That is Wendigo," said Martha.

"A what?" asked Kathleen. "I've never heard of a machine called that. What is it?"

"A wendigo comes from Algonquian mythology. It's a cannibalistic monster that's always hungry. Inez and I thought it was a hoot to name the shredder. Just a little whimsy to lighten the workday."

Trixie wasn't surprised Martha chose to name the antiquated shredder after a mythological eating machine. Made all the sense in the world.

Kathleen turned unsure eyes in the direction of the shredder. "It doesn't look safe. What does it shred, small cars?"

"Its primary use is to shred large cardboard boxes for recycling. Occasionally, books that are too damaged to be repaired and other paper items are run through Wendigo."

"It doesn't look up to code?" said Kathleen. "Someone could get hurt; there's no protection from those blades."

"Doubtful that it is up to code. If someone was not paying attention, yes, I imagine it could be quite dangerous. However, since you will not be operating the machine, you should be safe." Martha pointed to a dimly lit corner of the room. "The microfiche readers are over there. Should I assume neither of you know how to use them?"

"Let's just say it's been a while. We could use a refresher," said Trixie.

Martha blew out a frustrated breath. "It's not hard." She gave Trixie and Kathleen rudimentary instructions. "Now, is there anything else you need?"

"No. I think you've covered it. Thanks," said Trixie.

Martha turned to leave and then hesitated. She turned back to Trixie and Kathleen. "You do have a date range of when this girl disappeared, right?"

"Not exactly," said Trixie. "I thought we'd just take a stab at a date and flip through local newspapers."

"There are thousands of newspaper articles. You need a time frame to help narrow your search. Must I do everything for you two?" Kathleen opened her mouth. Martha held up a finger. "That was rhetorical." Martha pulled a walkie-talkie from her pocket. "Inez, could you come downstairs to microfiche? There are a couple of clients who could use your valuable input regarding Brookville history."

"Who's Inez?" asked Trixie.

"I believe I may have mentioned her before. She is a co-worker. Inez knows all there is to know about Brookville. If anyone can give you an idea of when the girl disappeared, it'll be her. She boasts of having an autobiographical memory. I'll admit, at times, Inez is impressive."

"What in the world is that?" asked Kathleen.

"Individuals with an autobiographical memory can recall past events with almost photographic detail. There are only a handful of such people in the world with this ability."

"Wow, that's quite a gift," said Trixie.

A few minutes later, a tall, slender woman walked toward them. She wore a black ankle-length full skirt and a turquoise short-sleeved sweater. Long multi-colored beads swayed with each step she took. Her gray hair was short, unruly, and streaked with purple. Bangles three inches deep jangled from each wrist, and huge dangly earrings swung from her lobes. Inez said, "How can I help you?"

"A young girl disappeared from this area approximately thirty years ago," said Trixie. "I have the impression she might have been in high school at the time of her disappearance. Does that sound familiar?"

"This must be about the bones found at the Brookville construction site. It's the hot gossip in town. Well, that and the murder of that poor woman— something else I get to remember. Anyway, I'm sure I can help. I've lived in Brookville all my life. Let's see, I was a junior in high school when," she paused, closed her eyes. "Yes, when Sara Adams disappeared."

Inez walked over to a wall of ceiling-to-floor shelving. Each shelf was filled with four-inch black binders. She removed a binder from the second row. "Each of these books contains microfiche sheets for specific date ranges. Sara disappeared around 1986. The information you are looking for may be in this volume." Inez pulled a sheet from the book and placed it into the reader. "And if memory serves me," she looked up, "and it usually does, the incident happened in the Spring around the middle of April."

Trixie couldn't help herself; she glanced at Martha, who was looking unimpressed.

Inez scrolled through the articles for a moment and then leaned back in the chair. "Voila. Here it is."

Kathleen's eyes widened. "That's impressive."

"It's a gift—most of the time," said Inez.

"Show off," muttered Martha.

* * *

Trixie and Kathleen had scrolled through several of the microfiche sheets containing news articles recounting the search for Sara Adams. Kathleen stopped scrolling. "I was astonished at Inez's ability to recall the dates of the girl's disappearance. She was quite impressive. Do you think it bothers Martha that Inez has this amazing memory?"

Trixie leaned back and stretched her shoulders. "It shouldn't. Martha has other talents, and when it comes to forensics, her wealth of knowledge is equally impressive."

"I agree. I've never met anyone quite like her."

Martha dropped into the chair behind Trixie. "That was kind of you to say."

Startled, Trixie rammed her forehead into the microfiche reader. "Son of a…how are you always so quiet?" She rubbed her head.

Martha held up her foot, clad in a navy tie-up. "Crepe-soled shoes. In addition to contributing to my stealth, they're extremely comfortable." She glanced down at Trixie's feet. "And they are good for your feet. I highly recommend them. You have the beginnings of bunions. You should get a pair."

Trixie glanced down at the hot pink strappy heels covering her feet. "I'll keep that in mind."

Martha leaned over Trixie's shoulder. "Find anything interesting?"

Kathleen picked up her notepad. "Actually, we have. According to one article, Sara Adam's parents told police she planned to hang out with friends the afternoon of her disappearance. Mr. and Mrs. Adams had a social engagement they were planning to attend that evening. However, they were unable to tell police who Sara was with or where she had gone. It was late when they got home that night, so they went to bed and didn't realize Sara was missing until the following morning." Kathleen looked up. "What horrible parents. I always knew where my kids were and who they were with."

Trixie grinned. "You just think you knew. I promise you your kids had a life you knew nothing about. They told you what you wanted to hear."

"Trixie Tanner, that is an awful thing to say."

"Ask them some time. I think you might be surprised."

Martha snapped her fingers. "Ladies, back on topic. Is there anything else? Did the articles mention any of her friends?"

"Do you honestly think her friends could be suspects?"

"As I mentioned earlier, everyone is a suspect."

"Okay, no need to be snippy. There was a brief mention of some of her friends being interviewed." Kathleen scrolled through the microfiche. "Yes, here it is. Police talked with two of her friends, Emily Carter and Alexandra Jeffries." Kathleen's head jerked up. "Isn't Alexandra Richard Jeffries's daughter?"

Martha nodded. "That's correct. An interesting coincidence."

"Maybe," said Trixie. "Personally, I don't believe in coincidence. Brookville is small. The odds of these kids knowing each other was good."

"What if the skeletonized remains really are Sara Adams? We may have solved a thirty-year cold case," said Kathleen, beaming.

"Making the leap to solving the case may be a bit premature," said Trixie. "At this time, we don't know if the remains are male or female. Nor do we know the PMI."

"PMI?" said Martha. "You know about PMI?"

"What's that?" asked Kathleen.

"Postmortem interval," said Martha.

"Which means what?" asked Kathleen.

"PMI is the time that has passed since the victim's death."

Kathleen turned to Trixie. "I understand how Martha knows that, but how do you?"

Trixie chastised herself. She had to be more careful. "I told you, I read a lot of true crime."

"Sometimes, Trixie, I'm not sure we know everything about you."

"I'm an open book. Besides, do any of us really know everything about our friends?" She turned back to the microfiche reader. Her mind churned. Was it possible they had found Sara Adams? Trixie couldn't imagine the peace it would bring the family. Hope rose inside her. She tamped down the optimism and pushed logic to the front. The odds were against the remains belonging to the girl, but what if they were?

Chapter Thirteen

Trixie touched up her makeup and scrutinized her reflection in the mirror. The navy linen slacks and pastel pink silk tank she'd worn to the library were wrinkled and limp. She smoothed her hands over the wrinkles, but they bounced right back. Trixie briefly entertained the notion of changing clothes, but she was too hungry to care. Besides, she barely knew anyone in Brookville, so what did it matter? She pulled a brush through her hair and grabbed her car keys.

Trixie's stomach growled at the thought of Emile's delicious shrimp and grits, and not for the first time, she was grateful he'd set up shop in Brookville. When she walked through the entrance of Emile's Café, she was stunned at the number of people waiting for a table. For a moment, she considered going elsewhere. But in the end, Emile's shrimp and grits won out.

Squeezing through the crowd of people, Trixie made her way to the hostess station. Kay, the hostess, waved. "Hey Trixie, just you tonight?"

"Yeah, what's going on? There isn't usually a wait at this hour."

"We had several large parties, and they've been slow to leave." Kay looked down at the seating chart. "It's going to be at least a thirty-minute wait. Is that okay?"

Trixie looked around the restaurant. "Sure. I'll wait at the bar."

She made her way into the bar area of the restaurant, found an empty chair toward the end of the highly polished counter, and ordered a Riesling. A television hung in the corner behind the bar. The scene of a camera panning across the landscape of a construction site caught her attention. It was the Brookville Corporation construction site. A white tent was set up in the background, and several law enforcement officers were stationed around the perimeter. Trixie motioned to the bartender, "Hey, could you turn up the volume?"

The news anchor, a young woman with perfect blond hair and makeup, said, "An anthropologist from the university has been brought in to examine the remains found at the Brookville construction site. A Sheriff's office spokesperson confirmed the remains are human." The woman said, "Now, in other news...."

Trixie took a sip of the wine and nibbled on a few nuts. She felt a hand on the back of her chair.

Doc's deep voice said, "I'm sure you have a theory."

Trixie gritted her teeth and turned. "Dr. Stone, I'm surprised to see you again. Are you following me?"

"Ms. Tanner, given that this town is very small, the odds of us running into one another are stacked against us." He motioned to the bartender. "Crown Royal on the rocks."

"There are other restaurants. Perhaps you should go to one of them."

"There are, but Emile's has the best shrimp and grits I've ever eaten. My decision to come here wasn't impulsive." He spun his chair to face her. "Ms. Tanner, I've had a very long day, and I'm looking forward to a quiet dinner and a few drinks."

"As am I, but you're the one who talked to me." She turned her back to him. Begrudgingly, she had to admit Doc looked good. In fact, handsome in a roguish way. Trixie took a long pull from the wine glass.

Doc leaned in close. "I think we may have gotten off on the wrong foot. I apologize if I was overly harsh with you and your friends."

Trixie spun to face him. "Doctor Stone, there is no need to apologize. We deserved your rage, and as for your snarky comments...well, not unexpected."

Doc studied her for a beat. "Rage and snark. Interesting choice of words. Ms. Tanner, I'm a perfectionist where my job is concerned. I take all aspects of it quite seriously and work hard to preserve the evidence so I can be the voice for the deceased. I hope you'll understand that my *rage and snark* wasn't personal."

"And what about our little encounter this morning at the park? Your behavior was less than stellar, no snark but rude."

"I'm not sure I agree with the rude comment. I think it was more curiosity."

When he wasn't yelling or being ill-mannered, Doc was attractive, and his deep voice with that slow, charming southern drawl was having the same effect on her as a good Tennessee whiskey. His words went down smoothly, leaving her with a warm burn that penetrated deep. She felt her cheeks flush and was thankful for the dim lighting. She gave herself a mental shake. Get yourself together. You're weak from hunger. You haven't eaten in hours. She said, "Apology accepted."

Doc gave her a curt nod and leaned in closer. "Thank you. Now that we've got that behind us, I hope we can be friends."

She felt the heat from his body, smelled his cologne—a blend of spice and the outdoors. She met his eyes—two chips of obsidian buried beneath black brows. Laugh lines extended from the corners of his dark eyes down into his cheeks. Obviously, he was capable of smiling. Maybe even laughing. "We can try." Her stomach growled in protest to the dinner delay. She placed her hand over it and drank more wine.

"Sounds like you're more than a little hungry. I imagine all that snooping builds up an appetite." Before she could respond, the hostess called Doc's name.

He stood. "Looks like my table's ready."

She held up her glass. "Always a pleasure."

He hesitated and let out a slow breath. "I'm certain I'll regret this, but if you promise to be on your best behavior, I'd be happy for you to join me for dinner."

Her stomach gave another loud rumble. Eating with this man was a bad idea, but she was starving. She stood. "Fine. But you need to know, if I wasn't so hungry, I wouldn't be eating with you." Her mother's words rang in her ear: *be nice, Trixie*. "Thanks for asking, and I'll do my best to behave."

"Not the most gracious acceptance, but I'll take it."

He placed his hand on the small of her back. The heat from his fingers penetrated the thin material of her blouse, and her stomach gave an unexpected flutter. Not from hunger.

Once settled into a corner booth, the waitress brought them menus. Trixie shook her head. "I won't be needing that. I know what I want."

Doc motioned to Trixie. "Please, ladies first." She ordered shrimp and grits. Doc handed the waitress his menu. "I'll have the same." When the waitress left, he said, "Hard to believe, we actually have something in common."

Trixie studied his face. The smile changed his appearance completely. He looked approachable. His dark hair hung loosely around his shoulders, and he wore a light blue V-neck sweater. The color emphasized the swarthiness of his skin. His body was lean, fit, and attractive. She fidgeted in the booth seat.

"Something wrong?"

He was watching her so closely that she was acutely aware of her appearance. Why hadn't she taken a few extra minutes to put on a fresh outfit? Seemed every time she saw this man, she never looked her best. She wasn't interested. So, what did that matter? She could appreciate a man's appearance without being attracted to him, right? Trixie tucked a strand of auburn hair behind her ear. "Nope, everything's great." She sipped more wine and watched customers come and go.

"Ms. Tanner, you're less than your usual verbose self. Are you sure you're okay? Or are you so weakened from hunger that you're having trouble with communication?"

She glared at him. "My name is Trixie. Why don't you use it?"

He folded his hands around his drink and looked thoughtfully into the tumbler, then at her. "I only call my friends by first name."

She cocked her head to the side. "Okay. Well, since we're keeping this professional, let's talk shop. What have you learned about Camille's murder?"

A smile touched the corners of his mouth, and he glanced at his watch. "Impressive, you managed not to ask about the case for a whole ten minutes. I knew you wouldn't be able to get through dinner without sticking your nose where it doesn't belong. Have you always been like this, or do you reserve your quizzical bad behavior for when you're around me?"

"It's not just you. I share my bad behavior freely, and I have an unbridled curiosity. Sean always said my curiosity would get me in trouble one day."

He tipped his drink toward her. "Smart man. Is he a friend or someone special?"

"That's none of your business."

"No, it's not. But I, too, have an inquisitive nature. Apparently, another thing we have in common."

She leaned forward propping her elbows on the table and lacing her fingers together. "I'll make a deal with you. How about we do an information exchange? I'll answer questions for you if you answer some for me." Doc leaned forward. His dark eyes met hers. There was a challenge in them.

"An interesting proposition. Is this your version of "Truth or Dare? And what are the rules?"

"I have questions, and you have answers. And I'm sure I could probably answer a few of your questions. Although, for the life of me, I can't imagine what you'd want to know."

Doc chuckled. "Ms. Tanner, don't underestimate the mystery you exude. I'm game, but the cases I'm working on are off-limits, agreed?"

She folded her arms across her chest, and her chin tipped slightly upward. "I'm not sure I can promise that. I have lots of case-related questions. Perhaps we could compromise. I'm sure there are some aspects you could share."

Doc sipped the whiskey. "I'll do my best to answer what I can—within reason."

"One more thing, the questions shouldn't be overly personal or invasive."

Doc held out his hand. "Agreed. Do we have a deal?"

She tucked her hand in his. "Deal." The warmth and pressure of his fingers against her skin sent a tingle up her arm. She pulled her hand from his grasp and picked up her wine glass. "You first."

Amusement flickered across his face. "I'm sticking with my original question."

Her forehead creased. "Which was?"

"Who's Sean?"

She clucked her tongue. "That's personal. I'll answer it if I get to ask you a personal question."

"Fair enough."

"He was my first husband."

"First husband? How many times have you been married?"

Trixie waved an index finger at him. "Oh, no, that's two questions. It's my turn." She looked at him thoughtfully. "Have you been married?"

"Came close one time, but she decided I wasn't the right guy." He took another sip of the whiskey. "Now, back to my question. How many times have you been married?"

"Three."

"Trying to find Mr. Right?"

"I had Mr. Right, but he died."

Doc leaned forward; the obsidian eyes softened. "I'm sorry. How long were you married?"

"Fourteen years."

His look was penetrating and thoughtful. Trixie shifted uncomfortably. "You must've been very young."

"Twenty-two. He was thirty-three."

"Quite an age difference."

"On paper, yes, but he was my soulmate. No one thought the marriage would last, but it would've lasted a lifetime had he not gotten sick."

"That must've been very difficult to be widowed so young."

"It was a very hard time." Her voice faltered. The raw feeling of loss that surfaced surprised her. Trixie cleared her throat. "My turn. Do you date?"

Stone's eyes widened. "Why, Ms. Tanner, are you interested?"

"I think not. I just can't imagine you have much time for such a frivolous activity."

He rattled the ice in the empty tumbler. "Even crusty medical examiners need companionship."

"I imagine the pay-by-the-hour date gets expensive."

He leaned back in the booth and let out a loud, deep laugh. "And she's back. My turn. Are you working on husband number four?"

"You've got to be kidding. I just got rid of number three. I'm done with the whole marriage thing." She didn't like discussing her personal life with him. She folded her hands on the table. "I know I promised to behave, but I have a few questions related to our case."

He looked at her incredulously. "*Our* case?"

"Yes, *our* case. We were first on the scene, and you must admit Martha did an excellent job of securing the area until your guys got there."

"No, I don't have to admit that. Ms. Kline is not a forensic professional and should not have touched anything."

"But she did secure the site correctly, didn't she?"

Stone looked at the ceiling. "Fine. Beyond tampering with a crime scene, I'll concede she didn't mess anything up."

Trixie slapped the table and grinned. "Ha. Wait until I tell Martha. She'll be thrilled."

"Please don't." Stone chuckled. "She doesn't need any encouragement. So, what is your occupation?"

"Professional blogger."

"Really? You can make a living doing that?"

"I can and do. My turn. Is it true that the site where the human remains were found is being considered a crime scene?"

Hesitating, his lips pulled into a tight line. "It's possible."

"Any idea when the victim was murdered?"

"Not at this time."

"What about—"

He held up his hand. "My turn. I bet you were a real brat as a kid."

Trixie rolled her eyes. "Fine."

"Do you have children?"

"No."

"Why not?"

"Maybe I didn't want kids, or maybe Sean and I didn't get a chance to have them." She spat out the words with a vehemence that surprised her. Children weren't something she allowed herself to think about. That fell into the woulda, coulda, shoulda category—not a place she chose to dwell. The bitterness of regret rose inside her. Her eyes met his, and for a moment, she wasn't sure whether she was going to cry or run.

He watched her for a beat. "I apologize. I believe I broke the rule. That's your business, and I'm prying."

Trixie rotated her shoulders. "You did, and now it's my turn. Do you have any leads on who killed Camille?"

"You'd have to ask Nelson; that's his arena."

The waitress returned and sat steaming plates of food in front of them. "Saved by the bell," mumbled Stone.

"Don't think the food is going to save you." Trixie breathed in the fragrant aroma. Her stomach growled loudly. "This smells divine."

Stone put a forkful in his mouth. "Eat. You're obviously starving, and it tastes as good as it smells."

For a few minutes, they ate in silence. Doc motioned to the waitress. "A whiskey for me and another wine for the lady." He glanced up at Trixie. "I believe it's my turn."

"Okay. Ask your question."

"Why did you leave the ATF?"

She skewered a shrimp with her fork and slid it into her mouth, then laid the utensil on the side of her plate. Her mind raced. Did she want to talk about the past now with this man? Not really. It wasn't something she cared to revisit. There were too many painful memories—things she had put behind her. She pulled bread from the basket and met his eyes. "Nelson couldn't hold water if his life depended on it," Trixie spread butter on the roll. "I'm retired."

"Aren't you a little young to be retired? What happened? You get burned out on the job?"

"No. I got shot. Because of my injury, I was no longer able to perform my duties as a field agent. They offered me a desk job, but pushing papers wasn't something I wanted to do, so I retired." She glanced at him. Saw the question in his eyes.

"What happened?"

Trixie leaned back into the booth seat. She picked up her wine glass and gave him her best, *why the hell does it matter to you?* look. "At the time, I was working in a field office in Houston, Texas. My team and I had been surveilling a group of known gun smugglers. You know, the type of guys who sell assault rifles, rocket launchers, grenades, anything that causes destruction. We'd received information that a large transaction was going down with an overseas buyer. Everything pointed to the information being good. We raided the warehouse at dawn. The weapons were gone, but the smugglers weren't. We were ambushed. I got shot in the back. The bullet was close to my spine, and the doc said it was more dangerous to do surgery than to leave it. Unfortunately, I have some residual issues because of the bullet's location. Lucky me. I got a souvenir to remember my time there. And don't get me started about going through airport security." Trixie scooped up the last of the shrimp and grits.

Doc laid his napkin on the table. "That explains why you weren't rattled at the crime scene. What made you decide to join the ATF?"

"Sean. I was a patrol officer at a small police station. ATF was working a case that sent them to our town. I was assigned to assist, which meant I was a glorified step and fetch. I saw what the ATF agents were doing, and it was so exciting. I wanted more from my chosen profession. I must have asked Sean a million questions. He answered them all. When the case was over, I applied to the ATF." She looked up at him. "And as they say, the rest is history."

"Any regrets?"

"Not one."

"I'm curious about something," said Doc.

"What's that?"

"Explain Ms. Kline to me? Most women would have reacted very differently to finding a body. They are visibly shaken, like Ms. Avery."

Trixie laughed. "Martha is a librarian by day, and by night, she's taking classes at the community college in forensics. And she probably has an unhealthy obsession with true crime." Trixie watched the flurry of expressions flash across Doc's face.

"By the way, dinner was delicious." Trixie gave a contented sigh, then cut her eyes at Doc. "And the company, tolerable."

"Thanks for the left-handed compliment." He leaned back into the booth seat. "I'll give you credit, all-in-all, you behaved better than expected. You realize this was just a temporary truce, right?"

Trixie swirled the wine in her glass. She looked up at him. "Absolutely, and if it makes you feel better, I promise I'll continue to be annoying. If anything, you've piqued my curiosity."

Stone tossed back the last of his whiskey. "I would expect nothing less. Would you like coffee and dessert?"

"I don't think I could eat another bite."

"What if we shared one? I hear the molten lava cake is to die for."

Trixie propped her elbows on the table and looked around the room. "I don't know. Dinner is one thing, but sharing dessert could start some serious gossip. We do live in a small town where tongues love to wag."

He motioned to the waitress. "I'll take my chances. And, if you think the gossip mongers haven't noticed us eating together, you'd be sadly mistaken."

Chapter Fourteen

Trixie rubbed sleep from her eyes and shuffled into the kitchen. She sniffed the air. Coffee was ready, and it smelled fabulous. She pulled a red mug from the cabinet, filled it with the steaming brew, and took the first sip. "Yep. Way better than a fourth husband."

As she dropped bread into the toaster, thoughts of Doc slipped into her mind. She had to admit he was pleasant company, and she had enjoyed the evening. But Stone wasn't the type of man she needed in her life. Men like him were trouble.

The toast popped up, and she yanked it from the toaster. Trixie grabbed peach jam and butter from the refrigerator. Besides, she didn't need a man to make her happy. Lord knows she'd been down that road. She slapped a spoonful of jam onto the bread and took a large bite. Jam and butter dribbled down her chin. Nope, she was fine the way she was. She swiped at the dribble with her index finger and stuck it in her mouth. Trixie finished the toast and placed the dirty dish in the sink.

What she needed was to get her mind busy. She didn't feel like working on the blog even though she was behind in her posts and had several deadlines dangling in front of her.

Trixie looked around her kitchen. It was a functional space but not quite what she needed. When she'd bought the condo six months earlier, she'd promised herself she'd have the kitchen remodeled to suit her needs. She wanted a small workspace added with a built-in desk.

As a blogger, she was often asked to sample different products. Many times, the samples were food or cleaning items. It always made sense to work in the kitchen, a place that was easy to clean in case there was a packaging mishap.

Trixie shuffled through her handbag and found the business card for Sandi Fields. "No time like the present." She topped off her coffee, settled back in the kitchen chair, and punched in Sandi's number on her cell.

"Fields Interior Designs, Jonathan speaking."

"Good morning, Jonathan. I'd like to schedule an appointment with Ms. Fields regarding some home renovations."

"One moment."

Trixie heard the quiet tapping of computer keys.

"Yes, we could fit you in next Wednesday morning at nine. Ms. Fields prefers to meet in the space you'd like to renovate. Would that be acceptable?"

"Sure. Sounds great." Trixie gave Jonathan her address and disconnected.

While she had Sandi Fields here, she should have her look at the rest of the condo. She would love to have her bedroom closet made into a larger, more functional space.

Trixie picked up a pad of paper used for keeping a running grocery list. She jotted down ideas for the kitchen, then started a slow walk through her home, critically looking at the space. She opened the door to the guest bedroom. It was filled with boxes and remnants of her past life with three men. She felt her excitement wane. This was a case of out of sight, out of mind, but she had to go through them before Wednesday. She'd procrastinated long enough. It was time to purge herself of the old baggage.

Trixie dropped to the floor pulled the closest box toward her, and opened it. This one was filled with odds and ends. As she sifted through the contents, she found a few framed sketches and a small original sculpture of a nude man. These were the belongings of husband number three, Alex, "the art collector." She wondered why she'd fallen for Alex. He was self-absorbed, incredibly handsome, and a wonderful lover, but after a time, she realized making love for him was all about self-adoration. It wasn't about pleasing his partner. Hence, why he felt the need to share his bed with so many. She pushed the box to the right, the discard pile.

As she made her way further into the room, she found boxes of dishes and linens that she moved to the left, useful items to keep. There were a few boxes containing books on archaeology and history. These belonged to husband number two, Martin. He was a kind man, just too old for her. After a few months of marriage, they both knew they'd made a mistake. The divorce was amicable, and they remained friends. She'd email him about the books.

There were still three boxes left. She glanced at her watch. It was nearly time for lunch. She pulled her cell from her robe pocket and dialed Kathleen and then Martha. They agreed to meet at Emile's for a late lunch. That would give her time to finish going through the last of the boxes and freshen up.

She pulled the three boxes closer and opened one of them. The smell of musty basement and the faint scent of cologne wafted toward her, Sean's cologne. Her heart hurt at the familiar scent. These were Sean's boxes. Items she'd lovingly packed away so many years ago. She pulled the box closer and carefully removed a tattered, blue flannel shirt. This had been Sean's favorite shirt. He'd called it his weekend shirt. She buried her face into the soft, worn fabric.

She recalled Sunday mornings spent lying together on the sofa, Sean reading the Wall Street Journal and her a mystery, and the sheer pleasure and contentment of feeling him next to her. If she'd known their time together would've been so short, would she have done anything differently? No. She'd loved him with every fiber of her being, and there would never be another Sean. She held the shirt to her face for a long time. Tears of a future together and what might have been soaked into the fabric. She breathed in the smell of Sean one more time, then put the shirt and the memories carefully back in the box. It was time; she moved all of it to the right.

Trixie pulled on jeans and a floral print blouse, washed her face, and pulled her hair into a ponytail. She gathered several of the boxes and placed them at the curb for trash pickup. The rest she put into the trunk of her car for the homeless shelter.

When Trixie walked into Emile's, Kay, the hostess, was standing at the door with several menus in her hand. "Back so soon?"

"Yeah, I'm meeting Kathleen and Martha. Have they arrived?"

Disappointment flashed across the younger woman's face. "Oh. I thought you might be meeting that handsome Doctor Stone again."

Doc was right; the gossip had started. "Okay. Dinner with Doc was nothing more than a chance meeting. It was not a date."

"Oh. Sure. Whatever you say." Kay cut her eyes at Trixie. "If you ask me, it looked like you two were getting along pretty well."

"Well, no one asked you," said Trixie, a little sharper than intended.

Kay pouted. "Your friends are at the table near the window." She handed Trixie a menu.

Trixie rolled her eyes and made her way toward the table. "Sorry, I'm late."

"Not a problem," said Kathleen. "We've just been catching up on the local news."

Trixie settled into the chair and opened the menu. "Anything interesting?"

Kathleen said, "You know how gossip is in this little town."

Trixie rolled her eyes. "You have got to be kidding. Have you been talking to Kay?"

"No. What did Kay say?" asked Kathleen. "We were talking to Emile."

Trixie laid the menu on the table. "Want to tell me what's going on?"

"Enough pussy footing around," said Martha. "Did you learn anything about our cases last night while having dinner with Doctor Stone?"

Kathleen leaned closer. "Forget the cases; how was dinner? I heard you shared dessert."

Trixie glared at Kathleen. "Seriously? We just happened to be here at the same time. The place was crowded, and I was starving. Doc was kind enough to share his table. Nothing more. And no, he wasn't exactly a fount of information. I'm assuming you heard the Sheriff's office brought in an anthropologist to examine the bones."

Martha waved at her dismissively. "Once it is on the evening news, it is old news. Did he tell you anything?"

"No. Not really."

Martha shook her head disappointedly. "You really need to work on your interrogation skills. I have a book that can help you. I will bring it to you this afternoon. You need to be prepared should the opportunity avail itself again."

Kathleen turned toward Martha. "You've got a book on interrogation?"

"Yes. It is an excellent read."

"I'll keep that in mind." Trixie opened the menu. "However, I doubt I'll need it as the odds of me having dinner with Doc again are slim to none. Now, what are you two eating?"

Once their orders were placed, Trixie said, "I've been getting lots of emails about the self-defense class. I know this sounds crazy, but we might have to turn people away because the room isn't large enough."

Kathleen's eyes widened. "Are you kidding?"

"No. There's a lot of interest. It's possible we'll need another instructor. I'm calling Deputy Williams this afternoon to give her a heads-up. She might know a few other officers who could come and help, just in case."

"I can't believe the class is tomorrow morning," said Kathleen.

Martha blew out an inpatient breath. "Can we continue discussing our cases? I have been thinking. We need a command center. You know, a place to meet, store information, and create a murder board. I would offer my spare room, only it is full of books. Do either of you have a place we could use?"

Kathleen shook her head. "Mine is set up for the grandkids when they come for sleepovers. I don't think a murder board would be appropriate." She looked at Trixie. "What about you?"

"With the exception of a large desk and a few chairs, my spare room is empty. So, what exactly do we need in our command center?"

A broad smile creased Martha's face. She pulled a small notebook and pen from her fanny pack. "We should make a list."

Chapter Fifteen

The next morning, Martha and Kathleen met Trixie in front of her condo. Martha lifted her arms to the side and did small circular rotations. "This cool air is invigorating. I am looking forward to class.

Kathleen zipped up her jacket. "I can't believe the first day of self-defense class is finally here. It feels good doing something proactive.

"We've done everything we can to make these classes a success," said Trixie.

Kathleen said, "Is an athletic prowess required to do self-defense?"

"Of course not."

"I'm sure your performance will be adequate," said Martha. She turned toward Trixie and let out a soft whistle. "Are you going to self-defense class looking like that? And what's up with the hair and make-up? Looks like you are going to a club."

Trixie's eyes widened. "A club? Martha, you've been holding out on us. How do you know about appropriate *club* attire?" She looked down at the green tee shirt and black yoga pants. "If people still went to clubs, this would never do. And there's nothing wrong with a girl putting on her best face." Trixie took in Martha's baggy gray sweatpants and sweatshirt. "Yeah, we've really got to do something about your wardrobe."

Martha looked down at her clothing. "What is wrong with my attire? I can move in it." She struck a karate pose.

Trixie slid into a lightweight black jacket. "We need to go, or we're going to be late."

"Was Deputy Williams able to recruit another instructor?" asked Kathleen.

"She said Deputy Nelson would help, and she was going to try and find one more instructor just in case we have a larger class than expected."

Kathleen stopped. "Deputy Nelson is coming—to class?" She chewed her bottom lip.

"What's wrong?" Trixie frowned. "Nelson seemed to take the discovery of the fishing line surprisingly well. What are you worried about?"

"You guys go on without me."

Trixie cocked her head and scrutinized Kathleen's face. "No, I don't think so. You're going to tell us what the problem is." Trixie folded her arms across her chest.

"I'm not very athletic, and I don't want to look ridiculous in front of... everyone." Kathleen lifted her chin. "Besides, I've lost interest in taking the class. You go on. I'm going back to my condo." She turned to leave.

Trixie grabbed her elbow. "Oh, I don't think so. "You're part of the reason this class was started, remember? We created it to help allay your fears and the fears of our community. So, we're sticking together, just like the three musketeers, all for one and one for all. And you won't look ridiculous." Worry etched Kathleen's face. Trixie touched her arm. "Seriously, what's bugging you?"

Kathleen drew in a deep breath and slowly let it out. "What if people think I look old."

"I don't think you need to worry about what other people think. And why would anyone think you look old? You look great."

"Well, I am in my fifties, and sometimes when a woman has had several children, and you throw in the natural aging process, things don't work as well as they used to. So, when you're jumping around, it can cause problems. You know what I mean?"

Martha frowned at Kathleen, then turned toward Trixie. "I got nothing. What about you?"

"I'm not sure where you're going with this. Just spit it out. What's the problem?"

Kathleen turned her back to Trixie and lifted her jacket. "I'm wearing a Depends. Does it make my butt look big?"

Trixie pinched her lips together, then burst out laughing. "Your butt looks fine. He'll never know."

Kathleen flushed and yanked down her jacket. She glared at Trixie. "I don't know to whom you are referring?"

"Oh, you know, *to whom I'm referring.*"

"What are you two talking about?"

"Never mind," said Kathleen.

Martha shrugged. "Fine. Don't tell me. No one tells me anything."

A few minutes later, they walked into the Brookville Club House. The compact athletic figure of Deputy Michelle Williams met them at the door. "Hi Michelle," said Trixie. "We appreciate you agreeing to instruct this class. I think it's going to help the residents feel safer."

"My pleasure. I love teaching self-defense, and I'm happy I could help. Nelson is here somewhere. I'm glad he was able to assist. There's quite a crowd." Michelle checked her watch. "Take off your shoes. We'll get started shortly."

Trixie, Kathleen, and Martha moved to the back of the room. "There certainly are a lot of people here," said Kathleen, slipping out of her tennis shoes.

"I do not see anyone I know," said Martha.

"Then this will be a great time for us to get to know some of our neighbors," said Trixie. "And speaking of friendly faces, hello, Deputy."

Deputy Nelson nodded at Trixie and Martha, then turned to Kathleen. "Ms. Avery, you look very nice this morning."

"Thank you. You look nice, too. You look different in street clothes, better." Kathleen blushed. "Not that you don't look handsome in your uniform. But who really looks good in beige, right?"

Nelson smiled. "Thank you, ma'am."

Trixie moved beside Kathleen and said, "Any information on the fishing line?"

"No, but on a hunch, Deputy Williams and I went back to the area where the fishing line was discovered. We found a footprint matching the print found at Camille Jackson's crime scene."

Nelson turned his attention to the growing number of people. "Looks like Michelle is ready to start. Ms. Avery, I hope we'll have time to talk later. If you need help with anything, you let me know."

"I'll be sure to do that. Thank you, deputy."

"Yes, ma'am." Nelson moved to the front of the room.

Trixie rolled her eyes. "I feel like I'm stuck in some old southern movie." In an exaggerated Southern accent, she said, "Why, Miss Kathleen, that deputy looks mighty fine when he's not dressed in that beige uniform." Trixie batted her lashes.

"Stop it."

Trixie whispered, "I don't think he noticed your butt."

"Ms. Tanner, would you come to the front," said Deputy Nelson, motioning to her.

Kathleen giggled. "Serves you right."

Trixie made a face at Kathleen and then moved to the front of the class. She glared at Nelson. "Really? What do you need me for?"

"You're going to help demonstrate the basic techniques. Michelle and I will assist the students with their form."

"Maybe you should've asked Kathleen to help out."

"I don't think Ms. Avery would appreciate having all that attention on her." He looked down at Trixie. "You, however, love the spotlight." Nelson turned toward the class. "Ms. Tanner will demonstrate the warm-ups while Michelle and I move amongst you to ensure proper form." He turned back to Trixie. "Face the class, bend your knees slightly, and straighten your back." Nelson addressed the class and gave instructions about the necessity of a solid stance. "Now, tuck your elbows into your sides, palms up. Make a fist. Punch forward while spinning your fist as you do so." He demonstrated the move. Trixie mimicked the maneuver. Nelson moved closer. "I heard you had dinner with Doc the other night."

Trixie stopped throwing punches. "Seriously? Was it on CNN, and I missed it? You'd think I'd accomplished world peace or something of equal magnitude."

"Around here, that is big news." Nelson turned toward the class. "Now, let's move to some hamstring stretches." Nelson demonstrated, and Trixie mirrored the movement.

"What's Doc's story? Is he always so bossy?"

"Doc is one of the smartest men I know. And yes, he is always in control. He's a highly respected member of our community, and he's earned that respect." Nelson turned toward the class. "Switch legs."

"Do you like Doc?"

"I don't have to like him. We have a mutual respect. Will you find us at a bar having a beer together, doubtful?" Nelson glanced around the class. "Mind if I ask you a question?"

"Sure." Trixie stood.

"Ms. Avery, is she involved with anyone?"

"Nope. She's a widow. Her husband passed away about a year ago."

"Oh."

"Jack, mind if I call you Jack? Move slow. She's willing, just a little unsteady. This is all new to her. With a little encouragement, I think she'll come around."

Nelson shifted his attention to where Kathleen was stretching. "Roger that."

* * *

After half an hour of punching and kicking at imaginary attackers, Nelson announced they'd take a ten-minute break. "Please help yourself to the refreshments at the back of the room, compliments of Brookville Condominiums." He turned toward Trixie. "Thanks for your help and for the intel."

"My pleasure." She turned to walk away, stopped, and turned back. "However, Jack, I'd suggest you drop the Ms. Avery. You sound more like a cop than a potential suitor. Her name is Kathleen."

Nelson gave a curt nod. "Noted."

Trixie made her way to the refreshment table. Several stacks of paper cups were arranged to one side of a large punch bowl filled with a red fruity beverage. Trixie filled a cup and watched Martha practicing punches in the corner of the room. Kathleen was talking to Nelson. Looked like the Deputy was moving faster than she expected.

A woman in her early thirties grabbed a few napkins from the table and mopped sweat from her face and neck. "I didn't think I'd be getting such a workout. This class is great, don't you think? I'm Audrey." She filled a cup with punch and took a sip.

"I'm Trixie. And you're right, the class is wonderful."

"It's such a shame someone had to die for it to be created."

"Did you know Camille?"

Audrey picked up a cookie. "No, I never met her, but she worked with my friend, Carrie. She's the administrative assistant for Dan Fields and Jason Knight."

Trixie sipped the punch. "Were they friends?"

"Camille had only been here a few months. I don't think they had a chance to get to know one another. However, I doubt they would've been friends."

"Why not?"

"From what Carrie told me, Camille had a reputation that preceded her."

"What sort of reputation? Was she hard to get along with?"

Audrey looked around the room and leaned in closer. "I don't mean to speak ill of the dead, but according to Carrie, there were rumors that Camille got the job because she was sleeping with one of the corporation's owners."

Trixie wondered if this was idle gossip or if there was an element of truth. "Does Carrie think the rumors were true?"

Audrey said, "Who knows? According to Carrie, Camille was always hanging around the office after closing."

"Maybe it was business."

"Maybe. However, about two weeks ago, Carrie overheard Camille and Dan having an argument."

"Dan Fields?"

"You know him?"

Trixie refilled her cup. "I recently met him and his wife."

Audrey motioned toward a tall blonde who was talking to a group of women. "You mean her?"

Trixie turned and saw the woman she'd met on the trail a few days earlier. Brittney's blond hair hung loosely around her shoulders. The white scoop-neck tee shirt and yoga pants did an amazing job showing off her attributes. You couldn't miss her. "Yeah, her. She's quite something."

"What she is, is a witch. You can't blame her husband for looking for love elsewhere, but I'm not sure Camille was a better choice."

"So, Camille was having an affair with Dan Fields?"

"According to the rumor mill."

Trixie watched Brittney for a minute. "How long have Dan and Brittney been married?"

"I don't know, maybe a year and a half. Anyway, long enough for her to spit out a baby."

Trixie choked on the punch. A spray of the fruity liquid dribbled down the front of her shirt. She grabbed a napkin from the table and mopped up the moisture. "Didn't take him long to get the wandering eye."

"How do you think he met Brittney? He cheated with her on the first wife."

"Were there kids with the other wife?" asked Trixie.

"Not that I know of. However, Brittney was either smarter than she looked or was dumb and let herself get knocked up." Audrey leaned in closer. "From what I hear, the ink wasn't dry on the marriage license before Brittney announced she was pregnant. If you ask me, she had a bun in the oven when they got married. Maybe Brittney thought a baby would provide Dan with a little incentive to hang around. Either way, he's tied up in a financial sling. And she's got a little crumb gobbler to make sure he doesn't go anywhere." Audrey tossed her napkin in the trash can. "I guess it's cheaper to keep her than get rid of her. You must think I'm horrible."

"You mentioned Carrie overheard Camille and Dan arguing. Did she say what they were fighting about?"

"Carrie couldn't catch everything, but she heard Camille tell Dan that it was time he had a talk with Brittney, and if he didn't, he'd be sorry. Carrie said things really started getting heated, so she left."

"Wow, Brookville is like a little soap opera. Who knew so much was going on?"

"I know, right?" Audrey sat the punch cup on the table. "It looks like we're getting ready to start back. It was great talking with you. We should do lunch sometime."

"Sure, that'd be great." Trixie watched Audrey jog back to her place on the floor. Apparently, Camille hadn't endeared herself to others. She looked over at Brittney. She didn't know Brittney but knew the type. If there was an affair between Dan and Camille, wouldn't that give Brittney motive? She couldn't wait to tell Kathleen and Martha what she'd learned.

Deputy Nelson clapped his hands. "All right, people let's get back to class. Line up."

As Trixie moved toward the front of the room, she replayed the conversation with Audrey. Was Audrey just a gossip and liked to embellish the facts to make herself sound like she was in the know, or was there truth to the story? If there was truth to the gossip, Brittney could take Dan for a pretty penny, which gave Dan a motive for murder.

Trixie took her position at the front of the room just as Doc Stone entered. Her heart hammered in her chest as she watched him move toward Nelson. The looks on their faces were grim. The men moved to the side. Nelson motioned for Michelle to start class. Trixie mimicked the maneuvers while Michelle gave instructions. From the corner of her eye, Trixie watched Doc and Nelson. Whatever they were discussing was serious.

Nelson returned to the front of the room, and Doc leaned against the wall and watched. His dark eyes found hers. Trixie's stomach gave a little lurch. Why was he here? It had been an enjoyable morning until now.

Amusement flickered across Doc's face. Trixie moved closer to Nelson. "What's he doing here?"

"He offered to help. With the size of the class, I accepted."

"And you didn't bother to mention it?" Over Nelson's shoulder she saw Doc watching her. "And how exactly is he qualified to help with any of this? He's a doctor, for crying out loud."

"Doc was Special Forces. I think that more than qualifies him, and I wasn't aware I needed your permission. Is there a problem?"

Trixie wanted to stomp her feet and yell, yes, there's a problem. He made her uncomfortable, and she'd told him too much about herself. "As long as I don't have to interact with him, I'm good. Now that he's here, you won't need me." She turned to retreat and nearly knocked Doc over. Strong hands gripped her shoulders.

"Ms. Tanner, we meet again. I enjoyed dinner. Perhaps we can do it again sometime."

She squeezed her eyes shut. He was determined to feed the rumor mill. Trixie felt eyes on them. She took a moment to compose her face, looked up at him, and said, "Doc, so nice to see you. Yes, perhaps we can." She walked past him and mumbled, "When hell freezes."

Chapter Sixteen

As the women walked back to the condos, Martha practiced punches and defensive moves. "Class was invigorating. I feel empowered." She punched the air again.

"What did you say?" asked Kathleen.

Martha stopped walking. "What's wrong with you two? You've been distracted the entire walk home."

"Sorry," said Trixie. "I've got a lot on my mind."

"Like what, Dr. Stone?" asked Martha.

Trixie turned toward Martha. "What? Why would you say that?"

"I saw you talking to him. From your facial expressions, I wasn't sure what was going to happen. One minute, you looked like you wanted to punch him, and the next...well, not so much."

Kathleen looked at Trixie. "What did he say to you?"

"He thanked me for having dinner with him."

"Really? That was nice of him and very interesting." Kathleen drew out the words with emphasis on the *very*. "He must have enjoyed the evening. Does he want to go out again?"

"Oh, for crying out loud, it wasn't a date. Can we move along, please?"

"We should talk about the case," said Martha.

"That's an excellent idea. In fact, I learned some information about Camille that I think you'll find interesting. We could go to the Café and have lunch."

"I'm ravenous," said Martha. "All that exercise has increased my appetite."

"We're close to my condo. I'll drive," said Kathleen.

A few minutes later, Kathleen pulled her silver Honda Accord into a parking space in front of Emile's Café. Getting out of the sedan, she said, "We should try another restaurant, don't you think? I mean, I love Emile's, but there's something to be said for variety."

Trixie stood beside her. "As my father used to say, if it ain't broke, don't fix it."

After they were seated and orders taken, Kathleen turned to Trixie. "So, what did you find out?"

Trixie recounted her conversation with Audrey.

Martha said, "So, we have a man with motive. That is interesting."

"Yeah, and don't forget about the wife. You know the adage, Hell hath no fury as a woman scorned," said Trixie.

"Did you learn anything from Doc on your non-date?" asked Martha.

Trixie waded her napkin and dropped it beside her plate. "Really? You too? He didn't tell me anything we didn't already know. But he did admit you did a proficient job of securing the site."

"Obviously. I didn't understand why he got so upset. I told him I was more than competent."

Kathleen nibbled the end of a pickle. "Interesting. Dan Fields had something to lose if Camille told Brittney about the affair."

"True, but is the situation dire enough for him to commit murder?" asked Trixie. Unfortunately, people cheat all the time. He's got money; he could've paid Brittney off."

Martha looked up from her plate. "People have murdered for less."

"Yes, they have, and even though Brittney may be a witch, that doesn't make her a murderer either."

"We need to do some digging—see what else we can find," said Martha.

Kathleen shook her head. "We shouldn't get involved. This is police business."

"Just because you and the deputy are chummy doesn't change the circumstances. There is a murderer out there, and none of us are safe until he or she is found," said Martha.

"The deputy and I aren't chummy."

"Your relationship with Nelson is not the point. Martha's right. None of us are safe until Camille's murderer is behind bars. Besides, a little research couldn't hurt. My first husband Sean always said when doing battle, it's important to be prepared." Trixie leaned forward. "Ladies, this is a battle we need to win."

Martha rubbed her hands together. Her eyes brightened with excitement. "We have our work cut out for us. The Brookville sheriff's department is small. They don't have the workforce to do the legwork required to get to the bottom of this." A grin spread across her face. "However, we can do what they cannot. I view this as our civic duty." She turned to Trixie. "We need to get our command center established. How soon can we start setting up your spare room?"

"Is today soon enough?"

"I don't know. I'm afraid we're biting off more than we can chew," said Kathleen.

"Kathleen, you worry too much. Besides, I have some happy news to report," said Trixie.

"Happy news?" said Martha. "I cannot imagine what that would be given the current circumstances."

Trixie turned toward Kathleen. "A certain deputy was asking about you."

"Oh. That is old news," said Martha.

"What do you mean, *old news?*" Trixie looked from Kathleen to Martha. "Someone needs to fill me in."

Kathleen blushed. "Jack asked me to go for coffee Tuesday afternoon. It's his day off."

"Oh, did he? He moved faster than I thought he would. And you've progressed from Deputy to Jack. Nice. Is he still calling you ma'am?"

"Yes, and I think it's sweet."

Martha shook her head and turned to Trixie. "Is there anything else to report?"

"Only that I'm having renovations done in my condo."

"And that is supposed to help the case, how?"

"The interior decorator is Dan Field's ex-wife, Sandi. She might be able to provide a little insight into Dan and maybe even Brittney." Trixie glanced at her watch. "If we're going to set up the command center, we need to run to the office supply store before it closes."

* * *

By late afternoon, Trixie's spare bedroom had been converted into a command center the FBI would have been proud to call home. The long desk was situated at the back of the room. A new computer sat on it. Three folding chairs made a semi-circle around the desk, and a narrow bookcase sat beside the doorway. Several packs of multi-colored dry-erase markers were stacked on the top shelf, reams of paper on the shelf below. A rolling double-sided six by eight-foot whiteboard was placed on each side of the room, and a small multipurpose printer, copier, and scanner was positioned in the corner. Martha labeled the board to the right *Human Remains* and the one on the left *Camille*.

Trixie propped her hands on her hips and surveyed the room. "This looks great. It reminds me of…" she hesitated, "the murder boards I've seen on TV." Her past had to stay in the past. Her time as an ATF agent was in another life. That person was long gone. Besides, explaining her history to Kathleen and Martha would require too much energy. Kathleen would be shocked; Martha thrilled. If Nelson was going to be dating Kathleen, she needed to remind him to keep his mouth shut.

Martha rubbed her hands together excitedly. "So, shall we start?"

Kathleen yawned and stretched. "It's been a long day. I really want a hot shower and bed."

"Why don't we start fresh in the morning," said Trixie. "Come around ten. I'll make a breakfast casserole, and then we can get busy."

When Kathleen and Martha were gone, Trixie wandered back to the spare bedroom. She smiled at the sign Martha had hung on the door. In precise lettering, she'd written *Command Center*. Trixie settled into one of the folding chairs and stared at the blank board with Camille's name written at the top. What did they really know about this woman? In reality, not much. Sure, maybe half of Brookville knew Dan and Camille had a thing, but was the affair over? Did Camille have a dark secret from her past that had caught up with her? Trixie opened the pack of dry-erase markers and removed one. She made a quick bullet-point list of what they knew, then added a few questions. She stood back and looked at what she'd written—nothing substantial. She erased the board.

Thoughts of Sean and her on another night long ago floated into her mind. She recalled them standing in front of a case board with little to nothing on it. She had been frustrated with the case and irritated with Sean for not being more concerned. He put his arm around her and kissed her temple. *Patience Trix. It'll come.*

Chapter Seventeen

Although it was another beautiful morning, Trixie couldn't quite bring herself to embrace it in her usual carefree way. She wanted to run and needed solitude and time to think. But the unsettling thought of a murderer still walking the streets gave her pause. Trixie scolded herself. Since when did she run from danger? That wasn't what she did. Kathleen was rubbing off on her. She wasn't going to let a murder or anything else keep her from living life.

Trixie went back inside the condo and retrieved the small revolver and a shoulder holster from her bureau. She strapped on the holster, checked the revolver to make sure it was loaded, then pulled on a lightweight jacket. Trixie patted the small weapon. "Much better."

She started off at a slow jog. Instead of running past the area where they'd found Camille, she decided to run toward the new condo construction site. It had been a while since she'd been on that side of the property and was curious to see the progress. Besides, forensics should have finished processing the area, which would give her a chance to do a little snooping.

Trixie, Kathleen, and Martha lived on the North side of the Brookville properties, where a small community of one-level duplexes formed a cozy, friendly environment. The Corporation had done a wonderful job of making each of the condos a little different on the outside and inside. The new condos were townhouses with no variation in design. The marketing for them was targeted at a younger demographic.

Trixie jogged into the construction site expecting the usual hustle and bustle of men working and found it deserted. She slowed to a walk. Where was everyone? As she moved down the street, a white pickup truck with Berkley Construction LLC printed on its side pulled to a stop. A man with a yellow hard hat got out and moved toward her. "Can I help you?"

Trixie raised a hand to shield her eyes from the sun. "Where is everyone?"

"We've been instructed to stop work."

"Why?"

The man pulled a handkerchief from his hip pocket, tipped his hard hat back, and mopped sweat from his face. "Lady, they don't pay me to ask questions. I just do what I'm told. Today, they want me to clear this area of Berkley equipment, and that's what I'm doing."

"You're kidding? That doesn't make any sense."

He shoved the handkerchief back into his pocket. "Maybe not, but those are my orders."

"So, this shutdown has nothing to do with the crime scene?"

"Not to my knowledge."

The Corporation had taken some hard hits recently, but was it enough to make them stop construction? She looked up at Hard Hat. "What about the properties that are sold? What's going to happen to them?"

"Lady, that's not my problem. I suggest you find another place to run."

Trixie watched the man climb back into his truck. She turned and jogged out of the construction site. Surely, they didn't stop all construction. A move like that would cost the corporation a fortune. The townhouses on this side of the property were eighty percent complete, and many sold; why not finish them?

Trixie ran further west to where ground was recently broken for the new condos and where the skeletonized remains were found.

As she approached the area, she saw the excavated site where the remains were discovered. An older woman and four twenty-somethings hammered wooden spikes into the ground and ran string from one stake to the next forming a grid pattern. Trixie watched them work. She must be the forensic anthropologist from the university and her grad students. Had they found something else? Gravel crunched, and Trixie spun to face the intruder, her hand automatically moving for her weapon. She stopped when she saw Doc.

"Oh, it's you."

"You are like a bad penny; you just keep turning up."

Trixie pasted a smile on her lips. "What can I say? I'm curious by nature." She motioned toward the activity. "What's going on? Have more remains been found? Did you know construction on the east side of the property has been stopped?"

Doc held up his hands. "Whoa. Where have civilities gone? There's no good morning or fancy meeting you here."

"Really? Just tell me what's going on, and then I'll leave."

Stone jammed his hands into his jeans pockets and watched the anthropologist and her students. "I seriously doubt that, but I'll tell you only because it'll probably be on the evening news. A femur was found several yards from the first remains. Dr. Cain and her students are setting up a grid to excavate the area. Based on topographical analysis of the site and data from ground penetrating radar, she believes there could be additional graves."

"What? More graves?"

Doc gave her a hard look. "Maybe, but we won't know until the area is excavated. You understand what I tell you goes nowhere, right?"

She crossed her fingers. "Of course."

He glared at her for a moment and then turned and walked away. "Never mind."

Trixie caught up with him and grabbed his arm. "It's a given I'm going to tell Martha and Kathleen, but that information will go nowhere beyond us." She held up three fingers. "Scout's honor."

Stone looked at her fingers. "Really? The scouts?"

Trixie shrugged. "Any port in a storm."

"Fine. Dr. Cain estimates the girl's remains have been in the ground approximately thirty to forty years."

"You said girl. So, the remains are female. What's the estimated age?" Doc shook a finger at her. "I know, I know, keep my mouth shut. So?"

"Mid to late teens."

Trixie took a moment to digest the new information. Facts clicked into place. "With the exception of the head, the girl's remains were intact." She met Doc's eyes. "What about the femur?"

"We don't know yet."

"Is it possible this was a Jeffries family cemetery?"

"Doubtful."

"What about a Civil War soldier?" The look Doc gave her spoke volumes. "Never mind."

Chapter Eighteen

K athleen sat back in her chair with a contented smile. "Trixie, that casserole was delicious. You've got to share the recipe."

"Yeah, sure."

Martha stirred sugar into her coffee. "You are not your usual effervescent self. What is troubling you?"

Kathleen eyed Trixie. "Now that you mention it, she is acting weird."

"I saw Doc today, and there's something strange going on with the condo construction. Bring your coffees and let's go to the Command Center."

"Why did you not mention this earlier?" said Martha.

Trixie called over her shoulder, "Because you would have been thrilled. Kathleen, not so much. And my delicious casserole would have gone to waste."

Once they were settled in the Command Center, Trixie told Kathleen and Martha about the femur and the possibility of more graves. She also told them about the construction site being closed.

Kathleen chewed her lower lip thoughtfully. "Why would construction stop? As you said, the townhouses are near completion and nowhere near the area where the skeleton was found. Something's not right about this."

Martha blew out a sigh. "Kathleen, the important issue here is the discovery of more skeletal remains. We need to stay on point. A femur was found. Who does it belong to? And the larger question, how many more graves are out there?"

"I'm not saying the remains aren't important. But maybe there are other issues going on with the Corporation that are relevant to Camille's death."

Kathleen crossed her arms over her chest, and her bottom lip began to tremble. "This is all very disconcerting."

Trixie pulled a marker from the pack and walked over to the boards. "Ladies, given that we don't know the Corporation's issues, I think we should stick with what we do know." She glanced at Kathleen. "However, I think it would be prudent to add a column on the board for the Corporation, just in case."

"Thank you, Trixie."

Trixie erased the heading, Human Remains, then drew a line down the center of the board. On the left side, she rewrote Human Remains, and on the right Brookville Corporation.

"There is someone we have not considered. What do we know about Fields's partner, Jason Knight? What was his relationship with Camille?" said Martha.

Trixie moved to the desk and opened the computer. "That's an excellent question. We know very little about Mr. Knight. In fact, I don't think I've ever seen him on the property. Let's see what we can find." She clicked on her favorite search engine and typed in Brookville Corporation. In seconds, a slick, professional website appeared featuring the elegant entryway to the corporate offices. A smiling Dan Fields and Jason Knight were positioned under the gorgeous hand-blown glass chandelier. Below them, the Brookville Corporation tagline, *Your vacation destination for everyday living.*

"I've never seen Jason Knight before," said Kathleen. "He's quite handsome."

Trixie moved the cursor to a set of tabs at the top of the page and clicked on the one labeled Images. Instantly, photographs of the Brookville condos, grounds, club house, and even a few shots of the trails filled the page. As Trixie navigated through the images, drawings of proposed floor plans for the new condos appeared.

She clicked the next tab labeled, *About Us.* Jason, Dan, Brittney, Camille, and Carrie stood in the entryway of the Corporate Office, each smiling, inviting potential customers to be part of the Brookville family. Trixie clicked on Dan Fields' name. A smiling photo and brief bio populated the page. She skimmed it quickly. "Beyond education, there isn't a lot of new information. Trixie clicked the back button and moved to Jason Knight's page. Jason is the Chief Financial Officer. She looked at Kathleen and Martha. "There's not much here. Let's dig deeper into their backgrounds." Trixie logged onto a website for background searches and typed in Jason Knight's name.

Martha leaned over her shoulder. "Nice. Do you have to pay for that service?"

"I do, but it's worth it. It's important that I thoroughly vet companies and their owners before I endorse them on my blog. Jason Knight's image and his personal information loaded. "Jason's credentials are impressive. An Ivy League education and an exemplary work history. No run-ins with the law, not even a parking ticket."

Kathleen's eyes widened. "Take a look at that annual salary. Is he married?"

"There's no mention of a wife." Trixie continued to search the internet; she found that two years ago, the Corporation was listed in Forbes as an up-and-coming company to watch. "There doesn't appear to be anything unusual." Trixie checked out the rest of the staff, but again, nothing concerning.

Trixie closed the laptop and returned to the board with the column labeled *Human Remains*. She drew a bullet point on the board, then turned toward Martha and Kathleen. "I know this sounds crazy, but what do you think the odds are that the remains are Sara Adams?"

"Statistically, the odds are not in our favor," said Martha. "However, stranger things have happened."

"Kathleen, do you have your notes from the archives?" asked Trixie.

"They're in my handbag." She walked back to the kitchen and returned with a small notepad. "Sara Adams was sixteen years old at the time of her disappearance. She had a boyfriend, Samuel Barlow; he was seventeen and from a neighboring town. He also disappeared around the same time." Trixie added a few more bullet points with the information.

Martha adjusted her glasses. "And let us not forget, Sara and Samuel were friends of Alexandra Jeffries. If this is Sara, I find it curious that her remains were found buried on her friend's property. And if the femur belongs to Samuel, that's an even more interesting coincidence."

Chapter Nineteen

Trixie drove into town. A large traffic circle formed the center of town with side streets extending from the circle outward, much like spokes on a bicycle wheel. A large, ornate fountain embellished the center of the circle. Several restaurants, boutiques, salons, and the Book Shoppe occupied space on the side streets.

Trixie parked and walked across the street to the Book Shoppe. She had admired its over-the-top signage, which looked like a large open book standing on its end with the name of the shop printed on the spine. She paused inside the store, stunned by what she saw. The room was circular and at least thirty feet tall. A ramp started near the entrance of the store and wound its way around the circumference of the room up toward the ceiling. Bookshelves loaded with every imaginable book encompassed the wall space. The store was a bibliophile's dream. Trixie closed her eyes and inhaled the scent of the books.

Books were her go-to when she needed to escape from her reality. As a child, her parents frequently took her to estate sales. Her books went with her, always a welcomed companion. Digital books might be convenient, but there was something about the real thing that couldn't be replaced. Not to mention the sheer pleasure of browsing the shelves of a good bookstore looking for an unread classic or a new mystery.

A few large, overstuffed chairs were dotted about the space. The old wooden floors creaked pleasantly as she walked across them. Trixie examined the flooring and the beautiful oriental rugs that accented the center of the space.

An older man with a mop of snowy white hair that drifted down onto his forehead moved toward her. "They're beautiful, aren't they?" The man's lovely Irish accent surprised her. Trixie looked up to meet the most brilliant blue eyes she'd ever seen. "Patrick O'Malley's the name, and you are?"

They shook hands. "Trixie Tanner."

On the south side of sixty, Patrick was shorter than Trixie. He winked at her mischievously. "Trixie, is it?"

Trixie pointed to the floor. "These floors are amazing. Given the width of the planks, I would think the flooring is at least a hundred-plus years old."

"Not just a pretty face, are you? You are correct; this flooring is closer to a hundred and fifty years old. This structure used to be a grain silo. Then, as time went by, it was converted into a variety of businesses until Robert and I bought it twenty-some years ago. We did much of the renovations ourselves, but when he died, it took the desire out of me to finish what we started."

Footsteps approached, and a tall, handsome man walked toward them. "Patrick, why is it beautiful women always gravitate to you?" The man held out his hand. "I'm Colin Delaney."

Colin had thickly lashed hazel eyes and curly light brown hair, and when he smiled, dimples creased his cheeks. Dear god, he's got dimples. She'd always been a sucker for dimples, and they looked especially nice on Colin.

Patrick leaned on the counter. "Anyway, Colin came along and convinced me to finish what Robert and I started. But don't be deceived by this handsome lad. He's not just a pretty face; he's also co-owner of this fine establishment. And without him, the Book Shoppe wouldn't have come to fruition."

Colin shook his head. "I'm surprised he gave me that much credit. Usually, he just calls me book boy and tells me to straighten the books on the bottom shelves." Colin mimicked Patrick's brogue, "Lad, be a dear and adjust the books on the bottom shelf." He burst into a deep, robust laugh.

Patrick shook his head. "It's true. I keep him around because he's got a bum you could flip quarters off."

"Flattery will get you nowhere, old man." Colin turned toward Trixie. "I rarely miss a pretty face. If you aren't new to the area, where have you been keeping yourself?"

"I've been busy getting settled after the move. There's not been much time to read."

"Do you live in town?" asked Colin.

"Yes, at the Brookville Condominiums?"

Patrick's brows furrowed. "The Brookville Condos? Isn't that where the young woman was murdered? I saw her picture in the paper. She was one of our regular customers. Loved a good cozy. Colin, what was her name?"

"Camille Jackson."

Patrick snapped his fingers. "Yes, that was it." He made the sign of the cross. "Poor woman. Did you know her?"

Trixie shook her head. "We never met."

Colin leaned against the counter and shoved his hands into his pockets. "She was a nice lady."

"How well did you know her?" asked Trixie.

"We used to chat when she came into the shop. I eventually convinced her to go out with me. We had a good time. Patrick's right; she was a nice lady."

"Was there a second date?"

"I was interested in getting to know her better. However, she wasn't interested in a second date. She said it wouldn't be fair. I assumed she wasn't over an old boyfriend." He pushed away from the counter. "Anyway, I've got boxes to unload. It was a pleasure meeting you."

Trixie and Patrick watched Colin walk away.

She said, "You're right."

"About what?"

"You could flip quarters off that bum."

Patrick gave her a devilish grin. "You are a cheeky lass. I think we're going to be great friends."

"Since you've lived in Brookville for a while, are you familiar with the Jeffries plantation?"

"I am. Lovely land with a sad story. I was sorry to see them develop it." Patrick lifted his shoulder. "But you can't stop progress. Do you know the history?"

"I've heard some of it. My friend said there were several Civil War battles fought on the land."

"Correct. The family had many struggles over the years. I suppose you heard Mr. Jeffries, one of the last in the line, died in a horrible way. Such a tragedy. Poor man wasn't in his right mind. He'd been sent to live in a nursing home. Authorities surmised he snuck out to return to his home place. The arson investigator believed Mr. Jeffries set the fire." Patrick shook his head slowly. "Just a tragedy."

"What happened to his wife and daughter?"

"The wife died several years before Richard passed. To the best of my knowledge, no one has seen the daughter in many years." Patrick waggled a finger at her. "You've fallen under our little town's spell. I have a book you might find interesting. Follow me."

He led her to the rear of the shop. On the back wall of the store, there was a small bookcase. On top of the case was a sign that read *History of Brookville*. The shelves were filled with a variety of books in all sizes. Patrick ran his index finger along the spines until he found the one he was looking for. He pulled it from the shelf and handed it to her.

Trixie examined the book's cover, *Fact or Fiction: A History of Brookville*. The book was old and well-used. She looked at Patrick. "I didn't realize you sold used books here?"

"We don't. I only loan these books to special customers. When you have time, you should take a spin through them. Most are well written and fascinating, others—not so much." He tapped the book in her hand with his forefinger. "However, I think you'll find this book particularly intriguing."

"Aren't these in the library?"

"Some are, but not this one. It's out of print and is one of the few remaining copies. I imagine you could find a book or two packed away in a dark corner of a basement or attic of some of Brookville's oldest families. The contents are fascinating, but the book itself has an interesting history. You should make time to visit the library's archives and research the scandal this little three-hundred page-book caused." He winked at her. "Once you've finished reading it, bring it back. There's no rush. I think you'll find it a fascinating read. When you're done, perhaps we could have coffee and discuss it." A small bell tinkled at the front of the shop. Patrick looked up. "I've got another customer." He patted her shoulder. "Take your time and browse." Trixie watched him shuffle away.

She settled into a comfy armchair and carefully opened the book. It smelled musty and old. The pages had yellowed slightly with age, and the edges were tinted brown where, over the years, many fingers had thumbed through them. Barbara A. Brown wrote the book in 1988. Trixie flipped to the first chapter titled, *In the Beginning*.

She was several pages into the book when she felt a hand on her shoulder. Trixie jumped and let out a little squeak. She pressed the book to her chest. "Sorry. I didn't hear you."

Patrick's eyes twinkled at her. "I told you it was a good read. It carried you away from the first page, didn't it?"

She patted the book. "You weren't kidding."

"Trixie, I'd like you to meet one of your neighbors. This is Sandi Fields."

Trixie turned to the woman who stood beside him. She was tall, slim, and attractive. Sandi's chestnut hair was cut into a sleek, short bob, and her makeup was done to perfection. She was impeccably dressed in navy slacks and a soft peach silk blouse. Her clothing was classic and expensive. Trixie had to give Dan Fields credit; he had an eye for an attractive woman.

Trixie stood. "I actually have an appointment scheduled with you for Wednesday."

"Then this is a fortuitous encounter."

The bell over the door tinkled again. "Ladies, please sit and chat. I've got work to do."

Trixie shook hands with Sandi. She noticed the beautiful bracelet encircling Sandi's wrist. "That is a fabulous bracelet. I don't think I've ever seen one quite like it."

Sandi toyed with the jewelry. "I doubt you ever will. My ex-husband gave it to me on our wedding night. He had it made for me." She looked up at Trixie and burst out laughing. "Your expression is priceless. My attachment to the piece has nothing to do with Dan. Just because the marriage didn't work doesn't mean I should give up something this gorgeous, right?"

Trixie laughed. "Good point. I understand you live in the condos. You and your ex must have a good relationship. I can't imagine living near any of my exes." Trixie returned to her chair, and Sandi sat in the chair opposite her.

Sandi smoothed a non-existent crease from her slacks. "I wouldn't say it's a good relationship; more we tolerate one another. The condo was part of the divorce settlement. It costs me nothing to live there, which allows me to use my money for things I enjoy. I view it as a win-win situation. My living on-site annoys Dan and his child bride, and I live there for the cost of utilities."

No love lost there. Sandi Fields was more than a match for Brittney, and Trixie was certain she took advantage of every opportunity to shove a dig into Dan and Brittney whenever possible.

Sandi leaned back in her chair and crossed her legs. Sophistication and self-assurance radiated from her. "So, what brings you to this thriving metropolis?"

Trixie laid the book on the table. "Divorce. I needed a change, and Brookville seemed like a good place to start over."

"It appears we have something in common. Divorce, that is." Sandi motioned toward the book. "I see Patrick's been filling your head with the sorted history of Brookville?"

"I have lots of questions about Brookville, specifically, the Jeffries plantation. I guess with the recent discoveries, he thought I'd find the book interesting."

"Discoveries? What sort of discoveries?"

"Haven't you heard? It's been all over the news."

"Oh, yes. Poor Camille. Such a tragedy. She will be missed."

Sandi's words held no sincerity. "You knew her?"

"Camille worked for the Brookville corporation for several years and had a dalliance with Dan, but that's history. Nevertheless, Camille wasn't a bad person. You look surprised, don't be. I know how the tongues love to wag in this town, and I'm fairly certain someone has already mentioned his infidelity to you. Would I be correct?"

"I might have heard something mentioned." Sandi's confirmation of the affairs explained Dan's reaction to Camille's death.

"I'm sure. I don't think Dan and Camille have been intimately involved for a while. At least, not since the child bride came into the picture. However, they did have a freakish connection."

"How does Brittney handle that?"

Sandi laughed. "Frankly, the child bride is so self-absorbed, she probably didn't notice. And, if she did, I doubt she viewed Camille as a threat to her marriage."

"I'm sure Camille's murder and the skeletonized remains have put a great deal of strain on Dan."

Sandi slowly uncrossed her legs. "I've been away for several days. What remains?"

"A partial skeleton was discovered at the construction site for the new condos. The forensic anthropologist from the university and Doctor Stone are working to identify them."

"That's more than a little unsettling."

"You aren't the first to have said that. My friends and I found Camille's body. Not something I care to experience again."

"I'm sure that was very traumatizing."

"Certainly not something I expected to find on my morning run. Are you familiar with the family? Did you know until the Jeffries property was sold to the Brookville Corporation, they had owned the land since the 1800s?"

"Can't say that I did. I haven't spent much time digging into the community's sorted past."

"Anyway, because of all that's recently happened, and with the help of the Brookville Corporation, we've started a self-defense class for the condo residents. You should think about attending."

"That sounds like something I'd be interested in."

"Great. The next class is on Saturday morning. You should come."

Sandi stood. "I will. Trixie, I hate to rush off, but I've got another appointment. It's been great meeting you, and I'll see you on Wednesday. Maybe we can have lunch sometime. We divorcees need to stick together."

"Yes, that would be great." She watched Sandi walk out of the store. During her time with the ATF, there had been times while working certain cases she'd get an odd little prickle at the base of her neck when something didn't feel quite right. She had that feeling now. Interesting.

Chapter Twenty

Trixie pulled into the parking lot of Emile's. She was looking forward to a quiet lunch and her book. Patrick had been spot-on when he'd said the book was a good read. The author had done a fabulous job of weaving Brookville's history into an engaging story that made you feel as if you were reading a mystery. She'd just stepped out of the car when she heard her name called.

"Trixie, hi, it's me, Audrey, from self-defense class."

Trixie waved. No way she'd forget this woman. Audrey was memorable and not in a good way. "Yes, I remember. How are you?"

"Great. Are you meeting someone for lunch?"

Trixie lifted her book. "Just me and Barbara."

Audrey looked past Trixie and into her car. "Who?"

Trixie shook her head. "Never mind. I brought a book to read."

"Oh. In that case, why don't you join me and my friends for lunch?" It'll give you a chance to meet some new people."

"I don't want to impose."

Audrey linked her arm in Trixie's. "Nonsense, I insist."

Trixie hesitated. "Okay, sure, why not."

As they walked into the café, Audrey said, "Emile's is the only decent place in this miserable town to eat."

"I don't know that I agree with that statement. Brookville has several good restaurants. However, I will say, Emile's is my favorite."

"Like so many things, opinions are subjective, aren't they?"

Regretting her decision to accept the lunch invitation, Trixie glanced over her shoulder at the exit sign. "I guess." She followed Audrey through the restaurant and wished desperately for a way to escape.

Audrey waved to a small group of women sitting at the back of the restaurant. As they approached the women, Trixie thought of how the adage, *Birds of a feather flock together,* fit these women perfectly. Sean would have said, *all show and no go.*

Audrey gave air kisses to the three women around the table and said, "Marla, Carrie, Sheila, this is Trixie. She's joining us for lunch."

"Thanks for letting me crash your lunch party."

Once settled into their seats, Marla said, "You were at the self-defense class last night, weren't you?" She leaned forward. "So, who's the good-looking guy with the long hair?"

"Good looking?" asked Trixie.

"Yeah, you know, the one talking to the deputy. He looks like a bad boy." A mischievous smile touched her lips. "And dangerous." She gave an exaggerated shiver. "I love a bad boy."

Trixie's eyes widened. "Oh. You mean Doc Stone." Good looking? That wasn't how she would've described him. Dangerous, maybe. She supposed he was attractive but not in a pretty boy way. Virile was a better adjective and roguish—definitely, roguish.

"Is he really a doctor?" asked Sheila, twirling a long blonde curl between her
fingers.

Trixie thought she resembled a cat toying with a poor, defenseless mouse. Doc was many things, but helpless wasn't one of them.

"Yes. He's the county's medical examiner."

Sheila leaned forward, exposing ample cleavage. "Is he married?"

Trixie thought back to her dinner discussion with Doc and wondered about the woman he almost married. What was she like, and why didn't they go through with the wedding? She said, "No, I don't think so."

Sheila licked her glossy pink lips. "Really doesn't matter. Personally, I hope he comes to the next class and gives me a little one-on-one instruction."

Trixie picked up her glass of water and took a sip to wash away the regret for joining these women.

"The classes are great, but the reason for them is disturbing," said Carrie.

Carrie was an attractive woman in a mousy way but seemed nice. Trixie wondered how she got sucked in with this pack of piranhas.

Carrie fidgeted in her chair. "Do you know if they have any suspects in Camille's murder?"

"Not that I know of. You worked with Camille, were you friends?"

Tears slid down her cheeks. "Camille really wasn't friends with anyone other than Dan."

For someone who claimed not to be friends with Camille, she was certainly upset.

"I'm sorry. I didn't mean to upset you."

"It's not that. I mean, I'm sorry Camille was murdered. It's just everything sucks right now. I might not have a job much longer."

Audrey put her arm around Carrie. "What's wrong?"

Carrie dried her eyes with a napkin. Looking to see if anyone was listening, she whispered, "Brookville Corporation is having some sort of financial problems."

"What? How?" asked Trixie.

"I don't know, but I overheard Dan and Jason talking—or I should say arguing. Dan said the Corporation was hemorrhaging money. And until he figured out what was going on, he was putting a halt to all construction."

"You're kidding?" said Audrey.

"No, I'm serious." Carrie absently tore her napkin into tiny pieces, forming a small pile of confetti beside her plate.

"How will that affect those of us who live at Brookville," asked Sheila.

"I don't know."

Trixie said, "Earlier today, I was out for a run and stopped by the construction site for the townhouses. They were moving the construction equipment out. Did Jason give Dan an explanation of where the money had gone? I would think, as CFO, he would know."

Carrie chewed her lip. "I heard him say he was looking into it. Then they shut the door."

Marla's blue eyes widened. "Seriously? I have friends who've bought townhouses. What's going to happen to them?"

Trixie shook her head. "I don't know, but I'm hoping the Corporation will make some sort of announcement soon. I don't think they'll have the luxury of keeping this quiet. And if the media catches wind of their difficulties, that could have disastrous consequences. Camille's murder, the skeleton, and now rumors of financial problems could be devastating to the Corporation's future."

"It feels like Brookville is going down the proverbial crapper," said Sheila.

"Carrie, tell Trixie about the argument between Dan and Camille," said Audrey.

Trixie leaned forward. "Audrey mentioned you'd overheard them arguing. What was it about?"

Carrie pursed her lips. "Audrey, you shouldn't have said anything. I told you about the argument in confidence."

"Stop worrying, Trixie isn't going to say anything." Audrey turned toward Trixie. "Are you?"

"Of course not. But if the argument was as obvious as you've described, others probably already know something was going on. Do you think they were having a lover's quarrel?"

Carrie jerked her head toward Audrey. "Oh, my God, you told her about the affair? I don't even want to think about Brittney knowing. Trust me, you don't want to be on Brittney's bad side. She may look like a Barbie doll, but behind the mascara and blush is a brain and very sharp teeth. She has an MBA from Vanderbilt." Carrie shook her head. "But it's not just her. The cops have been asking lots of questions. I know that's their job, and they're trying to find out who killed Camille, but it's compounding an already stressful situation." Her eyes scanned the restaurant. "I could really use a drink. Where's the waitress?"

Trixie asked, "Has law enforcement spoken with Dan?"

"Yeah, the deputy was in Dan's office for a long time." Carrie motioned to the waitress. "Bring us a couple bottles of wine." She looked around the table at the women. "That sounds good, doesn't it?"

"Any particular favorite?" asked the waitress.

"If it has alcohol, it's my favorite," said Carrie.

The waitress gave Carrie a curt nod. Within minutes, she returned with two bottles of wine.

Carrie filled her glass. "Thank goodness. Help yourself, girls."

After Carrie drank half the glass, Trixie said, "Audrey mentioned that Camille frequently hung around the office after hours. Was she there the evening before her murder?"

"I don't know, maybe." Carrie drank more wine. "Yes, she was there when I left for the evening.

"Do you recall what time that was?"

"I usually leave around six."

"Was that the same evening you overheard their argument?"

Carrie waded up what was left of her napkin and laid it beside the small heap of confetti. "No, the argument Audrey told you about happened a few weeks ago."

"Did Camille and Dan fight often?"

Carrie shook her head. "No, but a couple of nights before Carrie was murdered, I heard them talking loudly. Not really arguing—more like a differing opinion."

"Could you hear what they were saying?"

Carrie refilled her glass. "I don't know. I couldn't hear them that well. When Camille opened the door, she told Dan either he would do something about the situation or she would, and then she walked out and left. That was the last time I saw her."

Sheila sat her wine glass on the table. "Why all the questions? Are you a cop?"

Trixie turned toward Sheila. "I guess since my friends and I found Camille's body, I'm more than a little curious about the circumstances of her death. Aren't you curious why someone would want to murder her?"

"You know what they say about curiosity, right?"

Sheila's cavalier attitude grated on Trixie's nerves. "Did you know Camille?"

Sheila picked up her wine glass. "Nope. Never had the pleasure."

Trixie turned back to Carrie. "Did you tell the Deputy about the arguments?"

She shook her head. "I don't want to be any more involved than I am. That's Dan's story to tell." She threw back the rest of the wine. "Let's order."

* * *

When Trixie walked inside her home, the quiet was like a soothing tonic to her drained mind. Lunch with Audrey and her friends was exhausting. She had never been with a more shallow, tedious bunch of women in her life.

Generally, she preferred the company of men. Not necessarily in a sexual way, but she found them to be less dramatic. Kathleen and Martha were the exception to the rule. She was pleased and proud to call them her friends.

Trixie made a cup of herbal tea and settled into her reading chair with Patrick's book. There was no question the author, Barbara Brown, had been an integral part of Brookville's society. But who was she? Did she still live in Brookville? Another mystery for another day.

An hour later, she closed the book. Her herbal tea had long since turned cold, and now she had more questions than before and was anxious to get to the library's archives. She glanced at her watch, but that wasn't happening today.

Instead, she went into the Command Center and updated the board with the information she'd collected from Audrey and her friends. Once that was done, she retrieved a legal pad from the desk and scribbled several questions she needed to research.

Trixie needed to clear away the bad juju from Audrey and company and sort through the multitude of questions filling her mind. She pulled on her running gear and tied her shoes, confirmed the revolver was fully loaded, then strapped on the shoulder holster and left the house. She was running Brookville's trails today, and in her current mood, God help anyone who got in her way.

A mile into the run, the tension eased from her shoulders. Her stride lengthened, and the familiar euphoric feeling of flying took over. This was it. Right here. The reason she loved to run.

When she'd awakened in the ICU after being shot, her first concerns were her team members and the second, whether she could run. She was addicted, no doubt. Running was her go-to whenever life crowded in on her, when she had hard decisions to make, or when someone she loved so much it hurt, died. Running was what she did.

Trixie was reveling in the runner's high when she became aware of a presence closing in on her. Once a cop, always a cop. Instinctively, her hand went to the butt of the revolver. She pulled it from the holster and held it in front of her. Footsteps rapidly approached. Another runner or someone else? She pulled to a stop, turned, and aimed.

Doc dropped to the ground on his belly, hands over his head. "Don't shoot. What the hell are you thinking?"

"I'm thinking a woman was murdered here, and you should have called out to let me know you were there." She holstered the weapon.

Doc got to his feet and brushed dirt from his clothing. "Would you have shot me?"

She shrugged. "I guess we'll never know. Were you following me?"

"No. Like you, I enjoy variety in scenery and challenge when I run. Brookville's trails provide both."

Trixie arched a brow. "Aren't you concerned about running these trails? After all, a woman *was* murdered here."

"I'm more concerned about some crazy, gun-toting redhead running through the woods. You could've shot me."

"But I didn't." Trixie turned and started off at a slow jog.

Doc caught up with her. He gave her a side-eyed look. "Mind if I run with you? I would feel safer."

"Why? You worried about being attacked or that I might shoot you?"

"Both."

Trixie burst into laughter. "Fine. But if you run with me, we're going to talk about our cases."

"And there you go again, with our *cases.* May I remind you that you have nothing to do with them?"

"And may I remind you, Martha, Kathleen, and I are intimately involved. In fact, you might be surprised just how much so."

"This has the distinct ring of meddling."

"So, update me. Has Dr. Cain unearthed anything else? And before you say it's none of my business, you know as well as I do this information will eventually be all over the evening news. So, spill."

Chapter Twenty-One

Trixie woke up late. She'd read until the first rays of daylight had peeped through her bedroom window. Now, all she could think about was the book. She lay in bed for a few minutes longer, rehashing the incredible story. Was it true or just a brilliant work of fiction? She threw back the covers and got out of bed. Patrick O'Malley had offered coffee and a book discussion; Trixie was going to take him up on that offer. There were so many questions. She would start with him and then go back to the archives.

Trixie plucked the book from the nightstand and padded into the kitchen. She poured coffee into a bright blue mug and retrieved a legal pad and pen from the kitchen counter. Once settled at the kitchen table, she opened the book and started taking notes. Absently, she sipped coffee, re-read several chapters, and made more notes. When she'd finished, she was surprised to see it was nearly one o'clock. She called Patrick.

Patrick chuckled. "I knew you'd be spellbound once you started reading."

"The book was amazing. I'm surprised it didn't make it to the best-seller list. Do you have time for coffee this afternoon or even a late lunch? I'd love to discuss it with you."

"I'd be delighted. I could get away around two o'clock if that works for you. Let's have lunch. There's a little place I think you'll enjoy. I'll text you the address."

An hour later, Trixie was parked in front of Bernie's Burgers. She laughed as she got out of the car. The small brown A-frame structure was a salute to the Fifties. An arc of neon records glowed over the door. Elvis Presley's

"Jailhouse Rock" was prominently displayed on the label of the first album. Two large dancing neon figures glowed on each side of the door. A young girl dressed in a full skirt, her ponytail trailing behind her, danced with her partner, a young loafer-clad boy.

An older black Mercedes pulled into the lot and parked; Patrick stepped out of the sedan. Trixie waved. "This place is great. I didn't know it was here."

"If you like the outside, wait until you see the inside."

As they walked inside the restaurant, The Drifters' *"Under the Boardwalk"* played in the jukebox. "This is fantastic." Trixie admired the ceiling-to-floor memorabilia.

A tall, barrel-chested man moved toward them, a white apron tied around a still-trim waist. His hair was silver and brushed back into the style of the fifties. Golden brown eyes that had seen a lot of life studied her. Trixie estimated his age was somewhere between mid to late sixties. "Glad you like the place." The man turned his attention to Patrick. "It's good to see you. What's been keeping you away 'cause it can't be my food?"

"Thankfully, business has been good. Sadly, no time for going out to lunch."

The man turned toward Trixie. "You've brought me new business."

"This is my friend Trixie. Trixie, this is Bernie, the owner of this delectable establishment."

Trixie extended her hand. "It's nice to meet you. I love your place."

Bernie's thick hand engulfed Trixie's. His fingers squeezed her hand a little tighter than necessary. "Glad you like it. Grab a table." He crooked his index finger at a teenage girl who scurried over with two menus. "Tracy'll take your orders." Bernie studied Trixie for a moment and then turned and lumbered back into the kitchen.

Gooseflesh rose on Trixie's skin as she watched Bernie walk away. She turned to Patrick. "There's something about him I'm not sure I like."

"Not exactly welcoming, but he'll grow on you. However, this place has the best burgers I've eaten in my life. You must try the Carolina Burger. It's covered in chili, slaw, mustard, and onions. It's my favorite, and I've tried most of the burgers on the menu." Tracy arrived back at their table. Patrick looked up at Trixie. "Want to give it a try?"

"Sure, why not?"

Patrick ordered two Carolina Burgers with fries.

"I have a feeling I'm going to need an extra run today."

"Trust me, heaven on earth, and worth the extra calories." Patrick leaned forward. "Now, let's talk about the book."

Trixie pulled the pad of paper she'd written notes on earlier from her handbag. Patrick clapped his hands. "How wonderful, you took notes."

Trixie leaned forward. "Did Barbara Brown live in Brookville?"

"At the time the book was published, there were two people in town with that name, but they were both teenagers. We can only surmise Barbara Brown was a pseudonym. There have been many unsuccessful attempts to discover who the author really was." His eyes twinkled. "Another Brookville mystery waiting to be solved. However, as I'm sure you've noticed, the author had an intimate knowledge of Brookville. One can only assume he or she was a resident."

Trixie shook her head. "It's more than that. The author not only had an intimate knowledge of Brookville but also of Brookville society. In particular, the Jeffries family. They're very much a focal point of the book." Trixie tapped the end of her pen on the notepad. "The book was published in the late eighties, but the events in the book are focused on the seventies. Even though the country was coming out of the sixties and free love, this is the South." She lowered her voice. "I would imagine the scandal of an illegitimate child by a prominent family, such as the Jeffries, caused quite a stir."

"The seventies were the heyday for the Jeffries family, but suspicion of Alexandra's illegitimacy was whispered about in back rooms. No one dared say anything to the family. After all, Richard Jeffries owned this town, and he was a very powerful man."

Tracy returned with plates laden with fries and burgers the size of small saucers. Chili, mustard, and slaw dripped down the sides of the bun. Trixie's eyes widened. "Never in my life have I seen a burger like this. It looks fabulous."

"Tuck in. Tastes even better than it looks."

Trixie took a bite of the burger; juice trickled down her chin. She grabbed a napkin and caught the dribble. "Delicious."

Trixie and Patrick ate in silence for several minutes. Patrick leaned back in his chair. "I believe my appetite is sated enough to continue our conversation. As you read in the book, it wasn't just that the child was illegitimate; it was also the fact that Mrs. Jeffries had an affair with someone from the wrong side of the tracks. The community held the Jeffries to a higher standard than the rest of us." He picked up his glass of iced tea and took a drink. "And as we know, when someone is placed on a pedestal, it's a slippery slope."

"The book doesn't say who the biological father of Alexandra Jeffries was. Any idea?"

Patrick glanced at Bernie. "I have my own ideas." Trixie followed his gaze. The burly man was wiping down the counter. He looked up. His golden-brown eyes met Trixie's, but there was no warmth in them. An icy shiver rippled down her spine.

Trixie took a bite of her burger and chewed. "There is mention in the book of several disappearances. One of them, a young girl named Sara. Any idea what happened to her or, for that matter, any of them?"

Patrick dipped a French fry into the puddle of ketchup. "The disappearances caused quite a stir. If I recall, Sara was the first to go missing from Brookville. Her beau from a nearby town went missing as well. Then, a year or so later, a vagrant disappeared. The newspaper following the disappearance reported one of the vagrant's friends stated the last time he'd seen him, he was talking with an unknown woman. The vagrant was never seen again. Authorities found no evidence of foul play and assumed the man and woman left town together. Less than a year later, it happened again. Same sort of story. The disappearances in Brookville stopped for a few years, then they started back."

"But no bodies were recovered, right?"

"Not until last week."

"Do you think the skeleton belongs to one of the missing?"

"Maybe."

"What about Camille? Do you think her murder is related?"

Patrick dipped another fry into the ketchup. "I think anything is possible."

Trixie had the distinct feeling of being watched. She glanced up and met Bernie's golden eyes. The expression on his face was unreadable and disconcerting. Finally, he turned away and continued wiping down the counter.

Trixie leaned in closer. She tipped her head toward Bernie. "What's his story?"

Patrick glanced at Bernie and lowered his voice. "Now there's an interesting character. Rumor has it he showed up in Brookville when he was about eighteen years old, nothing more than a vagrant. He was a tall, broad-shouldered, good-looking lad. And quite the flirt. The mothers in town kept a vigilant eye on their young daughters when he was around. He worked odd jobs around town and for the Jeffries family. Then, a year or two after arriving in town, he was put in prison. I don't recall his crime. The interesting thing was when he got out of prison, he opened this place." Patrick chewed on a fry. "Curious, don't you think? How does a young man with no resources and fresh out of prison open his own restaurant?"

"That story isn't in the book, is it?"

Patrick tossed the rest of the fry into his mouth. "No, it isn't."

Trixie's eyes widened. "You think Bernie had an affair with Mrs. Jeffries, don't you? And if he did..." her eyes shifted to Bernie and then back to Patrick. "And if he did, it's possible he's Alexandra's father."

"Elizabeth Jeffries took that secret to her grave." He made the sign of the cross and then glanced at Bernie. "But if he is the father, he'll never tell." Patrick turned back toward Trixie. "A word of caution: if you're thinking about asking Bernie questions, don't. He's not a man to trifle with. At any rate, it appears you've got another mystery to solve."

Trixie watched Bernie. Richard Jeffries wouldn't want the world to know his wife had had an affair, let alone with someone like Bernie. Did Richard give Bernie the startup money to keep him quiet, or did Mrs. Jeffries give him the money to keep him close? "What happened to Alexandra?"

"I'm not sure. Rumor has it that when Alexandra was in her late teens, Richard caught her with a boy in her room. Apparently, a scuffle occurred, and somehow, the young man was shot to death. There was an inquiry, but authorities called it accidental, and no charges were pressed against Richard. A few months later, Alexandra was whisked away, never to be seen again."

"That's odd. You didn't hear anything through the gossip mill?"

"Lass, I was new to Brookville and knew very little of the gossip. But there's more." Patrick leaned closer. "Elizabeth died a few years after Alexandra was shipped away. The official story was that she had a heart attack."

"But you don't believe that, do you?"

"No. Not really. It was well known Elizabeth was, shall we say, mentally fragile. Gossip says she killed herself and because of the Jeffries name and standing in the community, it was covered up."

Trixie leaned back in her chair. "I think you could write your own Brookville history."

"Aye, lass, I could. Being a bookseller is a little like being a bartender; people come into the store and love to talk."

Trixie reached over and gave his hand a light squeeze. "And you love to listen."

"Indeed, I do. Nothing better than a bit of juicy gossip." He cocked his head to the side. "What are you going to do with all of these interesting tidbits?"

"Sounds like good fodder for more research."

Patrick's eyes grew serious. "You need to be careful. Sometimes, it's best for the past to stay buried in the darkness. It doesn't like being brought out into the light."

Sean's voice whispered in her mind. *Listen to him, Red.*

Chapter Twenty-Two

Trixie hadn't touched her blog since Camille's murder and the discovery of the skeletonized remains. And even though it was less than a week since her last post, she'd received emails from a variety of companies asking when she would review their products. Even her readers were sending emails wondering where she was. Like it or not, she had work to do.

She was in the middle of writing a review for Crispy Cheese Straws, a light and tasty snack when her doorbell rang. Why would someone come to her home this early in the morning? She wasn't expecting Martha and Kathleen. They were coming by later in the day.

Trixie dusted cheese straw crumbs from her shirt and opened the door. She was surprised to see Sandi Fields and a young man with perfectly coiffed dark hair and a clipboard standing on her porch. *Oh crap, it's Wednesday.* She smoothed back her unruly hair, fully aware of her disheveled appearance, baggy sweatpants, tee shirt, and orange fingers. "I totally forgot about the appointment. I'm so sorry."

Sandi gave her a tight smile. "We can reschedule if this is inconvenient."

"No. Of course not. I was working, and time got away from me. Please, come in." Trixie stood to the side. "Can I get you coffee?"

"No, thank you. We have a busy schedule. Perhaps we can get started with a tour of the house? As we walk, let's chat about your vision for the renovations. Jonathan will take notes."

"Let's move into the kitchen. This area is my priority." Trixie hurried ahead and tried to tidy the kitchen table as she went. "I'm not much on cooking. So, the kitchen is more my work area. I would love to have a place at the back of the kitchen with a built-in desk, some counter space, and a few drawers for hanging files. And maybe an overhead bin."

A furrow formed between Sandi's green eyes. "Wouldn't you prefer to convert the guest room into your office? You would have so much more space."

"No. The nature of my work at times requires me to sample a variety of company products. At times, the packaging isn't what it should be. The kitchen is easier to clean any mess that might occur."

Sandi walked around the kitchen. "Do you want a full kitchen renovation? I could make this space much more functional, which would help with resale if or when you decide to sell. Unfortunately, my ex-husband didn't consult me when he was constructing these condos. They could have been designed to be much more efficient."

"Sure. I'd love to hear your ideas and an estimate of the cost."

Sandi and Jonathan measured the kitchen. "I would move your refrigerator and stove to the same wall, add an island with stools to give you additional counter space and storage while providing an eating area. That way, if you use the kitchen table for your work, you wouldn't have to move anything. And I would also replace the faux granite counters with the real thing."

Trixie smiled. "I like it. What about the lighting?"

"We'd add some recessed lighting and a fun chandelier over the table." Sandi turned to Jonathan. "Did you get all of that?" He nodded. "Okay, let's take a look at the rest of the house."

Trixie led them into the master suite. She hurried over to her unmade bed and straightened the comforter.

"Trixie, relax. We aren't here to judge your housekeeping. The room is functional; however, if your closet is like mine, it could be converted into a more usable space."

"You read my mind."

Sandi shook her head. "You can tell a man designed the closet. You should come by my condo and look at mine. I'll make us a quick lunch and we can discuss the particulars."

"I'd love to." Trixie led Sandi and Jonathan out into the small hallway.

"What about your guest room?" Sandi paused at the door, looked at Martha's sign, and raised a brow. "Command Center?"

"Oh, ah, yeah, this is where my friends and I get together to indulge in our hobby."

"Which is?"

"Amateur sleuths. We've been researching Camille's murder. This space is fine. It really doesn't need any work."

"Amateur sleuths? Interesting."

Trixie's cell rang. "I'm sorry, I need to get that." She hurried into the kitchen and picked up the phone.

"So, what did Sandi say?" asked Kathleen.

"I'm showing her my condo now. I'll call you back." Trixie disconnected and hurried back to Sandi.

Sandi stood in the middle of the Command Center. "Wow, this is really something." She slowly moved around the room, pausing in front of each murder board. "Are you cops?"

Trixie laughed uncomfortably. "No. Like I said, it's a hobby. There isn't anything in here that needs work." She stood in the doorway and motioned for Sandi and Jonathan to follow her.

Sandi turned back to the whiteboard. "These notes are very detailed. You and your friends obviously take your hobby seriously. And there's quite a bit of information on the Jeffries family. How are they connected?"

"As far as we know, they aren't. We find their history interesting. Let's move along to the living room." Trixie made a mental note to lock the Command Center door.

When Trixie finished giving Sandi and Jonathan the tour of her home, Sandi said, "I'll provide you with drawings of my design suggestions and work up a quote. Jonathan will send them to you in a few days. Let me know when you want to come by to see my closet."

"I will. Thanks again." Trixie watched Sandi and Jonathan get into the sedan and pull away. Shutting the door, she leaned against it and let out a long breath. She wasn't sure if the tension came from thinking about the cost of renovating or that someone had seen the Command Center and all their notes. She gave herself a mental shake. Why did it matter? But something about Sandi's demeanor made it matter.

* * *

Trixie went back to her blog and finished the review of Crispy Cheese Straws. They were, in fact, a very light and tasty snack. Before she realized it, she'd eaten half of the box. The morning had flown by, and Kathleen and Martha would arrive in an hour.

Trixie was arranging cubes of cheese and assorted crackers on a tray when the doorbell rang.

Kathleen opened the door and poked her head inside. "Hello, anyone home?"

"Come in. I'm fixing snacks."

Kathleen and Martha walked into Trixie's kitchen. Martha grabbed a cube of cheese from the tray. "Excellent. Fortification, just what working detectives need,"

Kathleen held out a plate. "I made brownies. I thought detectives need the sugar to keep up our energy."

Martha's eyes widened. "Brownies? Truly, food from the heavens. Mind if I sample one?"

Kathleen peeled back the plastic wrap. "Help yourself."

Martha plucked a brownie from the plate and took a large bite. She brushed crumbs from her chin and shifted the brownie to her left cheek. "These are delicious."

"I'm glad you like them. The recipe was my mother's. I could send you a copy."

Martha shook her head and snatched up another brownie. "Not necessary. You make them, and I will consume them. It is the perfect symbiotic relationship."

Kathleen placed a hand on her hip. "How is that benefiting both of us?"

"Symbiosis is based on three relationships. One of which is commensalism, where one benefits and no harm comes to the other." Martha reached for another brownie.

Trixie shook her head and picked up the tray of cheese and crackers. "Come on. Let's get to work."

Once settled in the Command Center, Trixie recounted her discussion with Patrick.

"Do you think this Bernie fellow is the father of Elizabeth's illegitimate child?" asked Kathleen.

"I don't know, but you've got to admit for a man with no means, it's very suspicious he was able to open a restaurant right out of prison."

"What happened to Alexandra?" asked Kathleen.

"According to Patrick, no one knows," said Trixie.

"What a sad story. All that wealth and prominence, and it only brought them unhappiness," said Kathleen.

"Patrick mentioned that the other disappearances started shortly after Sara and her boyfriend went missing."

Martha picked up another brownie. "Interesting you should say that. Kathleen and I went back to the library archive this morning. Over the past thirty years, there have been over twenty suspicious disappearances."

Martha laid the remainder of the brownie on her plate. "Based on the available information, we should seriously consider whether there is a serial killer in Brookville."

"I think you're right. The evidence seems to be pointing us in that direction," said Trixie.

Kathleen shivered and folded her arms across her body. "What we found was more than a little disconcerting."

Trixie made bullet points on the Human Remains board. She turned to Martha. "Go on."

"Beyond a few brief articles, the archives were not overly helpful. We decided to use another source. As we have discussed and you have experienced first-hand, Inez has an uncanny ability for recalling Brookville history. Several years ago, she helped an investigative reporter who came to town to do research for a book. He was writing on crime in small-town America, specifically, the disappearances of people who society had forgotten or ignored. During their research, they stumbled upon quite a bit of information regarding missing persons in Brookville and surrounding small towns. At the time, they had suspicions that a serial killer was hunting in this area. The victims were typically prostitutes and vagrants; people that had no families or whose families had lost touch with them."

Kathleen chewed a cube of cheese. "But this is Brookville; we don't have prostitutes. And as for vagrants, I see a few panhandlers, but do we really have enough of a population for someone to have hunted them all this time?"

Martha said, "Your view of Brookville is unrealistic. This town is like any other. I am sure there are places where you would not feel comfortable. Think about the abandoned factories on the east side of town. I assume you avoid that area. I'm certain Nelson would confirm illicit activities occur there." Martha turned toward Trixie. "Wouldn't you agree?"

"Martha is correct. So, let's get back to Inez. If this information wasn't in the archives, where did she and the reporter find it?"

Martha nodded vigorously. "This is the fascinating part. It appears Inez used her feminine wiles to glean the information from a homicide detective. I was unaware this could be done."

Trixie burst into laughter. "Yep. Oldest trick in the book. Been around since biblical times."

"Apparently, I haven't read that book."

"Oh, for heaven's sake, stop it," said Kathleen. "There is nothing humorous about any of this." She pulled the plate of brownies toward her and dropped two of the chocolatey confections onto her plate. Martha and Trixie stared at her. "What? I'm an emotional mess. I need these. I can stop anytime I want." Kathleen shoved a brownie into her mouth. "The thought of a serial killer, here in Brookville…." She shoved the second brownie into her mouth. Cheeks burgeoning, she said, "Oh lord, do you really think Camille was murdered by a serial killer?" She reached for the platter of brownies.

Trixie pulled the plate out of reach. "Kathleen, breathe."

Martha said, "Doubtful. The serial killer hid his or her misdeeds. Whoever killed Camille did not try to hide her. However, if they were interrupted…."

Kathleen chewed faster; her eyes darted from Martha to Trixie. Trixie glared at Martha. "Not helping." She turned back to Kathleen. "And you need to relax. Let's switch subjects. Do we have any new information on Camille's case?" Trixie moved to the board labeled *Camille's Murder*. Who had motive to want her dead?"

"Brittney is an obvious choice. If she found out about Dan and Camille's affair, maybe she went into a jealous rage," said Kathleen.

"Maybe." Trixie wrote Brittney's name under the heading. "What about Dan? Maybe Camille threatened to tell Brittney, and Dan killed her to keep her quiet."

"That, too, is a possibility," said Martha. "And if Camille uncovered financial misdeeds, that could have gotten her murdered. Or was she embezzling money from the Corporation? Was she in cahoots with Jason Knight? He is the CFO."

Trixie added two more bullets and notations. "Good points."

"And there's always the possibility Camille had a fight with a lover, and things got out of hand," said Trixie.

"I doubt that is a valid point. To date, we have been unable to link Camille romantically to anyone other than Dan Fields."

"What else do we know about the Corporation's financial troubles?" asked Trixie.

Kathleen eyed a third brownie. "Not much. And, unfortunately, we don't have connections to provide us access to that information."

"Maybe we do," said Trixie. "Carrie works at the corporate offices. She appeared genuinely surprised and upset about their financial troubles. She might know something that could be helpful. It's worth a follow-up conversation."

Martha drummed her fingertips on the desk. "There is another person of interest that should be added to our list."

Trixie looked at the board. "Who?"

"Alexandra Jeffries."

"Why would we add her?" asked Kathleen. "No one has seen the woman since she was a teenager. For all we know, she's dead."

"While all that is true. I find it intriguing that her name and that of her family continue to surface, and we can find no record of her death. So, one must assume she is still alive."

Kathleen wiped her mouth with a napkin. "Unless she's buried in one of those graves on the Jeffries' property."

Martha stood and paced the small room. "Do we know who inherited the Jeffries estate?"

Trixie shook her head. "No, but that would be public record." She went back to the computer and opened the browser. After a few minutes of searching the records, she sat back in the chair. "Huh."

"What does that mean?" asked Kathleen.

"Richard Jeffries left his estate to the town of Brookville. The town sold a large portion of the property to the Brookville Corporation."

"Wonder why he did not leave his estate to Alexandra?" asked Martha.

"Maybe he knew she was dead," said Kathleen.

"Or maybe Richard Jeffries knew Alexandra was not his biological daughter. Maybe the rumors are true and maybe Alexandra was the daughter of Bernard Cooper," said Trixie.

Chapter Twenty-Three

T hree days later, Trixie sat at the kitchen table and reviewed the overwhelming materials sent from Sandi's office. There were sketches of several designs, paint chip samples, fabric swatches, and an estimate for each design scenario. One thing was obvious: renovating was not cheap.

She stuffed the materials back into the envelope. It was almost time for self-defense class, and Kathleen and Martha would be waiting for her. She hurried to her room and ran a brush through her hair. Giving her reflection in the bathroom mirror a final look, she dabbed perfume on her wrists and went outside.

"Sorry to keep you waiting."

Martha sniffed the air as Trixie walked by. "Are you wearing perfume?"

"Maybe. Why?"

"Why bother?"

"I like smelling nice."

"Is that the only reason? And what is up with the makeup? We *are* going to self-defense class, right?"

"Can we go, please? We're going to be late."

Kathleen took in Trixie's form-fitting teal tee shirt and black yoga pants. "Cute outfit, and your makeup looks especially nice."

"Don't start."

"Smell her," said Martha. "She's wearing perfume."

Kathleen leaned in closer to Trixie and sniffed. "And you do smell nice, too. Chanel? For self-defense class?"

* * *

Trixie, Kathleen, and Martha walked inside the clubhouse. The space was packed, and the noise deafening. Kathleen kicked off her shoes. "There are more people here this morning than last week. Are we going to have enough room to move?"

Martha stood on her tiptoes and looked around the room.

"What are you looking for?" asked Trixie.

"The maximum occupancy sign; we may have surpassed that number."

Through the crowd of people, Trixie saw Deputy Michelle Williams moving toward them. She motioned for them to go outside.

When they were outside the clubhouse, Trixie said, "Can you believe this turnout? What are we going to do?"

"Nelson is on his way. I told him to bring backup." Michelle pointed to a grassy picnic area behind the clubhouse. "We'll have to move some of the people out here."

Deputy Nelson joined the women. He winked at Kathleen, then turned to Michelle. "What's the plan?"

"We can move twenty-plus people out here. That should empty the room sufficiently. Did you bring any help?"

"Doc should be here any minute. I'll take the group out here, and Doc can help you."

Trixie wanted to protest, but the need for another instructor was real. The women went back inside the clubhouse, and Michelle gathered twenty participants and directed them outside. Across the room, Trixie saw Sandi Fields. How did she manage to do it? She looked just as gorgeous in yoga pants and a tee shirt as she had in her expensive suit.

Sandi waved at Trixie and moved toward them.

"Sandi, I'm glad you could join us." Trixie introduced Martha and Kathleen.

"This is a treat. I finally get to meet the rest of the Brookville sleuths. You have quite the setup."

"Set up?" asked Martha.

"Yes. The Command Center is quite something, a command center for the FBI." She laughed. "Depending on the outcome of your cases, this could be a new career path for you women."

"Wouldn't it be something if you solved the murder?" Sandi waved at a brunette across the room. "I've got to go. It was great meeting you all. Trixie, we'll talk soon."

Martha, Kathleen, and Trixie watched Sandi make her way through the crowd and over to a group of women. "I don't like her," said Kathleen.

Martha said, "Yeah, me either." She turned and glared at Trixie. "How does she know about our...hobby?"

Trixie picked at a non-existent hangnail. "If you recall, I told you Sandi was coming by my condo to give me an estimate on some renovations. She saw the room when I was showing her the house."

"Oh," said Martha.

The last of Michelle's group of twenty had moved outside. Martha made small circles with her outstretched arms. "Yes, this is much better." A smile stretched across her face.

"What's so funny?" asked Trixie.

"Someone is watching you."

"What are you talking about?"

Martha pointed at the wall across the room. "Dr. Stone is watching; no, scowling at you. Did you do something to irritate him?"

Trixie turned in the direction Martha was looking. "Me breathing irritates him." Stone was dressed in black sweatpants and a light blue tank. Trixie felt the now familiar flutter in her stomach.

Sure, there was a certain feral quality about Doc that she begrudgingly found attractive. But he wasn't her type, and she wasn't interested. Maybe she should introduce him to Audrey's friend, Sheila. She'd been blatant about her desire to meet him.

Trixie sucked in a breath. No point delaying the inevitable. "Damn the torpedoes." Trixie moved toward Doc.

Stone's arms were folded across his chest. His dark, brooding eyes tracked her movements. Self-conscious under his scrutiny, Trixie suddenly became the proud owner of two left feet. She stumbled, took three large steps, tried to regain her footing, and then tumbled to the ground. She was sprawled on the hard floor, trying to catch her breath, when Doc strode over to her.

Hands propped on his knees, he bent over her. "Need help?"

Trixie looked up at him. He was smirking. She hated smirking. "No. I don't need your help." She tried getting to her feet, but her right leg was numb. She looked up at Stone, who still wore the smirk. A crowd had formed. She mouthed the word "help."

The smirk turned to concern. He knelt beside her. "What's wrong?"

"My leg, I can't feel it." Normally, she felt pins and needles, and sometimes there was weakness, but this time there was nothing. It was like her leg was gone. Panic rose inside her, and Trixie fought to keep it at bay. She grabbed Doc's arm. "Please, I don't want anyone to know."

Kathleen hurried toward her, Jack Nelson in her wake. "Trixie, are you okay?"

Doc stood, providing a barrier between Trixie and the crowd. "Nothing to see. She's fine. Just knocked the air out of her. Give her some space to catch her breath." He looked at Nelson. "You and Michelle start class." Nelson's gaze moved from Doc to Trixie. He gave a quick nod and was gone. Moments later, class was in session.

Doc knelt beside her. "Can you feel anything?"

"No." Trixie heard the panic in her voice. Hot tears stung her eyes.

Doc lifted her and carried her to a cushioned chair. "Are you in pain?"

Trixie shook her head. "I wish it did hurt. Feeling nothing is way scarier."

Doc looked over his shoulder. "It appears Deputy Williams has a new assistant." Trixie turned her attention to the front of the room, where Martha was taking her new responsibility very seriously.

Trixie laughed. "Yep, you've been replaced. Good luck trying to get your position back."

Doc moved a chair across from her and settled into it. "That's fine. Besides, I only came for the entertainment." His eyes met hers. "And you didn't disappoint." He gave her a genuine smile—no smirk.

Despite herself, Trixie laughed. "Glad I could amuse you. If you insist on sitting here, want to explain the irritated look you were giving me prior to the entertainment portion of the morning?"

"What? Sorry, I was thinking about work."

Trixie pushed herself up in the chair. The sensation of pins and needles prickled her foot. A flood of relief washed over her. "Work? As in *our* cases." Stone narrowed his eyes. "You found something, didn't you?"

"The Sheriff's office will make an official statement later today."

"About?"

Doc blew out a breath. "Without a doubt, you are the most single-minded, determined woman I have ever met."

"I get that a lot. What was found?"

"Dr. Cain uncovered four more graves."

"Were the remains intact? Were they old or fresh?"

Doc leaned back in his chair. "Are you finished?"

"Sorry. Continue, please."

"None were fresh, as you say. Two of the skeletonized bodies are intact. We've set up an onsite lab to help with processing the remains. However, it's going to take Dr. Cain time to piece together the others. We'll try searching dental records; maybe we'll get lucky. Dr. Cain was able to extract bone samples from the base of the skull of two of the decedents. She sent them to a lab that specializes in extracting and enriching human DNA from degraded bone. Our hope is they will be able to find a match in CODIS."

Trixie contemplated a scuff mark on the floor while debating whether to tell Doc what they had uncovered in their research. Would he accuse them of meddling? Or would it save them time and be helpful to the case?

"Ms. Tanner, it appears you are struggling with some sort of thought process. Care to share?"

She looked at him. "Could you and Jack come to my home this evening? There's something you need to see. We may have uncovered information that could aid the investigation."

* * *

As they walked back to their condos, Martha said, "That was another excellent class." She looked at Trixie. "Why didn't you participate?"

"The conversation was more interesting."

"I saw you and Doc. The two of you looked very cozy," said Kathleen.

"Cozy is not the word I would use." Trixie stopped walking. "Doc told me the forensic anthropologist has uncovered four more skeletons."

Martha pushed her glasses up on her nose. "So, our suspicion of a serial killer appears to be more viable."

Kathleen's eyes shifted anxiously from Trixie to Martha. "Do they think he's still in the area?"

"Keep in mind the remains thus far have been between twenty and thirty years old," said Martha. "Whoever murdered these people may no longer be alive. It is also possible they are incarcerated or—"

"Or what?" said Kathleen.

"Never mind."

"You think it's possible they are still here, don't you?" said Kathleen.

"We can't rule it out," said Martha.

"Kathleen, relax," said Trixie. "Jack and Doc are coming over tonight. It's time we show them what we've discovered. It could help them.

"Personally, I think it is past time," said Martha. "When will they arrive?"

"After dinner."

"Excellent. That will give Kathleen time to prepare more of her delicious brownies."

"I'm not sure this is a good idea," said Kathleen. "And I don't know that I want to make brownies."

"That is too bad. I imagine Deputy Nelson would enjoy your brownies. You know, being a bachelor and all."

Trixie said, "Don't worry about it. I'm sure I can scrounge something from the kitchen. You know, crackers with a dollop of jam and a pot of coffee would be fine. Don't you think, Martha?"

Kathleen threw her hands up in the air. "Fine. I'll make the damn brownies, but I'm going on record that I'm not happy about it."

"Noted," said Trixie.

Chapter Twenty-Four

Trixie moved beside Doc and handed him a cup of coffee. He gave her a side-eyed look.

"What?" she asked.

He pointed to the murder board. "This is impressive. The detail and the timeline—well, it's...." He lifted a hand. "Well, it's quite something."

Trixie narrowed her eyes at him. "Do you mean that in a sarcastic, you women are a pain in my ass kind of way? Or more, you women have done an amazing job, and this will help our case immensely, kind of way?"

Stone rubbed the back of his neck. "It's a combination." He turned to face her, his expression serious. "Ms. Tanner, what you women have put together is amazing, but it's time to let Nelson do his job."

Nelson rubbed his eyes. He looked tired. "Besides me and Doc, who else knows you've been digging around in these cases?"

Martha adjusted her glasses. "We have not been quiet about our research. We've asked questions, and it's no secret that we've been looking through the archives."

Nelson shot Martha a look. "You women have been running all over creation without any regard for the consequences. I want names. Who knew you were investigating Camille's death and the skeletal remains?"

Martha beamed at Nelson. "I am pleased you see us as equals, co-investigators."

Nelson turned toward her. "I am using the term investigate loosely, *very* loosely."

Kathleen sat at the desk and pulled paper and pen toward her. Pen poised, she said, "So, let's make a list of people who know about our investigation."

"Brittney Fields," said Martha. "We met her at Camille's crime scene."

"Patrick O'Malley from the Book Shoppe knows I have an interest in Brookville's history and the dirty secrets of its residents," said Trixie. "Oh, and you should probably include the co-owner, Colin Delaney."

"And let's not forget Audrey from self-defense class," said Kathleen. "Trixie talked with her quite a bit."

"And if we include her, we should add her friends Sheila, Marla, and Carrie to the list. Especially Carrie," said Trixie. "And we can't discount Sandi Fields and her ex-husband, Dan."

"And if they know, it is possible Jason Knight knows," said Kathleen.

Trixie said, "Excellent point. We should add him to our suspects list as well."

"We should also include Inez from the library. However, I doubt she is a viable threat," said Martha. "Oh, and don't forget Sandi Fields saw our command center."

Trixie said, "And it's possible that Bernie Cooper may have overheard my conversation with Patrick. Although, I can't be certain, but the looks he gave me do make me wonder."

"Bernie Cooper?" Nelson rubbed the stubble on his chin. "Wow, I haven't heard that name in a long time."

"Yeah, he owns and operates Bernie's Burgers. It's just outside of town," said Trixie. "Great burgers, by the way."

Nelson's jaw worked. "Is there anyone in town who doesn't know about your," he made air quotes, "investigation?"

Martha said, "Deputy, I'm certain there are many people in Brookville who do not know us or what we have been doing."

Nelson pinched the bridge of his nose and shot Doc a desperate look. "You women realize that Camille's murderer and or the person or persons responsible for," he waved at the boards, "these other deaths, may also know you're poking around in their dark secrets?" He paced in front of the murder boards. "The murderer could be someone on Miss Kathleen's list, or it could be someone connected to a person on that list, or it could be someone not connected to any of the above. Gossip spreads in this town." He turned toward the women. "You must stop your investigation immediately. Do you understand?"

"Our hope was that the information would be helpful. Not send you into a panic," said Trixie.

Nelson's face flushed. "I'm not in a so-called panic." He glanced at Kathleen. "I'm concerned. You women are setting yourselves up as targets and possibly victims."

Kathleen's hand fluttered to her throat. "Jack? Do you really think we're in danger?"

Nelson moved beside Kathleen and put his arm around her. "Don't you worry. I'll take good care of you."

Trixie perched on the edge of the desk. "Maybe if you told us what you know, we could compare notes and work together."

"Ms. Tanner, the deputy is giving you sound advice. You should take it," said Doc.

Martha moved to the front of the room and shot Nelson a look. "While we are sharing information. We should also share a theory we have developed."

"Which is?" asked Nelson.

"We believe Brookville has a serial killer."

Nelson shook his head. "That seems a little far-fetched. Yes, there have been some disappearances over the years, but vagrants and prostitutes float from town to town. I'd have to dig into this further, go back into cold case files and revisit that information before I could make any determination, and frankly, I don't have the manpower or time."

"There is no need. Inez used her feminine wiles several years ago to retrieve much of that information. However, we could use an update of, say, the last five to ten years."

Nelson gritted his teeth. "Inez, who? And she used her what? On whom? What information?"

Doc moved beside Trixie. "Now would be a good time to jump in. I don't think Nelson has much left on that last nerve."

Trixie rolled her eyes. "And it was just starting to get interesting." She turned toward Nelson. "Jack, Martha's trying to tell you that we have the missing persons information from the Sheriff's department. How we received that information is irrelevant. You're missing the point. It would be helpful if we could go through your cold case files for the last five years. You just admitted you don't have the time or manpower. Using our energy would certainly save you time and be helpful, right?"

Color rose in Nelson's cheeks. "I can't just turn over case information to you women. And as for this Inez person, I'd like to know how she was able to get access to those files."

"I just told you how," said Martha.

"Jack, sweetie, try one of my brownies." Kathleen held the plate out to him. "I made them myself." He glared at Martha and then looked down at Kathleen. She looked up at him, her blue eyes widened. Nelson's face softened, and he took a brownie from the plate.

"These look delicious." He bit into the confection. "And they taste as good as they look."

"Let's get you a cup of coffee." Kathleen tucked her small hand in Jack's.

Trixie said, "And that, Martha, is feminine wiles at work."

* * *

After Nelson and Doc left, the women cleared away the dirty dishes. "I think that went well, don't you?" said Trixie.

"Agreed," said Martha. "However, it would have been nice to know if Nelson was going to let us see the cold case files."

Kathleen dried a flowered mug and placed it inside the cabinet. "Martha, Jack needs to figure out the best way to handle the situation. We don't want to get him in trouble with the Sheriff."

Trixie placed the last of the clean mugs into the cabinet. "Kathleen's right. We don't want Jack to lose his job because of us. Thanks for helping me clean up."

"I'm beat," said Kathleen.

Martha yawned. "Me too. And I've got the morning shift at the library."

Trixie walked Kathleen and Martha to the door. "Are you sure you don't want me to drive you home? It's getting dark."

Martha shook her head. "I'm fine." She punched the air with her fist. "I can take care of myself."

"And I need to walk," said Kathleen. "I ate too many brownies. Besides, there are plenty of streetlights. We'll talk tomorrow."

The evening had gone better than Trixie expected, but now, she was ready for bed. She had just turned out the lights in the kitchen when she heard the squeal of tires followed by a piercing scream. Instinctively, she grabbed her weapon from the kitchen drawer, then ran to her front door and yanked it open. Martha was running toward her; the color drained from her face. "Call 911. Someone just tried to kill Kathleen."

Chapter Twenty-Five

Nelson paced the circumference of the drab hospital waiting room several times. He stopped and jabbed a finger in the air. "If that sweet woman dies or is permanently injured in any way, I will find the one responsible, and I will make sure they are buried as deep in God's earth as I can get them."

Trixie stood and took hold of Jack's arm. "You need to calm down. The doctor doesn't think Kathleen has any life-threatening injuries. She's banged up, but otherwise okay. They're running scans as a precaution. Now sit down and chill, or you're going to be admitted."

"Fine." Nelson perched on the edge of a straight-backed blue vinyl chair, then jumped up. "I can't sit still." He turned to Trixie. "You want coffee? How about you, Martha, you want coffee? Never mind, I'll get all of us coffee. I'll be back in a few minutes." He stormed from the room.

Martha called to him. "Take your time." She watched Nelson hurry down the hall. When he was out of sight, she said, "Thank goodness, I was on the verge of asking the doctor to sedate him."

Trixie leaned back in the uncomfortable chair. "That makes two of us." She watched the doorway for a moment, then turned to Martha. "You okay?"

"I'm fine." Martha held out her hands. "At least my hands aren't shaking anymore."

"Do you feel up to going back over what happened?"

"Sure."

"You're certain this wasn't a distracted driver who ran up on the curb, when they realized what they'd done, took off?"

"Positive. This was not an accident. Someone tried to kill Kathleen."

"Start at the beginning, and don't leave anything out."

"Kathleen and I were walking back to our condos. I had started down my street when I heard an engine rev and tires squeal. When I turned, I saw the car bouncing over the curb, speeding toward Kathleen. I yelled for her to look out." Martha's expression was grim; her determined, tear-brimmed eyes looked up at Trixie. "The driver did not try to avoid Kathleen. He or she came barreling toward her. The intent was clear."

Trixie put an arm around Martha. Her stoic friend was shaken, and it worried her. She tamped down her personal feelings and let the cop-out. "Tell me about the vehicle?"

"It all happened so quickly, and it was dark."

"Trixie gave Martha's hand a gentle squeeze. "Martha, think. It's important. Close your eyes, take a deep breath in and let it out slowly." How many times had she sat with a victim or a witness, trying to help them relax and remember? Each time praying their shattered mind would give up a thread of the illusive memory. Trixie felt the tension ease from Martha's shoulders. "As the vehicle moved toward Kathleen, it went beneath several streetlights. Focus on what you saw?"

"I don't know; it all happened so fast."

"It's okay. You're doing great. Just relax."

Martha squeezed her eyes shut. "You are right; as the sedan came toward Kathleen, it did pass under a streetlight." Martha opened her eyes in surprise. "The vehicle was a white four-door sedan."

Trixie squeezed Martha's hand. She pushed down the excitement and gently urged Martha on. "You're doing great. You said it was a white sedan. What else?"

Martha gave a quick nod. "Definitely a white sedan."

"Foreign or American?"

Martha hesitated. "American."

"Were there any distinguishing marks on the body of the vehicle? What about make or model?"

"The front end of the vehicle will be very messed up. Did you know

Brookville's curbs are slightly higher than the average six-inch curb?

"No, I can't say I did. Do you recall anything else? Even if it seems insignificant."

It was so dark." Martha hesitated. "But maybe."

"Maybe what?" Trixie tried to keep the impatience out of her voice. "What did you see?"

Martha looked at Trixie. Her brows pinched together with worry. "You understand, I'm not sure, but as the car passed beneath the streetlight—"

"Martha, what did you see?"

"I had the impression the driver was a woman, and I think her hair was blond."

* * *

Nelson returned a short while later with a relieved smile on his face. "I just saw the doctor. He said Miss Kathleen was going to be fine. She can go home."

Relief washed over Trixie, and tears slid down her cheeks. "That's the best news I've had all day. Can we see her?"

An orderly pushed Kathleen's wheelchair into the waiting room. "That won't be necessary because I'm ready to go home." A white bandage covered the left side of Kathleen's forehead. Her arms were scraped and bruised, but otherwise, she looked wonderful. Kathleen turned to Martha. "I don't know how to thank you. If you hadn't warned me...Martha, you saved my life. Now get over here and give me a hug."

Martha gave Kathleen a brief embrace. "I am glad you are alive. I would hate to lose you so soon."

Trixie pulled Nelson to the side and gave him the information Martha recalled.

Nelson looked at Martha. "Let me see if I got this right. I'm looking for a white sedan with a jacked-up front end that may have been driven by a blond female."

"That is correct," said Martha.

Jack turned toward Kathleen. He cupped her bruised cheek. "I'm going to call this in then I'm taking you home."

Chapter Twenty-Six

Trixie had a miserable night's sleep, and she now sat at the kitchen table staring at a blank computer screen. She had zero focus and no desire to write about tasty treats or new cleaning products. Trixie replayed the events of the previous day. She had come too close to losing her friend.

Nelson was right. Moving forward with this investigation was dangerous. And as much as she appreciated Martha's and Kathleen's enthusiasm, she wasn't willing to risk their lives.

She closed the laptop, picked up her cell, and dialed Kathleen.

"Hello." Kathleen's voice was barely audible.

"Kathleen, what's wrong? Are you okay? Why are you whispering?"

"Just a minute."

"Kathleen, what's going on? Kathleen?" Trixie moved toward her bedroom. She pulled the revolver from her nightstand drawer. Her hand was on the knob of her front door when Kathleen returned.

"Trixie, I'm fine. I just didn't want to wake Jack."

Trixie raised a brow. "Excuse me? Deputy Jack Nelson is there? He spent the night? Well, I'm glad you got yourself that bed warmer."

"Stop it. Your mind is in the gutter. Jack slept on the couch. He wouldn't leave last night. He's such a wonderful man, but he can be a bit smothering."

"He means well. Yesterday terrified him. How are you feeling?"

"Sore, but that's to be expected? And I'm turning a lovely shade of purple— all over. My hip looks terrible. I'm lucky nothing was broken. All things considered, I feel fine. I just need to move around and work out the stiffness."

"You want to grab brunch?"

"I would love that. Where?"

"If you're up to it, we could walk to the Brookville Club. I haven't been there yet. It's not far from your condo, and walking might help loosen up those muscles."

"Sounds great."

"I'm heading your way now. I can't wait to hear all the juicy details about last night." Trixie disconnected before Kathleen could protest.

When Trixie arrived at Kathleen's condo, an irritated Jack Nelson opened the door. "You women are going to be the death of me."

"Jack, we can't stop living, and we have to eat."

"At least let me drive you to the restaurant."

"For pity's sake, you can see the restaurant from here," said Trixie. "We'll be fine."

"Do you have your weapon with you?"

Trixie patted her handbag. "Of course. Now, would you relax?"

Kathleen walked out the front door. She stood on her tiptoes and kissed Jack on the cheek. "Thank you for staying with me, but you have work to do. Lock the door on your way out. I'll be fine." She gave him a little wave, then linked arms with Trixie.

"Look at you being all independent. I'm so proud."

Kathleen giggled. "He's a keeper. I don't want to look. Is he watching?"

Trixie glanced back. Nelson stood on the front porch of Kathleen's condo, hands jammed on his hips. "Oh, yeah. He looks like an angry sea captain navigating his ship through stormy waters."

Kathleen giggled. "Good."

A few minutes later, Trixie and Kathleen were seated at a small table by a large picture window overlooking the Brookville golf course. A white linen cloth covered the table, and a small crystal vase containing two yellow rose buds was placed in the center.

Kathleen looked around the spacious restaurant. "This is very nice."

"It's also surprisingly crowded." Trixie glanced at her watch. "It's just a little after eleven. Do you suppose all these people live at the Brookville condos?"

A tall, slender, young man dressed in a white button-down shirt and black pants positioned himself by their table. "Good morning, ladies. My name is Eric; I'll be your server. May I take your drink order?"

Trixie looked up at him. "Is it always this crowded?"

"Yes, ma'am. We stay busy."

"Are most of your clients from the condos?" asked Kathleen.

"I wouldn't say most, but quite a few are. Now, what can I get you?"

The women placed their drink orders. As Trixie scanned the people in the restaurant, a tall, well-dressed man entered and took a table in a corner near the door. "Kathleen, check out the guy in the navy suit. Isn't that Jason Knight?"

Kathleen glanced over her shoulder. "I think so. His photo on the website did not do him justice; he's extremely handsome. And look at that glorious wavy hair. Wouldn't you love to run your fingers through that?"

Trixie laughed. "I think that bump on your head did something to you."

"Don't be silly; a girl can appreciate an attractive man, and he certainly is attractive."

A minute later, Brittney Fields entered the restaurant looking stunning in a fitted cobalt blue dress and matching stilettos. She scanned the room and charged toward Jason Knight's table.

"Whoa," said Trixie. "Look who just joined Jason."

Kathleen nibbled a bread stick. "What?"

"Brittney just walked in, and she is not happy. In fact, she looks very irritated."

Kathleen looked over her shoulder again and then turned back to Trixie. "Next time, I'm sitting on that side of the table." She rubbed her neck. "I'm getting a crick. Wonder what's going on?"

"I don't know, but it could be interesting. Scoot around to this side so you can see better."

The waiter returned with drinks and took their lunch orders.

The women watched Jason and Brittney. Kathleen said, "They work together. It is possible this meeting is work-related." Trixie rolled her eyes.

Jason put his arm around Brittney. Brittney slapped his arm away. "That doesn't look like work to me," said Trixie. "They look like they're arguing."

"And look at her body language. She's sitting ramrod straight, and there's a lot of finger pointing. She's obviously upset."

Trixie picked up a roll. "And look at Jason, he's completely unruffled. He's just sitting there saying nothing. Do you see his face and that smug look? I hate that look. Husband number three used to give me that same look." Trixie took a bite of the roll. "I can't tell you how bad I wanted to knock it off his face."

"He really does have a smarmy grin. Oh, oh." Kathleen patted Trixie's arm. "Did you see that? Now he tried to take her hand, but she jerked it away."

"Interesting."

The waiter returned with their lunches, effectively blocking their view. Trixie strained to see past him and finally gave up. She looked up at the young man. "Did anyone ever tell you you make a better door than a window?"

"Ma'am?"

"Never mind." When the waiter moved away from the table, Brittney stormed out of the restaurant. Trixie picked up her fork. "Wonder what that was about?"

Kathleen shook her head and took a bite of quiche. "Oh, my, this is delicious. Try yours." Kathleen scooped up another fork full. "Do you think there's something going on with Brittney and Jason?"

Trixie chewed. "You're right. This really is excellent. We need to come here for dinner. This place could give Emile a run for the money." She glanced in Jason Knight's direction and watched him pull his cell from his jacket pocket. "A lover's quarrel? I don't know, maybe."

Kathleen daintily dabbed at the corners of her mouth with the linen napkin. "Wonder who he's calling?"

"I don't know. But he doesn't look the least bit rattled after his encounter with Brittney. He's laughing and looks totally relaxed."

Kathleen pulled her cell from her handbag. "I'm calling Jack. He's been trying to get in touch with this man for days. She dialed and spoke briefly, then dropped her phone into her handbag.

"Is he on the way?"

"He is, he called me his little informant. Isn't he just the sweetest thing?"

"Oh, yeah, adorable," Trixie shoved another fork full of quiche into her mouth.

They watched as the waiter placed Jason's food order in front of him. "How long before Jack gets here?"

"Should be any minute," said Kathleen.

Nelson walked into the restaurant, looking very official. Trixie said, "Prince Charming has arrived." He gave Kathleen a subtle nod, then moved toward Jason's table.

They watched Nelson settle into a chair across from Jason and remove the notepad and pen from his pocket. Jason sat on the edge of his chair, his face flushed. "Jason doesn't look happy," said Kathleen. After a few minutes, Nelson closed the notebook and left the restaurant. "Well, that didn't take long."

Trixie got to her feet. "I'll be back."

"Where are you going?"

Trixie ignored Kathleen and continued out the front door. "Jack, wait up." Nelson turned toward her. "Not now, Trixie."

"What did he say?"

Nelson opened the door to the cruiser. "It's none of your business."

"I thought we'd gotten past all that. Aren't we working as a team? So?"

"So, I don't think he had anything to do with Camille's death. He has a solid alibi." Nelson slid into the driver's seat.

Getting information out of Deputy Jack Nelson was exhausting. "What's his alibi? And I'd like to point out we did share our information with you. You owe me." Nelson looked skyward. Trixie said, "The good Lord above isn't going to help you. You might as well tell me because I'm not leaving."

He glared at her. "I don't owe you anything. However, I will concede that you women were helpful. Jason Knight was working late with Brittney Fields."

Laughter and incredulity bubbled up. "Oh, right, like she's reliable."

"In my earlier interview with Dan Fields, he corroborated both their statements and confirmed they were working together on a project. Now, I've got work to do. Don't you have something else to do with *your* time?"

When Trixie returned to the table, Kathleen was scooping up the last bite of apple pie and ice cream. Her partially finished quiche was pushed to the side. "Why didn't you finish your quiche?"

"You know I'm an emotional eater. This stuff makes me nervous." Kathleen sat the empty dessert plate on top of what was left of her quiche. She leaned back in her chair with a contented smile.

"All better?"

"Much. Thank you."

"I never knew apple pie and ice cream were a cure for stress. I have other stress reducers that are quite effective."

Kathleen's lips compressed into a tight line. "What did Jack say?"

"Not much other than Jason has an alibi. Then he told me to keep my nose out of his business. Can you believe that? And after we shared with him." Trixie pushed her plate to the side. "Something's definitely going on with Brittney and Jason. Just not sure what it is." Trixie brushed crumbs from the table into her hand and dumped them onto her plate.

"Trixie, if Camille discovered financial hanky-panky, I wonder if she kept documentation somewhere."

"That's an excellent point. I'm sure Nelson has her computer. We should ask him if they found anything important."

"Don't you think we might be jumping the gun just a bit. I was just hypothesizing. We have no reason to think anyone was stealing from the Corporation."

"Not yet." Trixie picked up her cell and punched in Nelson's number.

"Now what?" Nelson barked.

"You don't need to sound so irritated. Did you find anything suspicious on Camille's laptop? Maybe questionable Brookville Corporation financials?"

"We've been through that computer with a fine-toothed comb. There's nothing there. We've checked her business and private emails, her phone messages, and texts; there's nothing suspicious. Now, if you don't need anything else, could you please let me get back to my day?"

Chapter Twenty-Seven

When Trixie returned home, she dropped her handbag on the kitchen counter and kicked off her shoes. She filled the kettle with water and had just put it on to boil when her cell rang. Riffling through her handbag, Trixie pulled it out.

"Is this Trixie Tanner?"

The voice of the caller was familiar. "It is. Who is this?"

"Carrie Newton. Audrey's friend. I met you at lunch the other day at Emile's. I hope you don't mind me calling. I got your number from Audrey."

"Of course not. I thought your voice sounded familiar. Is everything okay?"

"I'm fine, but wanted to know if we could meet for coffee."

"Sure. When?"

"Café au Lait in thirty minutes?"

"I'll see you there." Trixie disconnected. Why would Carrie want to meet? Was she looking to broaden her circle of friends? Doubtful. Women like the Audrey's and Carrie's of the world weren't interested in being friends. They were more interested in being part of the pack.

Trixie turned off the stove. Did Carrie know something about Camille's murder that she didn't want to share in front of her friends? Excitement fluttered in her stomach at the thought. More than a little anxious to get to the coffee shop, she slipped back into her shoes and grabbed her handbag,

* * *

In Trixie's opinion, coffee shops were some of the most magical places on the planet, after bookstores. Of all the coffee shops she'd visited, Café au Lait was at the top of her favorite's list. It was cheerful, cozy, and the aromas emanating from the kitchen were fabulous.

As she walked inside the small, comfy shop, the smell of freshly brewed coffee ignited her senses. Her mouth watered for an iced caramel macchiato. She ordered and reminded Ann, her favorite barista, not to skimp on the caramel.

Drink in hand, she pulled a newspaper from the rack and settled at a table near the door. Soft jazz played in the background. This time of day, there were very few customers. She sipped the sweet beverage and studied the variety of coffee-related signs hanging on the walls. Sayings such as *Life is Better with Coffee* and *My Favorite Gem is a Coffee Bean,* made her smile. The relaxing combination of soft jazz and the comforting aromas worked their magic. She leaned back in the chair and slowly flipped the pages of the newspaper.

Ann stopped by her table. "I've just taken a fresh batch of biscotti from the oven. Want one?"

"Are they vanilla almond?"

"Of course."

Trixie groaned. "You know I have no willpower."

Ann brought the cookie to her table. "Mind if I join you for a few?"

"Please do. My friend won't be here for a bit." Ann pulled out a chair and sat. "So, what's going on at Brookville? I heard an employee of the Corporation was found dead. Do the cops have any suspects?"

Trixie nibbled the fresh biscotti. "Not that I know of. It's all very sad. She was so young. Did you know her?"

"It's a small community, but I don't recall her coming in here. Is it true you found the body?"

"Not exactly." Trixie took another bite of the cookie. "This is delicious. You've perfected the recipe."

"Thanks. I think it's the extra almond extract. It really gives it a little something."

The little bell over the door at the front of the store jingled, and Carrie walked in. "Sorry, Ann. We'll have to catch up later. Looks like my coffee date is here." Trixie waved at Carrie.

Carrie checked her watch. "Hi, am I late?"

"No, I'm early."

"What can I get you?" asked Ann.

"Coffee with cream." Carrie settled into the chair Ann had vacated. "I hope I wasn't interrupting anything."

"No. We were just catching up." Trixie watched as the younger woman pulled a sugar packet from the sweetener container. She fidgeted with the packet.

Carrie looked around the cozy coffee shop. "This is the first time I've been here. It's a cute place."

"They have great coffee. You should try Ann's biscotti. They're the best." Trixie sipped her coffee and waited.

Ann sat a mug in front of Carrie. "Let me know if you need anything else."

Carrie tore open the sugar packet and stirred its contents into the coffee. "You must be wondering why I called."

"I'd be lying if I didn't say I was more than a little curious."

Carrie clutched the cup with both hands and looked at Trixie. "Can we keep what's discussed here between us? I love Audrey, and she's a wonderful friend, my best friend, but discretion is not her strong suit."

"I gathered as much." Trixie leaned forward, resting her elbows on the table. "Whatever you say will be kept in confidence."

Nodding, Carrie sipped the coffee. Her hands shook slightly. She gave Trixie a nervous smile. "You're right; the coffee's delicious."

"Did you want to talk about Camille? Is there something more you wanted to tell me?"

Carrie twisted a strand of her brown hair between her forefinger and thumb. "I don't know where to start."

Trixie reached out and gave the younger woman's hand an encouraging squeeze. "Start at the beginning. How long have you been with the Brookville Corporation?"

CHAPTER TWENTY-SEVEN

"I've worked with Dan and Jason for nearly seven years."

"Then you were with them before the condominiums were built?"

Carrie nodded.

"What's your position with the Corporation?"

"I'm a glorified office manager. I do some of the accounting and whatever else needs to be done."

Trixie finished the biscotti and dusted crumbs from the table. "Do you like working for the Corporation? Are they good to their employees?"

"In the early days, Brookville Corporation was actually a great place to work. Dan and Jason were more like family than employers. If the staff got in a bind, they'd pitch in and help. We'd have dinners together, and there were days when they would close the office early just so we could have a little extra personal time. Working at Brookville wasn't like work; it was fun, and you looked forward to coming in each day. But now, not so much."

"What changed?"

"Brittney. When she came to work for the Corporation two and a half years ago, everything changed."

"I thought she just gave tours of the condominiums. I didn't realize she was a paid employee. What's her role?"

"She was hired as a project management specialist."

Trixie pressed her lips together but kept silent.

"Brittney's not just a pretty face. She's intelligent and driven and should not be underestimated. She was hired to automate and streamline the Corporation's operations."

"Did she accomplish the assignment?"

"Oh yeah. She streamlined the Corporation and Dan Fields. Now, don't get me wrong, Dan's no saint, but before Brittney came, he and his wife, Sandi, were happy. They went through a rough patch several years earlier but seemed to have worked out the kinks. They'd go to lunch together almost every day, and I'd see them holding hands. You know, nice stuff. A few months after Brittney came to Brookville, I noticed Dan was having fewer lunches with his wife and more with Brittney. A year later, he announced that he and Sandi were getting a divorce."

"Did you like Sandi?"

Carrie looked thoughtful for a moment. "Let's just say she's a talented woman and deserved better than she got."

"I've met her, and I've seen her work. You're right, she is talented. Do you think Brittney was the reason their marriage collapsed?"

Carrie barked out a humorless laugh. "Brittney put her sights on Dan, and that was it. However, as I said, Dan's not blameless. He has a voracious wondering eye."

"I'm assuming his wandering eye was the cause of his marital troubles with Sandi."

"In the past, when his indiscretions ended, he always came back to Sandi, and she welcomed him with open arms."

"What happened this time? Did he actually fall in love with Brittney?" Trixie tried to keep the disbelief out of her voice."

"I don't know if it was love, but a bun in the oven can change a man's way of thinking."

"Oh, I thought Brittney got pregnant after she was married."

"That's what they wanted everyone to think." Carrie leaned forward and lowered her voice. "Dan's old school, and when a man knocks up a woman, he does the responsible thing and marries her. Personally, I think Brittney knew that, and it was her plan all along. As I said, she's not stupid."

Trixie looked out the window at the traffic moving past the shop. She let the information sink in, then turned her attention back to Carrie and said, "So, what happened to Sandi? Did she acquiesce?"

"What choice did she have? She moved on, and Dan gave her whatever she asked for. Since there weren't children, the property was split, and they went their separate ways."

"I thought it unusual that she elected to live in the condos her husband owns," said Trixie.

"I promise you, that's intentional—she likes poking the bear."

"Dan?"

"Brittney. Trust me, Sandi can hold her own."

"I have no doubt about that. How long after the divorce announcement before Dan and Brittney got married?"

"Maybe three months, she was the new Mrs. Dan Fields before the ink was dry on his divorce papers."

"Did you think it odd Brittney fell for Dan versus Jason Knight? I mean, you'd have to be blind not to notice how attractive Jason is, and he's closer to her age and certainly well off. I'd think a young woman like Brittney would've been drawn to him."

"You'd think, but they never seemed to hit it off. They bicker all the time. She'd get mad at him and go to Dan to complain, and of course, he'd take her side." Carrie drank the last of her coffee. "From the moment that woman walked through the door, Dan and Jason's relationship hasn't been the same."

Trixie swirled the coffee around in her mug and thought about the argument she'd witnessed earlier between Brittney and Jason. Co-workers, friends, something else? She looked up at Carrie. "I'm assuming when Camille started working at Brookville, the office dynamics changed again. Did Camille and Brittney get along?"

Carrie wiped the table with her napkin. "They were like oil and water. If their lives had depended on it, they couldn't agree on the sky being blue. You can't have two alpha females in the same space."

"You think Brittney viewed Camille as a threat?"

"Probably. Camille and Dan had an affair several years earlier."

"Was that the stuff that Dan and Sandi had to work out?"

"Yes. Brittney is an aggressive woman and would have viewed Camille as competition. Camille was an attractive woman but no match for Brittney. She didn't have the same killer instinct as Brittney."

Interesting choice of words, Trixie thought. "Had Dan and Camille rekindled their affair?"

"I don't know. When I think back to their conversations...maybe, or it could've been innocent. Either way, they definitely had a connection."

"Wait, when did Camille and Dan have their affair?"

"From what I understand, they were involved when the Brookville offices opened, but the affair ended soon after. When the Corporate office moved to New England, Camille went with it. Then, a little over four months ago,

Dan asked her to come back."

"Did you think that was odd?"

"Yeah. The New England office is much larger."

"What was her position there?"

"Officially, executive assistant, but Camille was way more than that."

"Why do you think Dan brought her back?"

"Dan trusted Camille and needed someone in his camp he could count on."

"Interesting. So, did Brittney hear the gossip?"

"Since having the baby, she hasn't been working in the office much. She's been too focused on getting herself back in shape for some competition. She's got the cutest little boy—curly blonde hair and big blue eyes. Sadly, I don't think she cares much about him. She hired a full-time nanny. All she's concerned about is getting her body back. On the upside, since she's been gone, the atmosphere in the office has improved dramatically. Even Dan and Jason seem to be getting along better."

"Why was the corporate office relocated to New England?"

"Brookville Corporation is a multi-million-dollar company. We have projects all over the country. The town of Brookville is home to Dan and Jason, and this is where the company was originally set up. The office was relocated to New England a few years after the creation of the corporation to put it in a more centralized location." Carrie stood. "I'm getting more coffee. You want something?"

Trixie shook her head. "No, thanks." She watched Carrie walk to the counter. As interesting as the history lesson was, she needed Carrie to get to the point.

Carrie returned to the table with a fresh cup of coffee and a slice of lemon pound cake. She put a forkful of cake in her mouth and closed her eyes. "This is really good."

Trixie propped her elbows on the table and leaned closer. "Why did you want to meet me? It can't be to discuss Brookville Corporation history and their dirty laundry."

Carrie stopped chewing. Her eyes darted around the small space. Anxiety tightened her lips. She pushed the pound cake to the side and clutched the coffee cup again. "I'm worried," she said, shaking her head. "No, that's not true. It's more than worry—I'm frightened."

"About what?"

Carrie leaned in closer and whispered, "Someone tried to break into my home. If it hadn't been for Bentley, my Rottweiler, I don't know what would've happened. Trixie, I'm terrified that what happened to Camille could happen to me."

Chapter Twenty-Eight

Trixie was straightening the house when her cell rang. "Ms. Tanner, this is Jonathan from Sandi Field's office. We have had an unfortunate scheduling issue arise. Would it be possible for us to start renovations on your home in the morning?"

Trixie looked around the kitchen. "In the morning? Wow, that's fast." She wasn't expecting renovations to start for another two months. "Sure, I guess that would be okay."

"If tomorrow isn't convenient, the next available date is," Trixie heard the tapping of computer keys. "Your rescheduled date would be in four months. Would that be better?"

Now that the plans were drawn up, Trixie didn't want to delay renovations. She sighed. "No. Tomorrow is fine."

"Excellent," said Jonathan. "Because we don't want to disrupt your schedule any more than necessary, would you have any objection to Ms. Fields having a key to your condo? That would allow us to come and go as needed, regardless of you being home. Obviously, we would call and forewarn you of our arrival. If that's not convenient, then you would need to be onsite in the mornings during the lunch breaks and at the end of the day."

This was Brookville, not Charlotte. Nothing happens here—except murder. "Who will be in possession of my key?"

Jonathan's voice held a note of disdain. "Only Ms. Fields or the job foreman. I can assure you all our craftsmen have been thoroughly vetted. Ms. Fields doesn't have riffraff working for her."

Trixie pushed down her internal cop voice and her cynicism. "I'll have a key for Sandi when she arrives."

"Very good. I'll let her know. The team will see you in the morning at nine sharp.

Trixie disconnected. She looked around the kitchen, and a flutter of panic rose inside her. There would be no time to sort through old pots and pans and crockery. She would basically be throwing everything into boxes. So much for organizing the process. She should have told Jonathan the later date was better, but she was anxious to have her new kitchen and workspace. Trixie sucked in a breath of resolve. This was panic of her own creation, so, claim it and get busy.

She expected Kathleen and Martha to arrive at her condo in a couple of hours. They had planned to spend time working on the cases. Trixie had time to start packing. She brought boxes in from the garage and began emptying the cabinet contents into them. The panic of earlier was replaced with a flutter of excitement. Once renovations were done, the kitchen would be much more functional, and the workspace she'd dreamed of would be a reality. Trixie threw more plastic bowls into a box.

She was busy wrapping wine glasses when the doorbell rang. Trixie looked up and saw Kathleen through the window. She motioned for her to come in.

Kathleen walked into the kitchen. The counters and table were filled with plates, glassware, paper products, cans, and boxed food items. "What on earth is going on? It looks like a tornado touched down."

Trixie placed the wrapped wine glasses into a box. "Renovations begin tomorrow morning. The kitchen must be cleared out so they can start work."

Kathleen grabbed a sheet of newspaper and a glass. "Weren't they supposed to start in a couple of months?"

"Yes, but there was a scheduling issue. If I didn't take the opportunity for them to start work tomorrow, I'd have to wait four months. I'm afraid we're going to have to delay our work on the case. By the way, where's Martha? I thought she was only scheduled to work for a couple of hours this morning."

"You know how odd Martha can be. She called about an hour ago and said she would be late."

"Martha, late? She's never late."

"She sounded odd on the phone. I'm a little worried about her."

Two hours later, Kathleen and Trixie had finished packing the kitchen. "Trixie taped the lid of the last box. Has Martha texted you?"

Kathleen pulled her cell from her handbag and glanced at the screen. "No. I'm calling her. Something's wrong. This isn't like her." She dialed Martha's number. A cell phone rang outside Trixie's door just as the doorbell sounded.

Trixie opened the door. Her mouth gaped open. "Martha? What happened to your hair?

Martha ran a hand over her closely cropped hair. "Why are you gaping at me? Can I come in?"

"Of course, you can, but your hair."

"I had to make an emergency stop at Inez's beautician." Martha's hand touched her head again.

Kathleen's round blue eyes grew to the size of small saucers. "Martha, what on earth? Did you do that on purpose?"

Martha dropped into a kitchen chair. "I realize it is not yet five o'clock, but do you have an alcoholic beverage? Is it acceptable to drink at," she looked at her watch, "one thirty?" She glanced around the kitchen. "Are you moving?"

"Yes, to alcohol and no to moving. You want whiskey?" asked Trixie.

Anything will do. At this point, I would consider rubbing alcohol."

Trixie poured whiskey into a tumbler. "Do you want water or ice?"

Martha motioned for Trixie to hand over the glass. "No. Nothing to dilute the beverage or its effects."

Trixie joined Kathleen and Martha at the table. Martha tossed back the liquid and coughed. Her face flushed, and tears ran down her cheeks. She blew out a breath. "Once the initial burn passes, it leaves a very pleasant warm feeling; just what the doctor ordered." She held out the glass. "Hit me again."

Trixie looked at Kathleen and then poured. "Better?"

"Yes, thank you."

"I'd suggest sipping this one," said Trixie.

Kathleen patted Martha's hand. "Sweetie, what happened?"

Martha shook her head. "You know the worst part?" She looked from Kathleen to Trixie.

"What?" asked Trixie.

"When Nelson got there, I cried like a baby. I will never be able to face that man again. I have lost all credibility." She shook her head. "He will never view me as a peer."

Trixie sat in the chair next to Martha. "Perhaps you should start at the beginning. What happened?"

Martha took another sip of whiskey. "You know, this stuff is not so bad." She placed the tumbler on the table, folded her hands in her lap, and took a deep breath. "Inez and I were clearing away large boxes, and there were several old books that were beyond repair. We were taking them to the basement to feed the Wendigo."

"The what?" asked Kathleen.

"You know, the large shredder in the basement." Martha blew out a breath. "Kathleen, we talked about that when you came to use the microfiche readers. If you recall, you were worried about the safety of the machine. Turns out, you were right. I was feeding several heavy boxes into the shredder when the lights went out. I heard footsteps running toward me. I thought it was Inez, although I could not imagine why she would be running. It was so dark. Whoever it was, shoved me hard. I fell backwards onto the shredder belt. My braid got caught in the teeth of the machine. The teeth were pulling me into Wendigo's jaws. I tried to pull my hair free, but it was too tangled. I must have screamed. The next thing I knew, the lights came on, and Inez was running toward me. She hit the emergency stop." Martha took a long pull from the tumbler; tears slid down her face. "I...I owe Inez my life. If she had not shown up when she did, my head would have been crushed."

"Oh, Martha, are you okay?" Kathleen pulled her into her arms.

"Kathleen, you are smothering me. I am fine." Martha ran a hand over her shorn head. "My hair, however, did not fare so well."

"What did Nelson say," asked Trixie. "Any idea who did this?"

"I couldn't tell him anything. When I went to the basement with the boxes, I didn't see anyone. There is a camera positioned in the hall just before the door leading to the basement. When I left the library, Nelson was having a tech download the CCTV video."

"Did anything unusual happen this morning? Was someone acting in a threatening or abnormal way?"

Martha sipped the whiskey. "Something did happen earlier in the morning. In all the excitement, I had forgotten."

"Go on," said Trixie.

"Brittney Fields came into the library."

"That doesn't seem odd. It is the public library," said Kathleen.

Martha shot an exasperated look at Kathleen. "Does she look like the type who reads?"

Trixie said, "Did Brittney see you or engage you in conversation?"

"She asked where the microfiche readers were. Brittney said she remembered me from that day on the trails and asked if we were still investigating Camille's murder. I told her we were." Martha looked up, a startled expression on her face. "Brittney said we should keep our noses out of Brookville business. I was busy at the time and ignored her comments. You don't think Brittney tried to kill me? She may be many things, but I doubt one of them is a murderer."

Trixie pulled her cell phone from her jeans pocket. "I'm calling Nelson." She punched in his number. "I don't know if Brittney is a murderer, but Nelson needs to know."

Nelson picked up on the fourth ring. "Is Martha okay?"

"She's fine, but she just recalled having a conversation with Brittney Fields earlier in the morning at the library." Trixie relayed what Martha had recounted. "Martha said you were looking at the CCTV footage. Did you see Brittney go downstairs?

"No. Someone in black sweatpants and hoodie went down to the archives shortly before Martha was attacked."

"Did you get a look at their face?"

"Unfortunately, Martha's assailant was aware of the camera. We found the hoodie and pants in the trash can in the women's bathroom."

"Are you bringing Brittney in for questioning?"

CHAPTER TWENTY-EIGHT

"Trixie, contrary to what you may believe, I do know how to do my job."

"I wasn't being critical, just curious."

"Trixie, hang on."

Trixie heard talking in the background. Nelson returned to the phone.

"I've gotta go. Someone broke into Camille Jackson's condo and tossed the place."

Chapter Twenty-Nine

"Maybe it's a coincidence," said Kathleen. "You know, there are people who read the obituaries looking for homes of the recently deceased to break into. Maybe that's what happened."

Trixie had learned long ago there was no such thing as a coincidence. "Maybe. But I find it odd that someone also tried to break into Carrie's home. I believe Camille Jackson knew something, and that something got her killed." Trixie stood and paced the kitchen. "Whoever tossed Camille's home didn't find what they were looking for, so they tried breaking into Carrie's." Trixie turned to Martha. "What are your thoughts?"

"I could use some food. I realize this is highly unusual, but I am ravenous. Logically, after such an experience, I would not expect to have an appetite, but I believe I could think better if I had something to eat."

Trixie grabbed her car keys from the kitchen counter. "You need comfort food, and I know just the place. I'll drive."

A short while later, Trixie navigated her red Mercedes sedan out of Brookville and onto the highway. They rode for several miles, then Trixie took an exit onto a deserted country road.

"Trixie, are you sure you know where you're going? Because we appear to be in the middle of nowhere," said Kathleen.

Trixie pulled into a parking lot. "We have arrived."

"Bernie's Burgers?" said Kathleen.

Trixie circled the lot, looking for parking. "Martha needs comfort food, and Bernie's Burgers is the best. Wow, this place is packed." Ahead, she saw a Camry backing out of a space. Trixie pulled into the vacated spot.

As they made their way through the parking lot to the entrance, Martha stopped to watch the neon figures on each side of the door dance.

"I didn't know this place was here," said Kathleen.

Trixie opened the door. Chuck Berry's "Johnny B. Goode" greeted them as they walked inside. "You're in for a treat."

A hostess dressed in a white blouse, blue poodle skirt, and saddle oxfords moved toward them, "It'll be a few minutes."

After a short wait, the hostess motioned to them. They made their way to a table in the corner. Once seated, the hostess said, "Veronica will be with you shortly to take your lunch order." She handed them menus and took their drink orders.

Kathleen opened the menu. "What a fun place. How did you find it?"

"Patrick brought me here."

Kathleen scanned the room. "Considering the crowd, the food must be good."

Martha opened the menu. "There is quite a selection of burgers. Who knew there were so many ways to prepare hamburgers? It is all quite overwhelming."

"What sort of burger do you normally like?" asked Kathleen.

"Cheeseburger, lettuce, tomato, and mayonnaise, but that seems very mundane given all the selections. However, after my near-death experience, I feel I should try something different—you know, live a little."

The waitress came to the table to take their orders.

"Carolina burger and fries for me," said Trixie.

"Same for me," said Kathleen.

"I would like a blue cheeseburger," said Martha. "This is a day for new experiences: Scotch, blue cheeseburgers, and almost being murdered. It really has turned out to be quite a day."

Trixie watched Martha for a moment. "Are you sure you're okay?"

"This is exactly the distraction I needed." Martha looked around the restaurant. "I have only seen places like this on television. I never knew they really existed."

Trixie leaned in closer. "See the man behind the counter? That's Bernard

Cooper; he owns this place."

Martha glanced at Bernie, then turned to Trixie. "Is he the man rumored to be the biological father of Alexandra?"

"According to Patrick, he was locked up for several years. When he was released, he opened this place."

Kathleen turned toward the restaurant entrance as a tall, sophisticated woman entered. "Isn't that Sandi Fields?"

Trixie looked over her shoulder. The woman was waving and smiling at someone. She made her way to the front of the restaurant. Bernie came from behind the counter. The smile on his face looked grotesque and out of place. He hugged Sandi.

Trixie let out a low whistle. "I wasn't expecting that."

"I wonder how she knows him?" said Martha.

"Never mind that," said Kathleen. "Did either of you notice if they have desserts? I need pie. Now that the excitement has settled down, I'm suddenly feeling very jittery." She looked up at Trixie. "You need to be careful. You could be next."

"Kathleen, we all need to be careful, but for now, let's relax and enjoy lunch. Besides, I doubt anything will happen to us in a crowded restaurant."

The waitress returned with food-laden plates. Trixie picked up the bottle of ketchup and squirted a puddle onto her plate. "Now, this is a lunch. I might have to eat yogurt for dinner, but it will be worth every bite."

Martha took a large bite from her burger. "This sandwich is quite satisfactory and far superior to the typical burger."

Sandi made her way to the women's table. "I see you've found the best-kept secret in Brookville. Dan and I found this place shortly after moving here. Bernie is a great guy. We've been friends since the first day we met."

Trixie had trouble imagining ever being friends with Bernard Cooper. There was something about him that was off. Not to mention, he was just creepy.

Trixie wiped mustard from her mouth. "Pull up a chair and join us."

"I wish I could, but I've got a final walk-through on another project in an hour. I dropped in to leave Bernie some fabric swatches. My team and I will be at your condo in the morning at nine sharp."

"I'll have the coffee on," said Trixie.

Chapter Thirty

Trixie stood in front of the murder boards. She added a column, *Attempted Murder,* on the back of the board titled *Camille's Murder.* She included a few brief notes detailing the attempts on Martha's and Kathleen's lives. Then flipped the board and added a bullet point about Camille's home being broken into and another for the attempted break-in at Carrie's house. She firmly believed the two break-ins were related.

Trixie picked up a crystal wine glass and sipped a delicious Merlot Patrick had recommended. She studied the boards. What was she missing? What was someone looking for? And what could Carrie and Camille potentially have in their possession that someone wanted so badly they were willing to commit murder? And if it was related to the Corporation's finances, why hadn't Jason Knight's home been broken into? Trixie added additional bullets with the questions. Her doorbell rang, disrupting her thoughts. When she opened the door, Jack Nelson stood in the doorway, his expression serious. "This is a surprise. What can I do for you, Deputy?"

Nelson jammed his hands into his pants pockets. "You got a few minutes to talk?"

Trixie opened the door wider. "Sure, come in. I was having a glass of wine. Would you like a glass? Or I could make coffee."

Nelson walked inside the condo. "No. I'm not staying long." He raked a hand through his salt and pepper hair. "Trixie, you women have got to stop your snooping. There have been two attempts on your friends' lives. This last one with Martha was...well, too close. If that librarian hadn't come along when she did..." He looked up at Trixie. "You understand what I'm saying, right?"

"Jack, I get it. I'll talk with Martha and Kathleen, but I'm going to continue *snooping*, as you say. It's gotten personal. Someone tried to hurt my friends, and I want to know who that someone is."

"Trixie, you're not a cop anymore. Let me do my job."

"I haven't been a cop for a long time, but that doesn't mean I can't take care of myself." Trixie held up her hand. "End of conversation. Now that we've cleared that up was anything missing from Camille's house? Any idea when the break-in occurred?"

"Has anyone ever told you you have a brick head?"

"Yeah. I get that a lot. So how about some answers?" She met his eyes. "I'm not going away, Jack, and I will see this through to the end, with or without your help."

"Yeah, I was afraid you were going to say that. My friend at the ATF said once you were focused on something, it was hell to get you off it."

"Who is this friend?"

Nelson shook his head. "Doesn't matter. Maybe you should put on that pot of coffee. This may take a while."

Trixie brought a tray holding a carafe of coffee, two mugs, and a plate of cookies into the Command Center. Nelson filled both mugs and handed one to Trixie. He motioned toward the boards. "You've added more information since Doc and I were here." Nelson poured cream into his coffee. "Truth is, our office is woefully understaffed, basically, because nothing really happens here." He hesitated. "I guess I should've said nothing happens that we know about." He picked up a cookie and took a bite. "I'm assuming you've talked with Doc, and he told you they've uncovered more skeletal remains?"

Trixie nodded.

"I went through old missing person files for the past ten years, and what I found was more than a little disturbing. There have been dozens of reports. Most of the missing were the homeless or prostitutes. I'm ashamed to say that back in the day, those cases weren't given the energy they deserved. Brookville's Sheriff's Department is small now, but back then, it was even smaller. He stood in front of the board titled *Human Remains*. "All of these people disappeared, and no one missed them. Just doesn't seem right."

"We can make it right. Let's find out who's responsible."

"Doc said it'll be a while before we'll know how long the remains have been in the ground."

Trixie tapped the end of the marker on the board. "Someone in this town knows what happened to the missing. We need to keep digging.

She moved to Camille's murder board and uncapped the marker. "Was anything missing from Camille's condo?"

Nelson shook his head and waggled an index finger at her. "We're not doing this. You aren't working this case."

"You just said you don't have the manpower. So, like it or not, we *are* working on this case together. You need my help, and we need to know who tried to kill Kathleen and Martha. Face it, Jack, you're out of options."

He blew out a long, tired breath. "Fine, but I don't want Miss Kathleen and Martha involved. They're civilians and don't have the skill set needed to keep themselves safe." He turned toward the board. "Camille's brother came to pack up her condo. Someone had been there and ransacked the place. We're not sure when the break-in occurred or if anything was taken. However, he did say that Camille had a few pieces of expensive jewelry their mother had given her. It was still in her jewelry box."

"What about electronic devices? Are any of them missing?"

Nelson shook his head. "She had a Blu-ray player, an expensive set of earphones, and a printer; none of that was touched."

Trixie paced the room. "Maybe they were looking for her computer. What did Camille know that cost her her life? And what is the link between Camille and Carrie?"

"Carrie?" asked Nelson.

"Someone tried to break into Carrie Fisher's home a few nights ago. Fortunately, her dog chased them away."

"That name is familiar."

"She's the office manager for Dan Fields and Jason Knight. You didn't know about the attempted break-in?"

Nelson's lips tightened into a straight line. "Our department is small, but that doesn't mean I know about every call that comes in. I'll find out which deputy responded and get the details."

"Whoever killed Camille wanted something she had, but they didn't find it at her place. Now, they're looking in another direction. I spoke with Carrie a few days ago, and she told me she was afraid." Trixie picked up the carafe and refilled her mug. "Camille was the executive assistant; I would assume she had access to the corporation's finances. And what about Jason Knight? Is he in danger? He is the CFO. There's talk the Corporation is having money problems. Trixie made a bullet point on the board and wrote, *Camille—Finances?* "Maybe the arguments between Dan and Camille weren't about their affair but about money?"

"What argument?" asked Nelson.

"Carrie Fisher overheard Camille and Dan arguing on several occasions. You should probably talk to Dan. It's possible Camille knew something about the company's money troubles. Maybe Dan Fields was taking money, and Camille found out. Maybe she was giving him the opportunity to come clean, or maybe she wanted a piece of the action. Wouldn't that be a motive for murder?"

"Hell, Trixie, people kill for less." Nelson stood. "I've gotta go."

"By the way, any luck finding the sedan that hit Kathleen?"

Nelson rubbed the back of his neck. "Yeah, we found it yesterday. It was abandoned in the next county over. Whoever stole it wiped it down, but we didn't come away empty-handed. We found a blond synthetic hair strand on the driver's side headrest."

Trixie sat her coffee cup on the tray. "Like from a wig?"

"Yeah. And something I haven't shared with you: we found a strand of the same blond synthetic hair on the hoodie found at the library."

Chapter Thirty-One

Trixie had just cleared away her breakfast dishes when the doorbell rang. She opened the door, and Jonathan hurried past her. A crew of men dressed in white overalls followed in his wake, and Sandi pulled up the rear, tall, elegant, and aloof in a cream-colored suit and coral blouse.

She opened a few of the kitchen cabinets. "Excellent. Everything appears to be out of the way." Sandi called to Jonathan, "Have them start ripping out the cabinets and countertops." She turned toward Trixie. "Are you staying?"

"Ah, no. I'm not sure I could stand seeing everything destroyed."

Sandi laughed. "It will get worse before it gets better."

"Give me a minute to collect my stuff, and I'll be out of your hair." Trixie hurried to her bedroom and grabbed her computer and handbag. Heading back to the kitchen, she was greeted with the sound of cracking wood followed by a loud crash. One of the countertops was being removed. Trixie turned to go out the front door.

Sandi followed behind her. "Trixie, don't forget to give me the house key. We're going to get most of the demo done today in the kitchen. If you aren't home when we're ready to leave, I'll lock up. We'll be back in the morning at the same time."

Trixie pulled the extra house key from her key ring and handed it to Sandi. "If you need me, you can reach me on my cell." A truck rumbled to a stop in front of her condo and deposited a large dumpster. She heard another loud crash. Two of the white overall-clad men carried out her old countertop and threw it into the dumpster. The thought of a nice quiet hotel with room service floated to the front of her mind, something to consider.

She'd planned to meet Kathleen and Martha at Café au Lait. The shop wouldn't be busy this time of day, and she needed to talk with them about Jack's visit. On the one hand, Trixie knew Jack was right, at least where Kathleen and Martha were concerned. They weren't safe, and Trixie would never forgive herself if something happened to them. Digging into Camille's murder and Brookville's past was making someone more than a little uncomfortable. But which case? She felt like a juggler with too many balls in the air. On the other hand, shouldn't Martha and Kathleen make up their own minds? All she could do was let them know it was okay to step away from the investigation and the danger.

Trixie walked inside Café au Lait. The comforting aroma of freshly brewed coffee and bakery items greeted her at the door. Kathleen and Martha were seated at a table in the corner. She watched them for a moment. Two women who a little over a month ago were strangers to her were now closer than any friend she'd ever had. These women meant the world to her, and she wasn't going to let anyone hurt them again. Nelson was right; they couldn't be part of this any longer. Trixie pasted on a smile and walked toward them. Martha looked up and grinned, crumbs dangled from her chin.

"These cheese Danish are delicious."

Kathleen giggled. "This is my new go-to place for dessert. You need to try the apple tarts; they are to die for."

Ann waved at Trixie. "What can I get you?"

"Coffee." Trixie settled into the vacant chair and turned to Martha. "You look like you've recovered from your ordeal."

"I am doing well. However, I will say the term near-death experience now has new meaning for me." She took another bite from the pastry.

Kathleen dabbed the corner of her mouth with a paper napkin. "What's up?"

Ann brought Trixie a coffee.

"Thanks, Ann. She stirred sugar into the coffee and took a sip. Martha and Kathleen watched her.

"What's wrong with you?" asked Martha. "As my co-worker Inez would say, your energy is off."

"Martha's right. Something is wrong."

Before she could answer, Trixie's cell rang. Saved by the bell. She looked at the caller ID and groaned. "Good morning, Jack."

"Trixie, I'm not calling you because we're working together. This call is a means to an end."

"Whatever. What do you need?"

"Carrie Fisher's home was broken into early this morning."

Trixie felt her heart skip a beat. Carrie had expressed her fear that what happened to Camille would happen to her. "Is she okay?"

"Yes. She was beaten, tied up, and locked in her bedroom closet. Her dog was drugged. Trixie, EMS is trying to get Ms. Fisher to go to the hospital, but she refuses to leave until the vet gets here to check out her dog, and she insists on talking to you. I'm texting you her address. I'd appreciate you coming as soon as possible."

Trixie stuffed the cell back into her handbag and stood. "I've got to go."

Martha and Kathleen got to their feet. "Not without us," said Kathleen.

Trixie grasped the back of the chair. "Listen. I think it's time you guys stepped away from these investigations. Both of you have almost been killed. Next time, you might not be so lucky. And I can't fathom life without the two of you." Trixie smiled brightly. "So, stay here, have another Danish, and I'll let you know what happens."

Kathleen and Martha didn't budge. "If you think it is that easy to get rid of us, you would be mistaken," said Martha. "Kathleen and I have discussed this issue. Yes, our lives were endangered, and that makes this situation very personal. We are not going anywhere except with you. This is *our* case, and *we* are going to be part of taking down the person or people who are responsible for so much misfortune." Kathleen's head bobbed in agreement.

"Look, I appreciate what you're saying, but this situation is dangerous, and you aren't equipped to deal with it."

"And you are?" asked Kathleen.

"Actually, yes."

Kathleen propped both hands on her hips defiantly. "What does that mean?"

"It means I am a retired federal ATF agent, and I know the risks. I'm not putting my two dearest friends on the planet in any more danger. So, it's time for you both to step away from this. Am I clear?"

Kathleen moved beside Trixie. "Like crystal, but that changes nothing. What's bringing this on?"

"Nelson came to my house last night. He is justifiably concerned about you two. And I agree with him. It's getting too dangerous." Trixie looked at Kathleen. "And what about your kids?"

"What about them? I've lived my life for my family and taken care of them. My husband is dead, and my kids are grown. For the first time, I feel alive and excited because I don't know what's going to happen each day I roll out of bed. It's no longer the same drill: go to work, clean the house, cook, do all the wife and mother things. I'm doing what I want to do with people I care about, and I love it. So, if today is my last day on this earth, just know I was where I wanted to be."

Martha nodded. "Well said, Kathleen. Until I met you and Trixie, I lived with my mother. Who, as we have discussed, is not a nice woman. You ladies brought light and love into a rather grim existence, and for that, I will be forever grateful. So, as Kathleen has so eloquently stated, if today is my last day, I, too, am where I want to be. We are the Lady Dragons of Brookville, and we stick together."

Love and pride bubbled up inside of Trixie. She pulled Kathleen and Martha into her arms. "I love you two, and I will do my best to protect you. For the record, Nelson is not going to be happy." Trixie looked at Kathleen. "Especially about you."

Kathleen lifted her chin and said, "Well, he'll just have to deal with it, won't he."

"Trixie, you realize we will be discussing your past more thoroughly?" said Martha. "I am more than a little intrigued with your life as an ATF agent."

"Let's go, Lady Dragons. I'll fill you in on last night's discussion with Nelson on the way to Carrie's house."

Chapter Thirty-Two

arrie's home was a small white Cape Cod structure with black shutters. As the women approached her house, law enforcement and forensic techs milled around the front yard.

Nelson stepped out onto the front porch and motioned them inside. His face was grim when he saw Kathleen and Martha. He pulled Trixie to the side. "I thought we discussed this last night."

"Yeah, well, they weren't interested in stepping aside."

Kathleen stopped in front of Nelson. "Jack Nelson, you are not the boss of me or Martha. If we want to be involved, that's what we're going to do."

Nelson's face flushed. "Miss Kathleen, this really isn't the place and time."

Kathleen looked around the bustling room. "Oh, I think this is a fine time. And if you're going to court me, you need to change your tune."

Nelson's Adam's apple bobbed, and his mouth gaped open.

"Now, where is *our* victim?" said Kathleen.

Trixie gave Kathleen a little elbow to the ribs. "I like the new assertive you."

"Well, something had to be done. He needs to know he can't push us around."

Nelson led the women into a small, comfortable living room. Hardwood floors covered with an inexpensive rug, two side chairs upholstered in the same floral print, a coffee table, and a brown leather loveseat filled the room. Carrie and her dog sat on the loveseat. She held an ice pack to her swollen face. Her left eye and cheek had turned a deep purple. Her lip was split and swollen; a large Rottweiler was curled on the loveseat beside her. His broad head lay in her lap, and his tongue lolled partially out of his mouth. Carrie looked up as they approached. She gave them a lopsided smile and winced.

"Trixie, thanks for coming."

"Who's your friend?" asked Trixie.

Carrie gently rubbed her hand over the dog's soft ears. "This is Bentley. He's had a rough time."

Trixie stroked the animal's head and looked up at Carrie. "It looks like he's not the only one. Is he going to be okay?"

"The vet stopped by a little while ago and said Bentley will be fine. He just needs to sleep off the drug, then he'll be right as rain. It's lucky he's such a big boy; a smaller dog might not have survived."

"Does the vet know what he was drugged with?" asked Martha.

"He took blood and is sending it to the lab for analysis."

Trixie sat on the edge of the coffee table. She leaned forward, propping her elbows on her knees. Forensics techs were busy collecting evidence and dusting for prints. "Carrie, what happened?"

"I was asleep. We're assuming the intruders tossed Bentley drugged meat, and of course, he ate it. They waited until he fell asleep and then came in through the kitchen window. At least that's what Deputy Nelson thinks."

"How many intruders?" asked Martha.

"Two." Carrie held her side and squeezed her eyes shut for a moment.

"Carrie, you need to get to the hospital," said Trixie.

Carrie gritted her teeth. "Not until I finish telling you what happened,"

Trixie shot a glance at Nelson, who motioned for her to hurry. "Did you recognize your attackers?"

She shook her head. "They wore black ski masks."

"What about their voices? Were they familiar?" asked Trixie.

"They never spoke. I woke to them duct-taping my hands together. When I started screaming, the larger of the two punched me in the face. The other one held up a paper with typed questions."

"What sort of questions?"

"They wanted my laptop and any flash drives I had."

"Did you give them what they wanted?" asked Kathleen.

"I gave them my laptop. I told them there was nothing important on it. But when I had no flash drives, they didn't believe me. That's when the bigger guy went to work on me." Tears ran down Carrie's swollen face. "I must have passed out. When I woke up, I was in the closet."

"Who found you?" asked Martha.

"The groomer came this morning for Bentley. The front door was open, and he saw Bentley lying in the foyer. When Bentley didn't respond, and I didn't answer his call, he phoned the police."

Nelson walked over to them. "Trixie, wrap this up. Ms. Fisher needs to get to the hospital. EMS is waiting.

Trixie turned back to Carrie. "Why did you want me here?"

Carrie looked at the techs and leaned closer. "Because I know you women are investigating Camille's death." Trixie raised a questioning brow. "Brookville is a small town; everyone knows everything about everybody. Whoever killed Camille did so because she knew something about the Corporation's financial difficulties. The night before last, I was in the office finishing up some letters. It was after hours, and I thought only Jason and I were left in the building. Dan came storming down the hall and burst into Jason's office, and slammed the door. There was a lot of yelling. I could hear just enough to know they were arguing about money." She looked down at Bentley and stroked his head. "I went over to Jason's door and listened." She looked up at Trixie. "I know that wasn't ethical, but I had to know what was going on."

"What did you hear?"

Carrie's face grimaced, and she grabbed her ribs again. "I thought I heard Dan accuse Jason of embezzlement, but I'm not completely certain because it was at that moment Brittney walked around the corner." Carrie shook her head. "Her expression spoke volumes. I didn't wait around. I grabbed my handbag and left. I didn't want to give her time to fire me. Although I'm sure that's coming."

"Thanks, Carrie, we appreciate the information. Now, you need to get to the hospital. Is someone taking care of Bentley while you're gone?"

"My neighbor will watch him."

Nelson motioned for the EMS techs. "That's it, ladies, Ms. Fisher has had enough. EMS is waiting."

Trixie, Martha, and Kathleen returned to Trixie's car. Once inside, Trixie turned in her seat to face Kathleen and Martha. "So, Lady Dragons, what do you think?"

Martha said, "It's interesting that the intruders never spoke. Which leads me to postulate, were they concerned Carrie would recognize their voices."

"Good point," said Trixie. "The ransacking of Camille's home and now the break-in leads me to one conclusion: Camille must have had dirt on someone in the Corporation. But whoever tossed Camille's home didn't find what they were looking for. So, they thought maybe Camille gave the information to Carrie."

"But she obviously did not," said Martha.

Kathleen pressed her hand to her chest. Her eyes darted from Trixie to Martha. "Which means whatever they were looking for could still be in Camille's home."

"Exactly," said Trixie.

Martha's eyes brightened. "I foresee a little B&E in our future." She rubbed her hands together excitedly.

"B&E?" squeaked Kathleen.

"Breaking and entering," said Martha. "And I have just what we need to accomplish our mission."

"I'm afraid to ask," said Kathleen.

Chapter Thirty-Three

The following morning, Carrie was released from the hospital. She had three broken ribs, a cracked orbital bone, and lots of bruising. Trixie dropped off a basket of goodies from her, Kathleen, and Martha with the promise they'd stop by in a few days when Carrie was feeling better. Carrie looked bad, but in Trixie's past life, she'd seen worse.

Trixie's next stop was the Book Shoppe. She pulled into a parking space directly in front of the bookstore. The old wooden floors creaked pleasantly as she walked inside, and the lovely scent of books, lemon furniture polish, and fresh coffee greeted her like an old friend. She closed her eyes and, for a moment, enjoyed the sensory experience. You can't buy that online.

"Nothing like starting the day with a good book and beautiful women," said Patrick O'Malley. He winked at Trixie.

She shook her head. "You are incorrigible."

"Darlin', I'm Irish. This is what we do."

Sandi moved toward the front of the store. She looked amazing in black yoga pants and a mint green tee shirt. Trixie looked down at her hastily arranged attire and was acutely aware she may have forgotten to brush her hair. "Ignore him, Trixie. He's full of blarney. I'm assuming Jonathan and the crew were at your home on time."

"Precisely at nine. And you're right, Patrick is full of something."

Patrick shook his head. "It's not right for two beautiful women, such as yourselves, to gang up on an old man."

Trixie laughed. "There's nothing old about you, and we might take your compliments more seriously if you weren't so full of blarney."

Patrick blew out an exaggerated sigh. "Even though I bat for the other team, that doesn't keep me from appreciating beauty when I see it." His eyes held a mischievous gleam. "I have work to do, so I'll leave you ladies to browse."

Sandi and Trixie watched him walk away. "Totally full of it," said Sandi. "And yet, he's one of my favorite people in the world. I love this place. You must be an avid reader to come back so soon."

"I am, and there's nothing I love more than a good mystery."

Sandi turned toward Trixie. "In fiction or in reality?"

"I guess both. A mystery is a mystery, right? But today, I need to pick Patrick's brain. I know he's lived in Brookville for quite some time and probably knows most of the town's gossip."

Sandi leaned against the counter. "I haven't resided here quite as long, but maybe I can help. What do you want to know?"

"As you noticed when you saw our Command Center, my friends and I are fascinated with mysteries, and Brookville has quite a few, including the Jeffries family and the disappearance of their daughter, Alexandra. Are you familiar with any of the family's history? I was hoping Patrick might have known them."

"Oh," said Sandi. "I'm not sure Patrick has lived here that long. Dan and I moved here about twenty years ago. I think the old plantation house burned down a few years earlier. What specifically do you want to know?"

"What happened to their daughter?"

"I don't recall hearing anything about her. Why are you so curious about Alexandra?" Sandi laughed. "Is she a suspect?"

"If you ask Martha, she will say everyone is a suspect. I'm just curious."

Sandi pushed away from the counter. "Wish I could help, but I've gotta go. My personal trainer is waiting."

"Where do you work out?"

"Ironworks. They have a fabulous gym."

"I've been looking for a place. I'll have to give it a try,"

"Well, if you're looking for a trainer. I can highly recommend Steven. He's great." Sandi walked over to Patrick and kissed the top of his head. "Behave yourself."

He winked at her. "Darlin', I'll give it my best effort. Don't be a stranger."

Patrick moved beside Trixie. "So, how about we have a cup of tea."

"Sounds lovely."

Patrick led her to the back of the store and into a kitchenette. A small microwave sat on the counter, and a dorm-sized refrigerator fit beneath it. A stove with two heating elements was situated in the corner, leaving just enough room for a round two-person table. "I'd just put on the kettle before you came into the shop." He poured tea into delicate china cups. Patrick sat a plate of scones on the table and settled into the chair across from Trixie.

"Patrick, this looks wonderful, and the china is beautiful."

"The china was my grans. Try a scone." He slid the plate toward her."

Trixie put one on her plate. "Did you make these?"

He gave her a sheepish grin. "I wish I could say yes. However, these are some of Café au Lait's creations. Ann is a fabulous baker."

"Agreed." Trixie took a bite of the scone. The rich, buttery taste with just the right amount of sweetness filled her mouth. Her eyes rolled heavenward. "Delicious."

"Darlin', about Sandi." Patrick busied himself with smoothing nonexistent wrinkles from the floral print tablecloth. "She's a nice lady, and I think a great deal of her. A little bitter after the divorce, but who could blame her?" His gaze shifted to Trixie. "The divorce between Dan and Sandi was ugly and taking place in a small town like Brookville, the gossip was rampant." He leaned forward. "Be careful what you say to her, love. As I said, nice lady, but bitter, and she holds on to a grudge." Patrick dunked a scone into his tea. "So, on to more pleasant topics. How is the investigation coming?"

"We've run into a dead end. Do you know what happened to Alexandra Jeffries? We haven't been able to find anything about her. There was a brief story about Alexandra's father killing an intruder, but nothing more. And when I say nothing, I mean we have been unable to find anything on Alexandra, no graduation, and no obituary. It's as if the girl dropped off the planet."

"And what is it about Alexandra that keeps you digging into her past?"

asked Patrick.

"I guess she's another mystery that needs to be solved."

Patrick held up a finger. "Give me a moment." He walked back into the store and then returned. "I've locked the door. We don't need anyone disturbing us."

Trixie arched her brow. "Patrick?"

"This is a two-cup story. How about a refill?" Trixie pushed her cup toward Patrick. He refilled her cup and returned to his chair and, for a moment, looked to be contemplating what he would say. Patrick took a sip of tea. "You understand what I'm about to tell you is a rumor, and in this town, all rumors start with a grain of truth? You've lived here long enough to know that during the Jeffries' heyday, this town was built with their money. The Jeffries name is on buildings, parks, everything. Approximately two years after Sara, Alexandra's friend, disappeared, there was a tragic accident at the Jeffries' home. According to the newspaper, Richard said he heard screams coming from Alexandra's bedroom. He rushed to her room, where he found a vagrant supposedly attacking her. He shot and killed the young man."

"Okay, that seems justifiable, but I get the feeling there's more to the story."

Patrick lifted his shoulder. "Here's the rest of the story. It was important to Richard Jeffries that his family embodied everything that said wealth and prominence and that their name should not be sullied in any way. Keep in mind this was the seventies when men controlled many aspects of a woman's life, and they also controlled the marriage. Richard's wife wasn't allowed to hold a paying job, but she was expected to be involved in charitable works. Once a week, she dragged Alexandra down to the mission to work in the soup kitchen and feed the poor. That's where Alexandra met the young vagrant." Patrick paused and took a bite of his scone. "They struck up quite the friendship. So much so, Mrs. Jeffries wouldn't let Alexandra come back to the soup kitchen."

"Okay. So, where's this going?"

Patrick grimaced. "You know an Irishman loves a good story. Be patient; I'm getting to the point. Fast forward to that fateful night. When law enforcement arrived at the Jeffries home, Richard met them in the driveway. He told them he'd shot and killed an intruder who was raping his daughter. But when EMS and the deputies went inside the house, Alexandra was sitting in the living room cool as a cucumber. No tears, no hysteria, nothing you would have expected from a young girl who'd just been assaulted. Her mother, however, was a different story; she was inconsolable."

"So, what happened? Didn't the responding officers think Alexandra's behavior was odd? Was she taken to the hospital for an exam?"

"They did think her behavior was highly unusual, but they assumed she was in shock. She was taken to the hospital for an exam. At that time, rape kits weren't the norm in emergency rooms, especially in a small town like Brookville. Anyway, the doctor confirmed she'd had sex, but could not conclusively determine if it was rape, and Alexandra refused to answer any questions. Now, for the interesting part. When law enforcement checked the father's hands for gunshot residue, there was nothing. Want to guess where they found it?" Patrick leaned back in his chair.

Trixie's eyes widened. "Alexandra."

Patrick pointed an index finger at her. "Bingo. It was believed that Richard paid someone a pot of money for the truth to be swept away. Shortly after the incident, Alexandra disappeared. There was speculation she was either sent to a sanitarium for the mentally ill or that she was pregnant and sent away to have the baby. The other tragedy in all of this was Mrs. Jeffries. She never seemed to recover and committed suicide less than a year later. The papers said she died of heart failure." Patrick looked down at his clasped hands. "That part was probably true. I believe she died of a broken heart."

"What a sad story. What about Bernard Cooper? What is his role in this tragedy?"

"He showed up for Elizabeth's funeral. You can imagine how the tongues wagged. I can't prove it, but I believe he and Elizabeth were still seeing one another."

"How did Richard react to Bernard showing up at the funeral?"

"As anyone who knew Richard would expect. He was the epitome of dignity."

Trixie studied the tea grounds in the bottom of her cup. "Do you think Bernard and Alexandra stayed in touch? That he knows where she is?"

"Maybe. And if there is anyone in this community that knows what happened to her, he does. But don't bother asking him. Many have tried over the years, and it never went well, if you get my drift."

Patrick's face clouded with worry. "I heard someone tried to hurt your friends. Do the police have any leads?"

Trixie looked up in surprise. How do you know about that?"

"Darlin', as we've been discussing, Brookville's an extremely small incestuous community. There are very few secrets here that stay secret. Eventually, they all surface, and the truth is revealed."

Trixie took a bite of the scone. "Sort of like the bones at the construction site."

"Very much like that. There's no telling what secrets they're hiding. You and your friends should be careful. You're digging into the past, and there are those who would prefer to leave the past buried, just like those old bones."

"What's that supposed to mean?"

He waved his hand dismissively. "Ignore me. It's just the ramblings of an old man full of blarney."

Chapter Thirty-Four

E arly the following morning, Trixie picked up Kathleen and Martha and drove them to the café. The rain was torrential, and the air held an unexpected chill. Inside the warm, cozy restaurant, they studied the menu. Emile came to the table. "Ladies, what brings you out on this miserable day?"

"Coffee and your amazing Eggs Benedict," said Kathleen.

"That sounds wonderful. I'll have the same," said Trixie.

Emile turned toward Martha and frowned. "And you, madam, will you be having an Egg McMuffin with *sauce* this morning?"

Martha hesitated. "I will have what they are having."

Emile sniffed. "Excellent choice. Your coffees will be out in a moment." He gave Martha a final look and walked back to the kitchen.

Martha watched him go. "He is still upset with me."

"He'll get over it," said Trixie.

"By the way, thanks for picking me up," said Martha. "This weather would have made for a very miserable walk."

"Martha, I've never seen you drive. Don't you have a car?" asked Kathleen.

"No. It has never been a necessity for me."

"How do you get to work?" asked Trixie.

"I ride the bus like everyone else. The proximity of the bus stop was a factor in making my decision to buy a condo at Brookville."

"For heaven's sake, I feel horrible. I didn't know you were without transportation. You should've said something," said Kathleen.

"Why? Bus is my preferred mode of transportation," said Martha. "Besides,

I have none of the vehicle expenses you have. And I can use my time for other things on the ride to work."

Trixie put her napkin in her lap. "What sort of other things do you do on the bus ride?"

"I like to read. And on occasion, I converse with other passengers, and sometimes, when the two of you have kept me up past my bedtime, I sleep."

"Okay, but do you know how to drive?" asked Trixie.

Martha studied her fork, scratched at nonexistent food residue. "I never got around to it."

"But in high school, they provided driver's education, right? Didn't you participate?" asked Kathleen.

Martha shifted in her seat. "I tried. However, there was a very unfortunate incident, and I was banned from driver's education."

"Banned? No one gets banned. What sort of incident?" asked Trixie.

Emile returned with their coffee. Martha busied herself with opening a sugar packet. She poured the contents into her cup and stirred. Trixie and Kathleen waited.

"Well?" said Trixie.

Martha picked up the pitcher of cream and poured a small amount into her coffee. "I wrecked the driver's training car."

"I'm sure you're not the first student to have a little bump up. Banning you from driver's education seems a little over the top," said Kathleen.

Martha looked at Kathleen. "Well, it might have been more than a little bump up. More like three little bump-ups. The last time, they had to bring in the Jaws of Life to get us out."

Kathleen's hand flew to her throat. "Was anyone hurt?"

Martha shook her head. "No. Nothing serious, just a few contusions. Although, I can confirm the literature on airbags is correct; they do save lives."

"Three cars—you wrecked three cars?" said Trixie. "Martha, you're like a cat.

Martha looked at Trixie over the rim of her cup. "I do not see how."

"You know, nine lives."

"Trixie, you do know that is an idiom, right? Cats really do not have nine lives," said Martha.

"Yeah, but they have an uncanny way of always landing on their feet." Trixie shook her head. "Never mind."

Kathleen fidgeted with her napkin. "What's wrong with you?" asked Trixie.

"Well, I have something I need to get off my chest."

"What is the issue weighing down your chest?" asked Martha.

"I spoke with my son, Dan, last night."

Trixie said, "Judging by your expression, the conversation didn't go well."

Kathleen took a sip of coffee, then returned the cup to the saucer. "I guess it was okay."

"But?" asked Trixie.

"He wanted to know what I've been doing lately. So, I told him."

Trixie's eyes widened. "You told him...everything?"

"Well, not everything, but I mentioned I was taking a self-defense class."

"I gather he didn't approve?"

"It's worse than that. He laughed at me." Kathleen pinched her lips together angrily and leaned forward. "Do you know what he said? He said he was glad I'd gotten my sense of humor back, and what was I really doing with myself."

"What did you say?" asked Martha.

Kathleen lifted her chin defiantly. "I told him I was making a quilt. That seemed to make him happy. Then I said I had to go because my quilting group was coming over, and I hung up. I was so furious with him. He is unable to see me as a person. He views me only as his mom, not as a woman who has a life."

"I'm assuming you didn't mention Jack," said Trixie.

Kathleen barked out a humorless laugh. "Are you kidding? The boy would've had a stroke."

"Want me to change the subject?" asked Martha.

Kathleen folded her arms over her chest. "Yes, please.

Martha leaned forward conspiratorially. "When are we breaking into

CHAPTER THIRTY-FOUR

Camille's condo? We should do it soon."

"I feel compelled to remind you two that breaking into Camille's condo is a crime," hissed Kathleen.

Martha waved her hand dismissively. "Only if we get caught." She looked at Trixie. "So, what is the plan?"

Kathleen closed her eyes. "Oh, good Lord, we've gone from bad to worse."

Trixie turned toward Kathleen. "Has Camille's family returned to pack up her belongings?"

"Why are you looking at me? I have no idea." Kathleen looked past Trixie. "I need a coffee refill. Where is our waitress?"

"You have an inside connection with someone who would know." Trixie leaned in closer. "You need to pump Nelson for information."

"Why me? You're retired from law enforcement. Isn't there some sort of code you people follow about helping each other?" Kathleen stood. "Never mind, I'll get my own damn coffee. You two are terrible."

Emile walked over to the table. "You ladies seem to be having a nice time."

Kathleen glared down at Trixie and Martha, then turned on Emile. She shoved her cup at him. "Could you *please* get me more coffee?"

Chapter Thirty-Five

Kathleen shook her head. "I don't like this—nope, not one little bit. I don't know why I agreed to participate in this B&E thing."

Trixie grabbed Kathleen's elbow and pulled her further into the shadows. "As a former ATF agent, I'm not thrilled with the prospects of breaking and entering. However, under the circumstances, we don't have much of a choice. We're here because we want to find Camille's murderer. There must be something in her house that cost Camille her life, and we need to find it." Trixie looked at the night sky. "This full moon is really making it hard to blend in with the shadows."

"You realize anything we find we can't give to Jack, right? And where is Martha? She's supposed to be part of this harebrained scheme."

"She's on her way. If we find something that has merit, we'll tell Jack to come back and do another search. Simple."

"There is nothing simple about this. We're all going to jail. I know it."

"We are not going to jail because we're not going to get caught," said Trixie.

Kathleen paced in the small, shadowed space. "Yeah, and I bet there are hundreds of people sitting in prisons all around the world who thought the same thing. Where did you say Martha was?"

"She said she had to make a quick stop and that she'd be here. Relax."

"I'm trying. If I can't eat pie when I'm nervous, I pace. Mac used to say I'd wear a hole in the carpet. I miss him."

Trixie put her arm around Kathleen's shoulders. "I know you do."

"But Jack's a great guy, and if I can't have Mac, I'd want Jack."

Trixie squeezed Kathleen's shoulder. "Jack's a great guy."

"Do you think he'll visit me in prison?"

"Kathleen, stop. We're not going to prison." Trixie squinted and pointed to the hedge closest to Camille's house. "Wait, is that Martha skulking in the bushes?"

"Where?"

Trixie pointed again. "Over there."

"Yeah, I think so. What's she doing?"

"She's motioning for us to come to her."

"How did she see us in the dark?"

Trixie and Kathleen jogged along the perimeter of the house, keeping to the shadows. Martha jumped out in front of them, a binocular-looking contraption strapped to her head.

Kathleen slapped a hand over her mouth, stifling a scream. "Oh, my Lord, you look like some alien creature. What are you wearing?"

"Vintage night vision goggles. Martha pushed them up on her forehead. "You want to try them? They are great. I can see everything."

"Martha, you scared the life out of me," said Kathleen. "And what is that black stuff on your face?"

Martha held out a small tub containing a black waxy substance. "The moon was so bright I thought it would help us blend into the shadows better. We should have checked the lunar calendar before our mission. But we are here now, so we must make the best of things." Martha shoved the tub at Kathleen. "Put some of this on your face."

Kathleen rubbed her fingers in the substance and smeared it across her cheeks. "I don't like this." She passed the tub to Trixie.

Trixie sniffed the tub's contents. "This smells like shoe polish. I'm not putting that on my face."

"You have to. We're in the middle of a covert operation. You do not want to be seen, do you?" said Martha.

"It's shoe polish. Football players don't put shoe polish on their faces," said Trixie.

"Football players use eye black—it's grease. You're better off with the shoe polish," whispered Martha.

"Fine." Trixie scooped up a finger full of the waxy black substance and smeared it across her cheeks, then shoved the tub back at Martha. "Did you remember to bring the lock picks?"

"Of course. I am anxious to try them. Follow me." Martha led them to the side door of the house, where the shadows were thick.

"I thought there was a light back here," said Kathleen.

Martha pulled out her lock picks, and seconds later, she turned the doorknob. "There was. I came by earlier today and loosened it. I thought it would make things better for tonight."

"Good thinking," said Trixie. "Where'd you get the goggles?"

"I have an acquaintance at the Army Surplus store. He calls me when interesting merchandise comes in. These babies are circa Vietnam War. They were in surprisingly good condition. I replaced the battery, and they work great."

"Martha, you constantly surprise me," said Kathleen.

The women walked inside the house. It was dark, and the air smelled stale. Trixie heard Martha unzip her fanny pack.

"Here," said Martha. "I brought these." She handed each woman a small flashlight.

"I'm not sure we should be using these," said Kathleen.

"We've got to have some type of light. It's so dark I can't see anything," said Trixie.

"These flashlights have been fitted with a special green filter that makes them an excellent choice for nighttime covert operations." Martha clicked her flashlight on, and a narrow beam of green light illuminated a small space. "However, it would be prudent to make sure the blinds are closed. Also, before we go any further, you two need to glove up." She pulled two sets of nitrile gloves from her fanny pack. "I do not think forensics will be back, but better safe than sorry."

Once the women were gloved, they turned on their flashlights. Kathleen swept her light across the room. "This place is a mess."

"It's no wonder. Everybody and his brother have been in here," said Trixie.

"We should split up. Doing so will be more efficient," said Martha.

CHAPTER THIRTY-FIVE

Kathleen stepped over a desk drawer. "What exactly are we looking for?"

"Camille found something she didn't want anyone else to see. Keeping it on her computer wouldn't have been safe. And when Carrie's condo was broken into, the burglars asked for her computer and any thumb drives she had. A thumb drive would be the obvious place to save important information, and it is small enough to hide. So, let's get busy. I'll take the kitchen," said Trixie.

"I've got the bath and bedroom," said Kathleen.

Martha sighed. "I guess that leaves me with the living room."

"What's wrong? Do you want the bath and bedroom?"

"No. The living room is fine. It's just that no one ever hides anything in the living room."

Kathleen shook her head and moved toward the bedroom. She stepped over bed linens heaped in the middle of the room. The drawer to the nightstand had been turned upside down, its contents strewn across the floor. She directed the narrow beam of green light to the bureau. The drawers were removed, and the contents dumped. Stepping over the pile of clothing and accessories, she opened the closet door. Clothing was scattered about the floor. Kathleen made her way into the bathroom. She lifted the lid to the toilet tank, opened the vanity cabinet, and checked inside the extra rolls of toilet paper. She called out, "Have either of you found anything?"

"There is too much chaos to find anything," grumbled Martha. "What about you, Trixie?"

Trixie slowly walked around the kitchen. "I'm still looking." She peeped in the boxes of food that had been emptied on the counters. Silverware, spices, and dish towels were strewn across the linoleum, the empty drawers piled in the middle of the floor. She remembered a movie she'd recently seen where the victim had hidden stolen jewels in the freezer. Trixie opened the freezer door. Empty. She moved to the pantry and felt under the empty shelves—nothing. Anything that had been stored here was now scattered on the floor and counters. She paused in front of the stove and opened the oven door. A stack of bake ware filled the inside. She lifted several of the baking pans; all were empty. "Yeah, I got nothing. Kathleen, what about you?" Trixie walked into the bathroom. Kathleen was on the floor gathering loose tampons and stuffing them back into the box. Trixie watched her for a moment. "What are you doing?"

Kathleen looked up. "This is one of my biggest pet peeves. When my daughter was a teenager, she would leave her feminine products lying all over the bathroom. I would tell her men don't need to know everything about a woman. I couldn't bear the thought that my husband, son, or one of his friends would walk into the bathroom and see her tampons lying around."

Trixie waved at the mess around them. "Kathleen, it doesn't matter. Most of Brookville's law enforcement has seen all of this."

Kathleen stood. "I don't care. It makes me feel better to clean it up." She gave the bathroom a final look and then blew out a disgusted sigh. "For crying out loud." She pointed to a shelf where a lone tampon lay between the cotton swabs and a can of deodorant. Kathleen picked it up and frowned.

"What's wrong?"

Kathleen handed the tampon to Trixie. "It doesn't feel right."

Trixie carefully felt through the wrapping. "You're right. There's not a tampon in here. It's something else."

"Do we open it?"

Martha joined them. "Do not open it. We must preserve the evidence until we decide how to proceed."

"It's possible this could just be a deformed tampon," said Kathleen.

Trixie rolled her eyes. "You don't really believe that, do you? She felt through the wrapper, then tested the weight in her palm. "I think we may have found the thumb drive. What a genius place to hide it and right out in the open."

"You have to give Camille credit for being resourceful," said Martha.

Kathleen said, "Yeah, but that also means she suspected someone would try to find it." She turned toward Trixie. "What do we do now? We can't just give it to Jack. Then we'll have to admit to breaking and entering."

Trixie held up her hands. "I know, I know. Stop chattering for a minute—I need to think." She closed her eyes and rubbed her temples. Martha and Kathleen stood quietly and watched her.

A floorboard toward the front of the house creaked. Trixie's eyes flew open. "Did you hear that?"

Kathleen clutched Trixie's arm. "Someone is here."

"Homes creak when they settle. You guys are too jumpy," whispered Martha.

The floor creaked again, closer this time. Trixie hissed, "That is not the house settling. Someone's in the house—with us."

"Turn out the flashlights," said Martha.

"What do we do?" Squeaked Kathleen.

"Is there a lock on the door?" whispered Trixie.

Martha fumbled with the doorknob. "Yes."

Another creak. "They're getting closer." Kathleen's words were barely audible. Heavy footsteps pounded down the dark hall, and a large figure charged toward them.

Trixie yelled, "Martha, shut the door. Now."

Martha slammed the door and locked it. The intruder threw his full weight against it and then twisted the knob. The women backed away from the door.

"Trixie, use your gun," said Kathleen.

"I didn't bring it."

Kathleen hissed, "Why not?"

"I didn't want to be in possession of a firearm if we were caught breaking and entering."

Martha flipped on the light. "There has to be something we can use to defend ourselves." She picked up a can of aerosol hairspray. "Does anyone have a match or a lighter?"

"No, why?" asked Kathleen.

"We could make a flamethrower," said Martha.

Kathleen wrung her hands. "Martha, how do you know this stuff?" The intruder threw his weight against the door again. A small yelp escaped Kathleen's lips. "Do something."

"I'm trying." Trixie pulled a can of spray disinfectant from beneath the sink. "We can use this, too." Trixie pulled Kathleen behind her.

Kathleen grabbed a handful of Trixie's shirt and held on. "What are we going to do? There's only one way out of this bathroom and…." She bunched more of Trixie's shirt into her hands.

"We need the element of surprise," Trixie whispered. "Martha, hand me the hairspray and turn out the light. And Kathleen, for the love of God, please let go of my shirt; you're choking me to death."

"Sorry." The intruder threw his body against the door again. The door frame made a sickening cracking sound. Kathleen squeaked.

Trixie whispered, "On the count of three, Martha, open the door. One." The intruder hit the door again.

"Trixie, it's not going to hold," whispered Kathleen.

"Two."

The assault stopped. Martha pressed her ear against the door.

Trixie moved closer. "What's going on?"

"I hear footsteps and…"

"And what?" whispered Trixie.

"A man's yelling."

"What's he saying?" whispered Kathleen.

"I can't make it out." Martha backed away from the door. "Someone's coming."

Kathleen bunched Trixie's shirt in her fist and pressed her forehead into Trixie's back.

Trixie pulled at the neckline of her shirt. "Kathleen, please, you're strangling me. You've got to give me some space to move."

The doorknob rattled, and someone pushed against the door. Trixie said, "Now, Martha."

Martha jerked open the door. Kathleen screamed, and Trixie leveled the spray cans in the direction of the intruder's head, dousing his face with the combination of hairspray and disinfectant. The man grunted and stumbled backward. Trixie continued spraying. The women ran out of the bathroom. Martha balled up her fist, screamed "kia" and delivered a punch to the man's forehead.

The intruder grunted, stumbled backward, and fell to the ground. "For crying out loud, stop spraying!" he croaked.

"Don't move, or I'll hit you again," said Martha.

The man raised his hands to protect his face. "Put down the spray cans," he wheezed. "I'm Deputy Jack Nelson from the BSD."

Kathleen pushed past Trixie and Martha. "Jack, sweetie, is that you?"

"Miss Kathleen? What in the hell are you three doing here?"

"What are you doing here?" countered Martha.

"Doing my job. Turn on the damn light."

Trixie felt for the light switch. She winced when she saw Jack's red, watering eyes and the large lump that had formed on his forehead. "You should probably flush your eyes with water." She turned on the spigot and stepped to the side. Jack filled his hands with the cool water and splashed it into his eyes.

After a few minutes, he dried his face with a towel. His eyes were red, and the area around them irritated and swollen. Kathleen examined his face and grimaced. "Oh, Jack, your eyes look terrible. You really should go to the hospital."

"No thanks to you three. I'm not going anywhere until you tell me what you're doing here." He sat on the edge of the tub and crossed his arms.

"You first," said Trixie.

"I'm here because a neighbor called dispatch and reported seeing lights and someone skulking around this residence."

"Did you see who was in the house?" asked Martha.

"I'm looking at them. However, the individual who was assaulting the bathroom door got away."

"Could you tell who it was?" asked Trixie.

"It was a man. That's all I can tell you. However, the individual knew the house and took off through the back door. Unfortunately, the light was out, and I couldn't get a good look."

Martha's eyes darted from Nelson to Trixie to Kathleen and then back to Nelson. "Oh, that is a shame."

He squinted at the women through watery eyes. "I've answered your question. It's time I got some answers. You did notice the yellow crime scene tape on the front door, right? And I'm assuming you realized this was still an active crime scene, correct? But the question that's burning a hole in my curiosity, apart from why you have black stuff on your faces, is how you got in here? I personally locked up this house."

Trixie waved her hand dismissively. "Jack, that's so unimportant. What you really need to ask is what we found. We think we have discovered the item that got Camille murdered. And if our suspicions are correct, this could be a win-win for all of us."

"Oh, it'll be a win for me because I'm taking the three of you to jail. I don't care what you found."

"Before you act on this knee-jerk reaction, you should really look at what we found," said Martha.

"Knee jerk?" Nelson thumped his forehead with the heel of his palm and winced.

Kathleen gently touched his forehead. "Oh, Jack, you've got a terrible bruise. How'd that happen?"

He glared at Kathleen. "How indeed. You women are either going to get me fired, or I'm going to die of a heart attack." He threw his hands in the air. "I give up. Tell me what you found?"

"You should be more grateful. After all, we are doing the job your forensic team should have done," said Martha.

Nelson's ears turned red, and his face contorted. He pointed a finger at her. "You..."

Trixie stepped in front of him. "Jack, we found this." She opened her hand.

He looked down at her palm, then gave her a blank look. "A tampon? You found a tampon. Great, that should make the boys in CSU sit up and take notice."

"Jack, sweetie, it's not what it seems. There's something else in the packaging. Look at the end—you can see where it's been glued shut. Perhaps you won't have to mention you saw us here, and then you could take this in and find out what's in this little package." Kathleen bent down and kissed his cheek. "Please."

"Don't try to sweet talk me, Miss Kathleen. It's not going to work."

Kathleen's blue eyes widened. "Jack, how could you say such a thing? I'd never try to sweet talk you." She pressed her small hand to his cheek. "Never."

He pulled in a deep breath and coughed. "It's late, and I'm tired. If you leave now, you'll save me a lot of paperwork. So, get out of here and take the back door. Did you touch anything?"

The women raised their gloved hands. Martha said, "We came prepared."

"Of course you did." Nelson turned toward Martha. "If I find out you are in possession of burglary tools, you are going to find yourself buried under the jail. Do you understand me?"

Martha said, "Well, of course, I—"

Trixie grabbed Martha's arm and squeezed. "Jack, don't be ridiculous. Of course, she doesn't have that type of equipment. Why would you ever think a nice middle-aged librarian like Martha would own such a thing." She shoved Martha toward the door. "We're leaving now, so you can call this in."

He pressed his fingers to his watering eyes. "Please leave, or I might change my mind."

Chapter Thirty-Six

Trixie stepped out of the shower and dried off with a thick white towel. She pulled on a peach robe, then wiped away condensation from the mirror. She leaned closer to the mirror and frowned; remnants of shoe polish still stained her face. That was the last time she'd listen to Martha. The next time they had a covert operation, she'd take her chances on being seen. At least if they were arrested, she'd have a clean face for the mug shot. A giggle bubbled out at the thought of them posing for police, their faces smeared with black shoe polish.

As she moved through her bedroom, she glanced at the closet. Construction was well underway, and as fast as Sandi's team worked, Trixie expected the closet would be finished in another day or two.

In the kitchen, she flipped on the light. For a moment, Trixie stood and admired Sandi's handiwork. She had done a fabulous job of reconfiguring the kitchen into a beautiful, functional space. The granite countertops, and beautiful oak cabinets were better than she'd expected. And the workspace tucked into the back of the kitchen was exactly what she had envisioned. Sandi had an eye for detail and an artistic flare. She'd covered the kitchen chairs with a colorful geometric patterned fabric, which amped up the cheerful, stylish feel of the kitchen. Trixie recalled the plethora of fabric swatches Sandi had asked her to look through. She'd been overwhelmed with the choices and, in the end, asked Sandi to select one. Without hesitation, Sandi seemed to instinctively know what would work best.

Grabbing the red tea kettle from the counter, Trixie filled it with water and set it on the stove to heat. She removed a porcelain cup and saucer imprinted with a delicate floral pattern from the cabinet, sat them on the counter, and dropped a chamomile tea bag inside the cup.

As a teenager, whenever there was drama in her life, her mother would sit her down at the kitchen table and put on a kettle to heat. She would tell her hot tea was a cure for many ills. The thought of her mother was comforting. She missed her mom and dad, both gone too soon. With no siblings, there were days when she felt very alone.

Trixie was lost in her gloomy thoughts when her cell rang. She jumped. "For crying out loud, it's just the phone." When she picked up her cell, she was greeted by Kathleen's unsteady voice.

"What's wrong?"

"I'm jumpy. You know what I mean? I have an uneasy feeling like I'm waiting for the other shoe to drop."

Trixie gave a humorless laugh. "I know exactly what you mean. It's just now sinking in how close we came to being in serious trouble. If Jack hadn't shown up...I don't know what would have happened. Did he stop by your house?"

"He did," Kathleen hesitated. "He was still upset."

"You can't blame him. Jack Nelson has a soft spot for you. I'm sure when he realized the danger you were in, it didn't sit well with him. And it didn't help that we broke into his crime scene."

"If you recall, I didn't want to go to Camille's house because we'd be *breaking* the law. Do you recall that conversation?"

"I may have a slight recollection of you mentioning that little detail."

"I hope he's not going to be in trouble with the sheriff."

"I'm sure he'll be fine. Did he get medical attention?" asked Trixie.

"Yeah, he stopped by an Urgent Care. The doctor said his eyes would be okay. He flushed them again and gave Jack drops to help with the inflammation and irritation. He should feel better in a few days."

"Thank goodness."

"Do you mind if I come over? I don't want to be alone."

"Sure, come on. Wear your PJs. We'll have a slumber party."

"Thanks. I'll be there in a few minutes."

The tea kettle whistled, and Trixie pulled it from the stove. She filled the cup with the hot water and turned to go into the living room when, from the corner of her eye, she noticed movement in the kitchen window. It was too soon for Kathleen to be here. Heart pounding, she slowly turned toward the window. A mop of gray hair and a round face, the nose smashed against the window, stared back at her. Trixie yelped, and the cup crashed to the floor, sending shards of porcelain and rivulets of tea in all directions. "Damn."

Martha waved. Trixie stepped over the mess and opened the door. Martha stood on the top step wrapped in a white terry cloth robe. "Why didn't you ring the doorbell like everyone else?"

"Why? You could see me. Anyway, I cannot sleep. I thought we could talk."

Trixie motioned Martha in. "You aren't the only one. Kathleen's on her way. We're going to have a slumber party."

"What is the point? I wanted to talk about the case."

Smiling, Trixie pulled a broom and dustpan from a small utility closet. "Would you like a cup of hot tea?"

"I am not big on hot tea. Do you have hot chocolate?"

"I'm sure I could scrounge up a cup." Trixie dumped the contents of the dustpan into the trash. The doorbell rang. She glanced at Martha. "Now, that's how company announces their presence. It's Kathleen. Could you get the door?"

Trixie was pouring milk into a saucepan when Kathleen and Martha walked into the kitchen. "I was about to make hot chocolate. Or, if you prefer, the kettle is hot, I could make hot tea. Your choice."

"Do you have the little marshmallows?" asked Kathleen.

Trixie opened a cabinet. "Maybe." She rooted around until she found a partially filled bag. "The answer is yes." She squeezed one of the marshmallows. "I'm not sure how fresh they are, but do marshmallows really go bad?"

"Doubtful. I'll take hot chocolate." Kathleen looked around the kitchen. "Sandi has done an amazing job. Your kitchen is beautiful. I might need to give her a call and have her do some work for me."

Martha shrugged. "It does look nice, but I only eat in my kitchen. I don't see the logic in remodeling."

Trixie added more milk, cocoa, vanilla, sugar, and a dash of nutmeg to the pan and set it on the stove.

Martha hovered over Trixie's shoulder. "I thought you would just open an envelope of instant hot chocolate mix. That is how I make mine."

"You've got to be kidding. My mother would turn over in her grave. This was her recipe. It's delicious. Have a seat. It'll be ready in a minute." Trixie slowly stirred the warming milk. "You know, if this was a real slumber party, we'd order pizza. What do you think?"

"Actually, I am hungry. I was too nervous to eat earlier," said Kathleen.

"I like pizza." Martha looked at her watch. "I do not recall ever eating pizza at ten o'clock at night."

"You never went to sleepovers when you were a kid?" asked Trixie.

Martha shook her head. "My mother was very strict."

"Well, you're in for a treat. Kathleen, my cell is on the table. Call in an order for pizza."

* * *

Thirty minutes later, the women sat around Trixie's kitchen table, eating pizza and laughing. "I know it's not funny, but the expression on Jack Nelson's face when Martha punched him in the head was priceless," said Kathleen. "I don't think I've ever seen him look so stunned."

"Self-defense classes have been very beneficial," said Martha. "After tonight's events, I realized I can take care of myself. It gives one a very empowered feeling." She turned toward Trixie. "And speaking of empowered feelings, I want to know more about your life as an ATF agent."

Kathleen chewed the end of a pizza crust. "Oh, me too."

"Really, there's not that much to tell."

"We don't believe that, do we, Martha?"

"Not for a minute. So, spill the beans."

Trixie leaned back in her chair. "I was a freshman in college planning to follow in the footsteps of my parents. They dealt in antiques, and I don't mean the consignment shop sort. They bought and sold the good stuff. All I ever wanted to do was work in the family business. But then, I took a criminal justice class in college. I thought it would be fun, you know, something different. It turned out to be more than a lark. Next thing I knew, I was a criminal justice major."

"I graduated in three and a half years and went to work for a small police department in Virginia. When our police force was asked to work with the ATF on a special case, I realized I wanted more. So, I applied to ATF. They accepted me, and I moved to their training facility in Glynco, Georgia.

"Why did you retire?" asked Martha. "You aren't old."

Trixie picked at the pizza crust on her plate. "I was shot in the line of duty. It was too risky to remove the bullet, so I was left with a parting gift. As a result, I occasionally have numbness and or pain in my right leg, which took me out of field work. I was offered a desk job, but by that time, law enforcement had lost its luster. I've been retired for six years and haven't looked back."

Kathleen's eyes widened. "Your leg gave out on you in class the other morning, didn't it? That's why Doc had to help you."

"It's getting worse as time goes by. The surgeon told me I might not have a choice about the surgery. But it's not without risk, and right now, I'm not ready to take the risk," Trixie said brightly. "Now, you know all about my sordid past."

Kathleen yawned. "Thank you for letting us intrude on your evening. I think I can sleep now."

"Me too," said Trixie. "You two can fight over the couch."

Chapter Thirty-Seven

The next morning, Trixie walked into the living room. Kathleen was sprawled out on the couch, and Martha was lying on the air mattress wrapped with blankets, looking very much like a human burrito. She stepped around Martha and made her way into the kitchen and the freshly brewed coffee. Trixie filled a mug and was adding cream when her cell rang.

Carrie's anxious voice greeted her. "Trixie, I'm glad I reached you. Something terrible has happened."

Trixie rubbed sleep from her eyes. "Are you okay?"

"Brittney was attacked early this morning. She's in critical condition at Brookville Memorial."

Trixie dropped into a kitchen chair. "What happened?"

"I don't know the details. I thought you should know."

"Thanks, Carrie." Trixie disconnected.

Kathleen shuffled toward the coffee maker. "Is something wrong?"

"Brittney's been attacked. She's in critical condition."

Martha joined them in the kitchen. "We should go to the hospital. It's possible Camille's killer may have been Brittney's attacker."

"I'm calling Jack." Trixie punched in Nelson's number and put the phone on speaker.

After three rings, he answered. "Trixie, I don't have time to talk."

"So, it's true Brittney was attacked?"

"Yeah. She's in bad shape. The doctor isn't sure she'll pull through."

"Do you have any leads?"

"We have two witnesses, but neither got a good look. Her attacker was tall, dressed in camo, and wore a ski mask."

"There was only one attacker?"

"Correct. Fortunately, one of the witnesses was an EMT. If they hadn't come along when they did, I'd be investigating another homicide. We're still processing the scene, but so far, there's not much to go on. I've gotta go."

"Before you go, what did the tech guy find on the thumb drive?"

"Financials for the Corporation. What it means at this point, I have no idea. We have a forensic accountant going through the information. Hopefully, we'll know something soon. Trixie, you, and your friends, stay out of this. I'm not going to ask again." Nelson disconnected.

Trixie dropped the cell into her handbag. "I'm going to the hospital."

"Didn't Jack just tell us to stay out of his investigation?" said Kathleen.

"Yeah, but when has that stopped us?"

"Give me fifteen minutes, and I will be ready to go," said Martha.

"Fine," said Kathleen. "But let's make it twenty minutes."

"Then we'll meet back here in twenty minutes," said Trixie.

* * *

Trixie pulled into the parking deck of Brookville Memorial Hospital. As the women entered the lobby, they saw Dan Fields sitting on a bench. He was bent over, elbows propped on his knees. His hands covered his face as if shielding him from the outside world and the tragedy.

"He looks terrible," said Kathleen.

Trixie sat beside him. "Dan, how are you holding up? How's Brittney?"

He turned toward her and wiped his tear-stained face. "Ms. Tanner? I wasn't expecting to see you here." He ran a hand through his hair. Stress lined his face. "Brittney's in a coma. The doctors aren't sure she'll regain consciousness, and if she does, there's the possibility of permanent brain damage. We have to wait and see." A sob escaped him, and a fresh flow of tears streamed down his face. He looked away.

Trixie put an arm around his shoulders. "We were heading to the cafeteria for coffee. You look like you could use a cup. Come with us."

Trixie bought coffee and a pastry for Dan. They settled at a table near the window, looking out on the side entrance of the hospital. Cars circled the drive, dropping family members off and picking up discharged patients. She slid the pastry toward Dan. "You should try and eat something. Brittney's going to need your strength."

He pushed the plate to the side. "Thank you, but I'm really not hungry." Dan sipped the hot coffee and then cradled the Styrofoam cup in his hands. "I don't know if you knew it, but Brittney was preparing for a triathlon. She's quite the athlete."

"She mentioned her training the day we met her on the trails."

Dan let out an anguished groan. "I told her to stop running the trails, but she insisted she could take care of herself." He turned toward Trixie. "Only she couldn't."

"What happened?" asked Trixie.

Dan studied the liquid in the cup. "There's a place on the trail where two large oak trees grow on either side. That's the spot where Brittney always finishes her run. She pretends it's the finish line. She increases her pace to a sprint to practice that lasts 25 to 30 yards of the race. This morning, someone strung a fishing line across the trail."

Trixie looked at Kathleen and Martha.

"Brittney was clotheslined. Two witnesses saw it happen. At first, they thought she had fallen." Fresh tears ran down Dan's face. "Her attacker came from behind one of the Oaks. He was standing on her neck." Dan's voice broke into a mournful sob. The witnesses yelled and ran toward her, but her attacker got away. Dan wiped his face with a napkin. "When the witnesses got to Brittney, she was gasping for air. Fortunately, one of them was an EMT. If he hadn't been there, she would have died."

"Could the witnesses give a description of Brittney's attacker?" asked Trixie.

"Nothing helpful."

Kathleen's hand fluttered to her throat. "That's horrible. Dan, I'm so sorry."

"Brittney's a strong woman. She's going to pull through this," said Trixie.

Dan shook his head. His face contorted. "I've got to get back. Thanks for the coffee."

Trixie watched him walk away. She turned toward Martha and Kathleen. "Brittney wasn't a victim of chance. What do you want to bet the fishing line is the same weight and brand as what we found near those same Oaks? This was a premeditated attack by someone who knew her routine. Beyond the Corporation, what else do Brittney and Camille have in common?"

Martha rearranged the sugar packets in the small container, grouping the packets by color. When she was done, she sat the container in the middle of the table and looked up at Trixie and Kathleen. "Dan Fields."

"What about Dan?" asked Kathleen.

"That is what both women have in common," said Martha.

"You're right," said Trixie.

"But Carrie didn't have an affair with Dan. So, how does she fit into the scenario?" said Kathleen. "She was beaten, but not murdered. And let's face it, if the intruders had wanted her dead, they had the opportunity."

"Maybe we're looking at this all wrong," said Trixie.

"What is that supposed to mean?"

Trixie's eyes narrowed. "It means I need to think about it. I've just had a very bad thought?"

"What?" asked Kathleen.

"What if the murderer comes back to finish what he or she started."

"A logical consideration," said Martha. "However, the individual may wait to see if Brittney is going to recover before taking such a risk."

"Either way, Nelson needs to put a guard outside Brittney's room." Trixie pulled her cell from her handbag and punched in Nelson's number.

"Trixie, you continually interrupting my day is making my job more difficult. What is it now?"

"Do you have a guard for Brittney's room?"

"I realize I'm only a lowly deputy from a small town, and you're a retired federal agent, and I'd like to emphasize the word retired, but I do know how to do my job. If you'd get off the damn phone and let me do it."

"You didn't answer my question."

Nelson blew out an exaggerated breath. "Of course, there's a guard. Carter's there now."

"Good. I promise I won't call you again, at least for the next hour," said Trixie.

"You women are going to be the death of me. Where are you now?"

"The hospital cafeteria."

"Stay put, I'm on my way."

Chapter Thirty-Eight

"What did Deputy Nelson want?" asked Martha.

"No idea. He said he was on his way," said Trixie.

"Perhaps we have pushed him to his breaking point, and he is taking us to the hoosegow. I find that an interesting word. Did you know it comes from the Spanish word *juzgado*, which means "panel of judges or courtroom? You must admit etymology is fascinating. Would you not agree?"

"What?" squeaked Kathleen.

"Jail," said Martha. "We will be jailbirds and in the system with a rap sheet."

"Martha, you aren't helping," said Trixie.

Several minutes later, Nelson strode into the cafeteria, looking tall and official. Kathleen sighed. "He is such a handsome man. If I'm going to be hauled off to jail, Jack is the man I'd want to take me there. I wonder if he'll visit me in lockup."

Trixie rolled her eyes.

Nelson took the empty chair at the table and laid a manila envelope in the center.

"What's in the envelope?" asked Trixie.

"I've been thinking about our conversation from the other night. Maybe if we go back to the beginning and review our case, we'll see something we missed earlier."

Trixie arched a brow. "*Our* case?"

Nelson pointed an index finger at her. "Gloating is very unbecoming. I'm asking for a fresh perspective. And…yes, I guess I'm asking for your help."

210

"We are at your service. So, what's in the envelope?"

"I couldn't bring the evidence box, so I brought the next best thing: crime scene photos." He pushed the envelope in front of Trixie, then turned to Kathleen. "You might not want to look at these."

"Jack, I'm not a shrinking violet. If you'll recall, I found poor Camille."

Trixie pulled the photographs from the envelope and slowly flipped through them. Martha hung over her shoulder. She pointed to a photo of several fabric swatches. "Where did you find those?"

"They were in Camille's pocket. Why?"

"It's possible she met with Sandi Fields at some point the day of her death. Sandi remodels homes, and she showed me a bunch of fabric samples like this when I was planning my home renovation. If Camille and Sandi met that day, maybe Sandi could help tighten up your timeline leading to Camille's death. Or maybe someone was with Camille when Sandi met with her."

Nelson pulled a pad from his breast pocket and made a note. "That's good. Anything else?"

Trixie finished going through the last of the photos, then returned them to the envelope. "Nothing. Do you have any more information on Brittney's attacker?"

"The fishing line used to clothesline her was the same weight line as what you ladies found earlier. It's been dry lately, so there were no footprints at the scene, and my two witnesses can't tell me anything more than Brittney's assailant was tall and dressed in camo. I've got my guys searching the area, hoping the attacker pulled off the ski mask and tossed it in the bushes or a nearby trash can." Trixie gave him a doubtful look. "Yeah, I know. Like that's going to happen. Basically, I've got squat on these damn cases." He glanced at Kathleen. "Pardon my language, ma'am."

"What about Jason Knight? What's his story?" asked Trixie.

"He's an interesting fellow, and there's something about him that bothers me. I just can't put my finger on it yet."

"Is he on your suspect list?" asked Martha.

"Everyone is on my list, but I think it's unlikely he murdered Camille." Nelson picked up the envelope and stood. "I've got work to do. Let me know if you run across anything of interest, and thanks for your help."

Kathleen watched Jack walk away. She turned back to Martha and Trixie. "So, what's next?"

"I don't think there's anything more we can do here," said Trixie. "I'm going to check on Dan before we leave."

When Trixie walked into the Intensive Care waiting area, Dan Fields was sitting in a chair with a young blond curly-haired toddler asleep in his lap. She took the chair beside him. "What a beautiful child. What's his name?"

"Ian."

"Don't you have anyone to watch him?"

"My sitter had an appointment, but Sandi has offered to take care of him. She's gone to get coffee, and then she's going to take him to her house for a few hours."

"Sandi?" She and Dan must have had a better relationship than she thought. She was struggling to see the aloof woman sitting on the floor playing blocks with a toddler.

"You sound surprised."

"Maybe a little. I didn't get the impression you two were on amicable terms."

He kissed the top of Ian's head. "I guess tough times can make people see past their difficulties."

"I guess so. How's Brittney? Has there been any change?"

"The same. She's resting comfortably."

Sandi walked into the waiting area with two coffees. She hesitated at the door and then entered the room. "Trixie, what a surprise. I wasn't expecting to see you here." She handed a Styrofoam cup to Dan. "If I'd known you were coming, I would've gotten you coffee." She gave Trixie a tight smile. "So, what *are* you doing here? I didn't realize you knew Dan and Brittney that well." She took the chair on the other side of Dan.

Trixie stood. "My friends and I heard what happened. We wanted to see if there was anything we could do to help. Dan, if you need anything, please let me know. Deputy Nelson is doing everything he can to find out who did this to Brittney." Trixie turned to Sandi. "By the way, my kitchen looks great. Did you do any work for Camille?"

"We'd talked but hadn't confirmed any plans. Why?"

"Just curious." Trixie turned back to Dan. "Let us know if you need something."

"Thanks again for coming."

"I'll see you in the morning," said Sandi. "My team will finish your closet this afternoon. I'll be there for the final inspection at nine." Sandi put her arm around Dan.

The comfort of a friend? Or were there still feelings? Was it one-sided or reciprocal? Trixie thought as she moved toward the door.

Trixie had just stepped into the hall when Jason Knight ran past her and burst into the waiting room. He dropped into the chair Trixie had vacated. "Why didn't you call me? I just heard someone tried to kill Brittney. What happened? Is she going to be okay? Do they know who attacked her?"

Dan handed the toddler to Sandi. "Jason, calm down. We don't know anything yet. For now, she's in a coma. All we can do is pray." Trixie looked at the scene before her. Sandi was holding the adorable, curly, fair-haired little boy. Dan was dark-featured. Her gaze went to Jason Knight, frightened and worried. His usual coiffed wavy hair was a tangled mass of light brown curls. She looked from Jason to the toddler and then back to Dan. Trixie couldn't see any resemblance to Dan, but Jason was another story.

Jason leaned back in the chair. "Coma? I wasn't aware she was in a coma. Oh my God, this can't be happening—not now."

Trixie cocked her head to the side and watched the Brookville Corporation co-owners. Jason Knight was obviously distraught. She thought back to the day at the restaurant when she'd seen him with Brittney. He had been cool, perhaps even a bit cavalier toward her. He'd tried to kiss her hand. At the time, Trixie hadn't given it much thought. Carrie had said Brittney and Jason couldn't stand each other. But the Jason Knight she was watching now was a far cry from the one she'd seen that afternoon in the restaurant. And what did he mean by *this can't be happening now*? She watched him. There was more to this story. Did Dan feel it, too? Did he see the resemblance in his child to Jason? Or did he choose to ignore it? And had he forgiven his wife for her transgression?

Trixie slipped out of the waiting area as Dan recapped the events for Jason. She moved into the hall as Nelson exited the elevator. "Why are you back so soon?"

"I'm here on official business."

Trixie's eyes widened in alarm. "Is Brittney dead?"

"No. I'm here to arrest Jason Knight."

"What? Why?"

"Not now, Trixie." He strode past her. She followed.

Nelson walked into the waiting area. "I'm sorry to intrude. However, I am here on official business. "Jason Knight, I'm arresting you on the charge of murder and embezzlement. Please stand. You have the right to remain silent."

Chapter Thirty-Nine

Trixie, Kathleen, and Martha huddled around a small computer screen in a vacant conference room of the Brookville Sheriff's Department. They watched Nelson volley one question after another at Jason Knight.

Jason sat at a rectangular table in a small interview room. Nelson sat across from him. Jason's red-rimmed eyes were exhausted. He ran a hand through his unruly hair. His voice cracked over the microphone. "Deputy, I've told you repeatedly Brittney and I had nothing to do with Camille Jackson's death. We had no reason to murder her."

"Really? No reason? Didn't Camille uncover evidence that you and Brittney Fields were embezzling money from Brookville Corporation? That sounds like a motive to me. Where were you the night Camille was murdered?"

"I was with Brittney."

Nelson stood and leaned against the wall, arms crossed over his chest. "That's convenient. Did you toss Camille's home after her death?"

Jason knuckle-rubbed his eyes. "Yes, I did, but not Brittney."

"I'm assuming you were looking for the evidence Camille had on you."

"I wanted to make sure there wasn't a trail leading back to us." Jason met Nelson's eyes. "I did not murder her. I swear it."

"Why did you break into her home a second time?"

Jason blew out a breath. He looked up at Nelson. "Because Carrie didn't have what I was looking for either. You obviously hadn't found any damning evidence on Camille's computer. So, that meant evidence was still somewhere in Camille's house. Only when I got there I saw those women going inside her home. Are they the ones who found the flash drive?"

Nelson chuckled and looked up at the camera. "They sure did." Jason slid down in the chair and stared at a spot on the wall. "So, Jason, I've got you on embezzlement, assault, breaking and entering, possibly the murder of Ms. Jackson and the attempted murder of Brittney Fields. Have I left out anything?"

"I told you; I did not murder Camille."

"Did Brittney get cold feet and decide to come clean to Dan? Is that why you attacked her?"

"I would never harm Brittney. We love each other and our son. We were supposed to take Ian and leave the country this weekend. With the money, we were going to make a fresh start in Montenegro."

"Why there?"

"It's beautiful, and there is no extradition treaty with the US. I've got our plane tickets. I can show them to you."

"Jason, you aren't going anywhere except prison, and if Brittney dies…well, let's just say your situation becomes even more dire."

Jason let out a mournful wail. "She can't die. We're supposed to be together."

Nelson pushed away from the wall. "That's not going to happen either." He opened the door and left the room.

Nelson walked into the conference room. "Well? How do you think it's going?"

Kathleen smiled up at him. "You were marvelous. So strong and assertive and very sexy."

Nelson flushed. "Miss Kathleen, that kind of talk isn't for here."

"You are doing an adequate job of interrogation," said Martha. "However, I am doubtful he is your murderer."

Nelson jammed his hands on his hips. "What? Sure, he is. He's got motive and no credible alibi for the night Camille was murdered."

"I've got to side with Martha on this one," said Trixie. "Jason has admitted to B&E of both homes and even to assaulting Carrie, but I don't think he murdered Camille, nor did he attack Brittney."

Nelson dropped into a vacant chair. "If he didn't murder Camille or attack Brittney, who did? What's the motive? And are the two incidents related?"

"Those are great questions," said Trixie. "Unfortunately, I don't have answers."

* * *

Back at her car, Trixie pushed the key into the ignition but didn't start the engine. "Trixie, honey, you okay?" asked Kathleen.

"Yeah, it's just been a very unusual morning. With all that we've learned, there are more questions than answers. By the way, I forgot to tell you something I saw in the waiting area. Dan and his little boy were there."

"What was the baby doing there?" asked Kathleen. "Doesn't he have a sitter?"

"Apparently, the sitter had a previous obligation. He's an adorable little boy who looks just like Jason Knight. You'll never guess who was going to take care of the child."

"Sandi Fields," said Martha.

"How did you know?"

"Logic. Sandi has always been the jilted partner, and despite Dan's many transgressions, she always waited for him to return. And eventually, he came back to her. It stands to reason she would take care of his offspring."

"Martha, you're right. You really are brilliant," said Trixie.

"You say that as if there were doubts about my intelligence."

"Absolutely none. But you do make a good point. I hadn't given Sandi's situation much thought."

"I can't see that woman being maternal," said Kathleen. "Can you visualize her snuggling on the couch, reading to the child? I certainly can't."

"Nor I," said Trixie. "I need time to think." Trixie dropped Kathleen and Martha at their condos and drove home.

She maneuvered her vehicle behind the renovation team's van. The front door of her condo stood open, and two men walked out carrying wooden planks. Trixie waited for them to pass and then hurried inside and followed the sound of banging. Her bedroom was covered in sheets of plastic, and two men were standing in her closet hammering.

"Ms. Tanner, we weren't expecting to see you this early," said a burly man in overalls.

"Hey Roger, I'll be out of your way in just a minute. I'm here to get my running gear." Trixie looked around her bedroom and took in the bedlam. "Sandi said you would be finished today, but it looks like you've still got a bit to do."

Roger took his cap off and ran a hand over his shiny, bald scalp. "Yeah. We've been balls to the wall trying to get this job done. We'll finish today, but we'll be here later than usual, will that be a problem?"

"Nope. Stay as long as you need." Trixie hurried to her bureau, stepping over planks of wood and dodging a few of the workers. Lifting the plastic tarp, she pulled running gear from one of the drawers, grabbed her shoes, and darted into the guest bathroom to change.

As excited as she was to have her condo renovated, she was equally excited to have it finished. It felt like someone had been in her home for months when in fact it had only been a little over a week.

Trixie warmed up and then started toward Raven trail, the longer of the three Brookville trails. She would finish on Hummingbird, the shortest trail at half a mile and where Brittney was attacked. She wasn't worried about the assailant. She was more concerned the attacker would be at the hospital, but Jack had that covered. Still, she wasn't foolish; she felt the comforting weight of the shoulder holster and revolver.

Running was just what she needed. She hadn't realized how stressed she was until the tension in her shoulders eased and her stride lengthened, followed by glorious peace. It was a drug she couldn't live without.

Floating on the wave of calm, she relaxed. She was nearing the large twin oaks. She slowed her run to a jog and stopped between the trees. Fishing wire was still tied to one of them. She walked around the area. There were ample places to hide and wait, and disappearing into the dense wooded area would have happened in seconds, especially when witnesses were busy trying to save a life.

The crunch of gravel and an all too familiar voice said, "You aren't able to stay away from mayhem, are you?"

Trixie turned slowly to face Doc Stone. "I haven't seen you in days. Where have you been keeping yourself?"

"A medical examiner's work is never done. Especially lately. What are you looking for?"

Trixie turned back to the trees. "I don't know. Something. Maybe nothing. I can see how the witnesses were unable to tell Nelson much about Brittney's attacker. Even in bright sunlight, the foliage here is dense and blocks out a lot of the light. Anyway, I guess it was more my curiosity than anything else." She looked at his jeans and black tee shirt. "You obviously aren't running, and there's no dead body, so what brings you here?"

"As we established some time ago, I have a curious nature as well." He cocked his head to the side. "Want to get coffee? My treat."

Trixie narrowed her eyes at him. "Why?"

"There has to be a reason; I can't just want coffee with an intriguing woman?"

"With anyone else, I might be flattered. With you, not so much."

He sighed loudly. "Fine. I could throw in a biscotti."

She said, "Now you're just bribing me."

Chapter Forty

Café au Lait in the afternoon brought a steady stream of customers looking for a late-day pick-me-up. Doc and Trixie settled at a small table for two at the back of the shop.

Trixie dunked a biscotti into her coffee and took a bite. "This is unexpected. What's going on that you wanted my company?" She took another bite of the cookie.

"Maybe I got tired of self-flagellation and decided I'd let someone else give me my flogging."

Trixie gave him a cheeky grin. "Funny." Her expression sobered. "Seriously, what's going on?"

"Frustration. Forensic anthropology takes time. There's a process that has to be followed, and I know that. But I'm tired of waiting, and I want some answers."

Trixie stirred sugar into her coffee. "That sounds like a Jack Nelson response."

"He and I are on the same page. We vent to each other because we know this stuff takes time and there's nothing to do but wait."

"What has Dr. Cain been able to tell you thus far?"

"She and her team have been piecing together the skeletonized remains of four bodies. But trying to establish PMI is difficult."

Trixie watched him for a moment. "Okay. But?"

Doc swirled the remains of his coffee in the cup. "Alas, she is not only attractive but perceptive. A drone was flown over the area where the remains were found. Depressions in the landscape were compelling enough that

Jack obtained satellite imagery of the property for the past forty years. Topographical changes to the property suggest there may be additional graves. In some of the more recent images, there appears to be fresh graves." He rubbed his eyes with his thumb and forefinger, then looked up at Trixie. "We are potentially looking at months of excavation."

"How many graves?"

"Upwards of twenty or more."

Trixie laid the biscotti on her plate and pushed it to the side. She had lost her appetite. Twenty-plus lives were taken and discarded, and no one knew or looked for them. Her attention moved to the sign hanging on the wall in front of her: *Life is Better with Coffee.* Was it? She wanted out of the coffee shop and away from its trivial signs and the happy, unaware people.

"I need to get out of here." Trixie shoved back her chair and was on her feet, moving toward the door. She was faintly aware of Doc following behind her. Outside on the sidewalk, she closed her eyes and tipped her face toward the sun. It felt good. When she opened her eyes, Doc was staring at her.

"Ms. Tanner, I shouldn't have shared this with you. I didn't mean to upset you. I assumed since you had a law enforcement background…." Doc shoved his hands into his pockets.

She spun to face him. "That what? I'd be okay with people being murdered and their bodies dumped in unmarked graves, their families never knowing what happened to them." She shook her head. "No, I'm far from okay. This right here, this emotion I'm experiencing, is something I can't explain to you, but it's why I became a cop. I want to find the individual responsible for causing so much sadness. I want them to pay for all the pain and suffering they caused. No, Doc, you haven't upset me. You've just made me more determined than ever to find who's responsible." Trixie turned on her heel and jogged down the sidewalk.

"Where are you going?" Doc ran to catch up with her.

"The Sheriff's station. I need to talk with Jack."

Doc grabbed her elbow. "That's not a good idea,"

She spun to face him. "And why not?"

"At present, Jack has more on his plate than he can handle. Your energy would be better spent elsewhere."

She, Martha, and Kathleen had everything that was needed to solve these cases. It was all there; she just needed to examine the facts. "You're right. You're absolutely right. Thanks for the coffee." She took off running in the direction of the Brookville Condos.

"Ms. Tanner, let me drive you home."

Trixie called over her shoulder, "I'm fine. We'll talk later." She waved and then picked up her pace. Her mind was overloaded with information and emotions. Someone tried to murder her friends. Was it the same someone who attacked Carrie and Brittney and possibly killed Camille? And who had been hunting in this area for so long, taking the lives of teenagers, the homeless, and the prostitutes. Trixie increased her pace and pushed the tumultuous thoughts from her mind. She focused on the rhythm of her breathing, how the sun felt on her skin, and on the feeling of flying.

A few miles into the run, she relaxed. The cacophony of thoughts quieted. She let the peace wash over her for a moment longer and then slowly began pulling out individual threads of information from her mind's filing cabinet. She examined each of them carefully, looking at the facts from different angles. Once satisfied, she returned them to the cabinet and pulled out another. She continued doing this until all the facts had been examined. It all seemed so clear now. How had she not seen it before? She ran up the sidewalk of her condo and opened the front door. Stepping over boards and equipment, she moved past several workers, ignoring their greetings. Trixie maneuvered herself down the hall and into the command center and closed the door. There was work to do.

She was so engrossed with reorganizing the facts of the cases she hadn't realized how late it was or that the workers had left long ago. Her stomach growled loudly. She was famished. She gave the murder boards a last look and opened the door. Her condo was dark. As she moved down the hall toward the kitchen, the hairs at the base of her neck rose. As a cop, the feeling that she wasn't alone or that something wasn't right had saved her life more than once. Sean had preached to her that when she was in the field: always maintain situational awareness. But she wasn't in the field; she was in her home, a safe place. The feeling persisted. She'd left her weapon in the Command Center. The living room and the front door were closest. She darted into the living room and was swiftly moving toward the front door when her elbow was grabbed. She was spun around, and a large fist crashed into her face. She was briefly aware that her knees buckled, and then there was nothing.

Chapter Forty-One

Trixie wrinkled her nose to the revolting odor, and her eyes fluttered open to blackness. The smell of rotted organic matter, stagnant water, and something else equally bad filled her nostrils. Laying on her left side in the small, cramped space, she was acutely aware of an intense discomfort that radiated from her head down to...the toes of her left foot. For the right foot, there was nothing; no feeling, no pain, just nothing. An overwhelming dread settled over her. She pulled in a deep breath of the foul air and tried to push down the fear and rising panic. Her mind was an incoherent flurry of thoughts and emotions. *Think, Trixie.*

Who hit her, and where was she? Trixie shifted her head slightly to the right. The simple act caused pain to ignite in her neck and shoulders. Bad idea. She lay still for several minutes and waited for the agony to ease. How had she gotten to wherever here was? Pain or not, she had to sit up and assess the situation. She couldn't do it lying in the water and mud.

Trixie tried to shift her body into a sitting position, but her left arm was useless. The pain radiating from her shoulder could mean it was either broken or dislocated.

She shifted her body until she was on her back. The movement was sheer agony. She lay in the filth for a moment, then rolled onto her right side and pushed herself into a sitting position with her right arm. She was covered in mud and the foul stench. Gasping for air from the exertion, Trixie leaned against the wall of her prison and waited for the pain to ease. A wave of nausea overtook her, and she vomited onto her lap. She leaned her head back against the moss-slickened stone wall and closed her eyes.

When she awoke, small shafts of light cut through the darkness. Her prison was a narrow cylindrical space. The opening was approximately twenty feet above her and maybe four feet in diameter. She was in an old well. What appeared to be a wooden well cap covered the opening. Missing slats allowed streams of sunlight to enter the darkness. If she had two good legs, she might have been able to shimmy her way up the walls of the well, but with the moss-slickened walls and only one good leg and arm, the odds were against her. Her head pounded. She wanted nothing more than to sleep, just for a few minutes. She promised herself she'd only close her eyes for a moment, and then she'd be able to think more clearly.

When Trixie's eyes fluttered opened, only faint rays of moonlight filtered through the small openings of the well covering. She was cold, hungry, and frightened. She wanted out of this place, and she wanted her cozy bed and clean sheets. She wanted her friends, and more than anything, she wanted to live. Hot tears ran down her cheeks, stinging the abrasions on her face. She had to get out of this. This couldn't be how she died; not here, not now, not this way. "I will get out of here." As the words left her lips, she felt the futility of them.

Trixie screamed. "Help me, please help me." Her screams reverberated off the sides of the well. Could anyone hear her? She gritted her teeth and put her right hand into the water to push herself into a more comfortable sitting position. Pain rocketed through her body with the effort, and in the water, something wriggled over her fingers. Screaming, she jerked her hand out of the water. The sudden movement caused another wave of nausea. She dry-heaved a few times and then sat still and waited for the feeling to pass.

How long had she been in the well? Days? Hours? She had no way of knowing. Would someone be looking for her? Who dumped her in the well, leaving her for dead, and why?

The exhaustion returned. Fatigue wrapped its arms around her, and her eyelids slowly drifted closed. The soothing comfort of the blackness engulfed her once again.

Trixie woke to water droplets pelting her face. She looked toward the well cap, shielding her eyes from the rain. At least it was daylight. Trixie tipped her face upward and opened her mouth, welcoming the cool, fresh droplets of rain. How long could she last without water or food? Would the rain cause the water level in the well to rise, and if so, how much? A fresh wave of panic washed over her. *Stop it. You aren't going to drown.*

In the dim lighting, movement in the water caught her eye. A large rat scuttled toward her outstretched leg. She watched it heft its weight out of the water and onto her leg. She stared at the creature for a moment. It cocked its head to the side; black beady eyes studied her, and its nose lifted in the air and twitched. The rat took a few tentative steps forward. Trixie felt the scream form deep inside, and then it erupted out of her mouth in a long, high-pitched shriek. The volume surprised both her and the rat. The rodent dove back into the water and scampered over to a hole in the well's wall. Hysteria fueled her scream.

She thrashed about in the putrid water. Then, from the corner of her eye, something bobbed briefly to the surface of the murky water and then sank. She dove her hand into the water after the object. Holding it up in the dim lighting, it appeared to be a bone—perhaps that of some poor animal who had fallen into the well. Maybe the unfortunate creature had been thrown into the well to die, just like she had. Would someone find her skeletal remains twenty years from now? Would they take the time to find out who she was, and would her murderer be brought to justice? No, she wasn't going to die in this God-forsaken well.

She rubbed her fingers over her find turning it from side to side. It appeared to be a jawbone. Several molars were still connected to the mandible. Trixie rubbed her index finger over the teeth, and gooseflesh rose on her skin. She held the bone up in the dim lighting and could have sworn there was a glint of silver. Was it possible the jawbone was human? Trixie pushed the mandible under the waistband of her pants. In case she was rescued, she wanted the world to know that another poor soul's remains had been tossed into the well. She couldn't help wondering, was it Sara's jawbone?

She was so thirsty. All she could think about was an icy cold glass of clear water. She looked down at the muck, and a hysterical bubble of laughter rolled from her mouth. Samuel Taylor Coleridge's *The Rime of the Ancient Mariner* popped into her mind. *Water, water everywhere, and not a drop to drink.* She laughed until tears rolled down her filth-covered cheeks, leaving narrow trails on her skin as they dripped off the end of her chin into the foul water below.

When the hysteria subsided, she was more exhausted than before. *I'll lose my mind before I die. Maybe that's not such a bad thing. I won't know where I am or what I'm doing.* She looked down at the water. *If I took a little drink, would it really hurt me? I'm going to die anyway. Stop it! Occupy your mind. Someone will find you. Think.*

She recalled the day she, Martha, and Kathleen had been on their way to Camille's crime scene. They had passed the well that provided water for the Jeffries' plantation home long ago. Was she in that well? Martha told them the well had been dry for decades. She had to admit, it was a genius idea to throw her in the well. No one would think to look here. "Why would someone want me dead? I never hurt anyone."

"Babe, it's not about who."

The voice was familiar. Wiping the tears and snot from her face, she looked up toward the well's opening, but the lid was still firmly in place. Reason told her it couldn't be, but the voice sounded so much like Sean's. That was impossible. He was dead. "Well, this is just freaking great. Now, I really am losing my mind. I'll die in this miserable place, and no one will ever know what happened to me."

"Red, this isn't you. Remember, you're my unsinkable Molly Brown. You've been in tougher scrapes. You'll survive this one. Besides, you promised to live for both of us. Remember?"

"Sean, is that you?" She reached out her good hand into the dark, dank air, seeking his familiar form.

"Trix, I told you I'd always be here when you needed me."

Her throat constricted, and the tears came again. "I remember, and I'm really trying, Sean. I really am, but this jam is tough. I'm not sure I'm going to get out of it."

"You'll find a way, baby. I know you will. Hey, Trix, you know it's okay, right?"

"What's okay?"

"It's okay for you to love again. You need to find a Yang to your Ying."

She laughed softly. "Oh, Sean, I had that with you. I miss you every day. I love you. You were my everything."

"Red, we each have a timeline. Mine just ended sooner than I would have liked. You, in this world, makes it a better place. Stay strong. You've got this. And give him a chance."

"Sean, don't leave me."

Sound from above caused Trixie to jerk her attention upward. The cover of the well was being removed. Relief flooded over her, and the tears of sadness changed into joy. "Thank God, you've found me. I'm down here. Please, help me." Trixie's voice was little more than a hoarse whisper. Would they hear her? Could they see her? She grabbed a rock from the bottom of the well and pounded the wall. The sound reverberated up the well; the effort was exhausting and painful. She pounded the wall three more times and stopped too weary to continue.

In the fading light, Trixie saw the silhouette of a man or maybe a woman leaning over the side of the well. A beam from a flashlight hit Trixie in the face. She lifted her hand to block the light. She heard a man's voice say, "It won't be long." Who was he talking to? Surely, he was going to get help. He couldn't, wouldn't leave her here. Hot tears streamed down her face as the well cover was moved back into place.

* * *

That night, rain pounded the well cap. Water poured through the small openings like a mini waterfall. The water in the well was almost waist-high. If she was lucky, maybe she would drown. She wasn't getting out of this miserable place. She thought about Sean; maybe she was losing her mind—talking to her dead husband. Her heart ached for him. She wanted nothing more than to go to sleep and never wake up. She closed her eyes and whispered, "I'm sorry, Sean, I tried. I won't be able to do any more living for either of us."

The rat returned. Its hairless tail acted as a rudder, navigating the creature toward Trixie. It warily climbed onto her lap. She no longer cared. She didn't have the energy to chase it away. Its nose constantly twitched, and he cocked his head at her. Tentatively, he climbed up her shirt and perched on her shoulder. Trixie felt the weight and warmth of its body. The rodent sniffed into her ear. Its whiskers brushed against her cheek, and then sharp little teeth took the first nibble of her earlobe.

Chapter Forty-Two

Trixie was aware of large hands sliding beneath her. Pain seared through every cell of her body. She was being moved. She heard voices and wanted to call out, ask who was there, but nothing more than a moan escaped her parched lips. She hurt so bad tears seeped from the corners of her closed eyes. When the pain seemed at its worst, she felt a gentle caress across her cheek and her hair smoothed from her face. Had Sean returned? Had he come back from the dead to save her?

"Thank God you're alive. Trixie, I've got you. I'm going to get you out of here."

She wanted to open her eyes, but they wouldn't obey her command. Her tongue licked at her dry, cracked lips. "Sean, is that you?"

"Relax, baby, I'm getting you out of here." The hand smoothed her hair again, and she felt a gentle kiss on her forehead. "Trixie, this is going to hurt. I'm so sorry. I'll be as gentle as possible."

Something was being tugged around her waist and shoulders. The pain caused her to moan again. "Honey, not much longer." She felt her body being lifted upward. Scalding pain seared through every fiber of her body, and then consciousness drifted away.

* * *

When Trixie opened her eyes, sunlight filtered into the room from between the partially opened white mini blinds. Small dust moats drift lazily along the rays of light. She watched them for a moment. She was dry and warm and clean. Was this heaven? It felt like it. She sighed and drifted back to sleep.

The next time Trixie opened her eyes, she heard muted voices. The room was dimly lit. She looked down at her shoulder and the blue sling that held her arm securely. IV tubing ran from her good arm's hand to an IV pole holding two bags of clear liquid—one small, the other much larger. For a moment, she watched the liquid drip into the tube. Not heaven, but a hospital. How had she gotten here? Did it matter? The cool, clean sheets felt wonderful; she nestled down in them and closed her eyes.

When Trixie awoke, sunlight filled the room. Movement caught her attention. Kathleen rose out of a chair and stood beside her. "Welcome back, Sleeping Beauty. How do you feel?" She gently brushed Trixie's hair to the side and tucked it behind her ear.

Trixie opened her mouth to speak, but her voice came out in a croak. "Like I fell in a well. Where am I?"

"Good to see you've kept your sense of humor." Kathleen bit her lower lip and squeezed Trixie's good hand. "Oh, honey, we thought we'd lost you, but the doctor says you're going to be just fine."

A lopsided grin flickered across Trixie's face. "Can't get rid of me that easily." She tried to clear her throat. "Can I have something to drink?"

Kathleen poured water from a small pitcher into a Styrofoam cup and then dropped in a bendy straw. Holding it close, Trixie greedily pulled in the liquid. "Slow down, or you're going to make yourself sick. The nurse said to sip it."

Trixie frowned at Kathleen and reluctantly released the straw.

Martha burst into the room. "Finally, you are back from the grave. What took you so long to wake up? We have questions."

"Martha Kline, what is wrong with you? This poor woman has literally returned from death's door. Your questions can wait. We're lucky she's alive." She gave Trixie a reassuring pat on her hand. "Don't let her stress you."

"Well, I missed her too, but I have questions. And there is still a murderer out there."

"How long have I been here?"

"Almost a week. Honey, you've been through quite an ordeal. You were in that well for five days. Frankly, it's a miracle you're alive."

Martha nodded vigorously. "And don't forget about the concussion. Remember the doctor said her—"

"Martha, you *are* not helping."

For a moment, Trixie's mind traveled back to the dark well: the smell of the dank air and putrid water and the weight of the rat as it climbed up her shirt. It wasn't real. She knew it couldn't be real, but the rat's beady black eyes held hers. Its stiff whiskers brushed against her cheek. Shivers ran through her body, and her hand involuntarily lifted and felt the bandage that covered her ear lobe.

"Trixie, honey, are you okay? Are you cold?" Kathleen pulled another blanket over her. Her eyes held worry.

"I'm fine. Did they do surgery on my shoulder?"

"No, the doctor was able to maneuver it back in place. But honey, they had to remove the bullet from your back."

Panic rose inside of Trixie. Her eyes darted to her legs. For a moment, she was terrified. Was she paralyzed? Even if she wasn't, would her leg function properly? She tentatively tried to wiggle her toes. She could. Relief rushed over her. "Why did they do the surgery? Who did the surgery?"

"The fall caused the bullet to shift," said Kathleen. "According to Doc, it was either remove it then or risk losing the use of your leg."

"Doc called a specialist he knew and had him flown in to do the surgery," said Martha.

This time, Trixie recalled strong arms cradling her and gently kissing her forehead. "How did I get here? Did Sean save me?"

A concerned look passed between Kathleen and Martha. "Trixie, honey, you do remember Sean is dead, right?"

"Of course, I remember, but Kathleen, he came to me in the well. He talked to me and told me I'd be okay." She looked from Martha to Kathleen. "I'm not crazy. I know what I heard. He got me out of the well."

Kathleen patted her hand. "You're not crazy, but your concussion was severe, and you were very dehydrated. The doctor said that you may have some distorted memories and headaches for a while."

Trixie turned toward the window. Tears rolled down her cheeks. She wasn't crazy. Sean had been in that well with her. He'd told her she was strong and she would survive. "I know what I heard. So, if it wasn't Sean, who pulled me out of the well?"

"Doc," said Kathleen.

Martha let out a snort. "Yeah, if you thought he was a pain at Camille's crime scene, you should've seen him directing the search for you. He wouldn't go home, or sleep, and he barely ate. And don't get me started about the yelling."

"He was more than a little determined," said Kathleen.

"Somehow, I'm having trouble seeing Doc as my hero." Weary dark eyes, tender and single-minded, flashed before her. She recalled large, gentle, competent hands cradling her body and soothing words whispered in her ear. "How did he find me?"

Kathleen frowned. "I'm not sure how he knew you would be in the well. He never explained that part, and frankly, we were so thankful you were alive no one asked."

"Well, I'm sure if he fished me out of the well, it was only to torment me later."

Kathleen gave her a thoughtful look. "Maybe."

"Let us get down to business. Who did this to you?" asked Martha.

"Martha. You know what the doctor said—no questions."

Trixie yawned. "I'm sorry, but I'd like to take a nap."

Kathleen fussed over the blanket, tucking it in around Trixie. "We've tired you out. You get some rest. We'll come back later."

"Yeah, get some rest. The way your brains were scrambled, you need sleep."

Kathleen pulled Martha from the room. "Not helping."

Yes, rest was exactly what she needed.

* * *

233

The gentle sound of rain patter on the roof was soothing, and Trixie felt herself being lulled into a deep sleep. In a short while, the rain intensified and was pounding the roof. But how could she hear it in the hospital? She opened her eyes and realized she was no longer in the hospital but back in the well. The rain drummed the well cap, and a stream of water cascaded through the narrow openings. She heard splashing, felt waves of water lap over her legs. Something big was in the well with her. She tried to see what it was, but it was too dark. Out of the darkness, a large, black, formidable figure rose from the water. It towered over her fierce and ominous. It was going to kill her. She had to get out of the well. Trixie tried to stand, but she was being held down. Why couldn't she stand? Had she lost the use of her leg? The dark mass moved closer. Its yellow eyes stared at her from the blackness. The creature reared back. Its claws white and sharp in the dim lighting. It lunged at her. She gathered her strength and screamed.

Strong arms wrapped around her. She fought against them. The monster wasn't going to kill her. She wasn't going to die that way.

"Shh, Trixie, it's just a dream. Wake up, it's not real." When she relaxed, the arms loosened their grip on her. She felt a familiar large hand smooth the sweat-moistened hair away from her face. Panting, she stopped fighting and slowly relaxed into the warmth beside her. When she opened her eyes, Doc was lying next to her on the bed. He cradled her against his chest and gently rocked her. "You're okay. You're safe."

"Doc? What happened?"

"It was a bad dream."

Doc went to stand. Trixie clung to him—balled his shirt into her fists. "No. Stay for a little longer, please."

Settling back on the bed, Doc held her. Trixie closed her eyes and buried her face into his shirt. As she breathed in his comforting woodsy scent, her fear dissipated, and her breathing returned to normal.

"Better?" asked Doc.

His warm breath drifted across her face, and his steady heartbeat soothed her. She snuggled against his chest. "Yes, thank you. It was such a bad dream. The monster was going to kill me in the well." Trixie looked up at him. "I wasn't going to die in that well."

A soft chuckle rumbled in his chest. "I don't think the monster would've stood a chance. And, if you'd had two good legs and arms, it would've been done for."

Trixie looked up at him. Weariness etched his face with new lines, and there were shadows under his eyes and something else she couldn't quite discern. "Are you making fun of me?"

He smiled broadly. The smile reached his eyes, not their usual dark and foreboding but relieved. Trixie's breath caught in her throat. She looked away and struggled to control her breathing. "I'm okay now."

"Is that your way of telling me to get out of your bed?"

Color rose in her cheeks. "Sometimes you really are insufferable."

Doc laughed loudly and stood. "Now that the spunk has returned, I think you'll be fine." He squeezed her hand gently. "Get some rest."

"Hey, Doc, how did you know where to find me?"

He leaned over the bed and cupped her face in his hand. His thumb gently stroked her cheek. "That's a story for another time."

"Thanks for everything."

Doc straightened. "I'm very happy you're alive. The world would be a much duller place without you." He turned toward the door and then stopped. A slow smile tipped the corners of his lips. "Besides, now you owe me."

Chapter Forty-Three

When Trixie awoke, the sun was just peeping over the horizon. And for the first time in many days, she felt like herself. Her mind was clear, and she was able to think. She wanted to think, to remember. She closed her eyes and went back to the hours prior to being thrown into the well. She was running, and for a moment, she let her mind linger on the remembrance of the run and the joy. She wiggled her toes and feet and felt the call of the run.

She thought about Doc. No matter what he said or did in the future, she would forever be grateful.

Trixie moved past the intense feeling of gratitude and focused on piecing together the fragile gossamer threads of her memory. Slowly, the events of that evening came back, and she remembered what she'd been trying so hard to recall. A smile slid across her face, and her eyes flew open. "Gotcha."

Kathleen came into her room shortly after breakfast. "You look like a new woman." She studied Trixie for a beat. "And maybe a little like the cat who ate the canary. How are you feeling?"

"Like myself. And the shower I just had was divine. I never knew hot water could feel so wonderful."

"Emile said to tell you hello, and when you're feeling up to coming into the Café, anything on the menu is on the house. And Michelle said hello, and she's looking forward to seeing you back at self-defense class."

"Does everyone in town know what happened?"

"It is a small town, and you know how people love to talk. Besides, a Brookville resident being tossed into an old well and left for dead is big news. By the way, Patrick also sent his best wishes."

"Anyone else, perhaps the sales clerk at the grocery store?"

"People care about you. Don't be so grumpy."

"I'm not grumpy, just enjoying teasing you. Anything else going on in town?"

"There was some mild curiosity about you and Doc—"

"Oh, for crying out loud. Doc was part of the search party. I'm grateful he found me. Brookville residents need something else to focus their attention on."

Kathleen reached into her purse and pulled out several envelopes. "These were in your mailbox."

Trixie shuffled through the stack. "Thanks." She held up an envelope. "There's a card here from Dan Fields. How's Brittney?"

"She regained consciousness, and the doctors say she should recover. There might be some residual vocal issues, but overall, she's going to be fine."

"What about her legal troubles?"

"Dan doesn't want Brittney charged, but I don't think the DA feels the same way. However, as benevolent as he was about her criminal activity, he's not as forgiving about her infidelity. He filed for divorce."

"Let me guess, Sandi was there to pick up the pieces." Trixie opened the envelope and read the card, noticing it was signed by Dan, Ian, and Sandi. She held it out to Kathleen.

"Yep, Sandi didn't waste any time."

"Do me a favor and let Dan know I'm doing much better and that I've figured out who murdered Camille and attacked us. The Sheriff's office is expecting an arrest in the next few days."

Kathleen's eyes narrowed. "Trixie? What are you up to?"

"And when you talk with Dan, be sure to mention I'm being sent to a special out-of-state rehab facility in the morning. And let him know how much I appreciated the card from him and Sandi."

"Are you really being sent to an out-of-state rehab facility?"

"No, but Dan doesn't know that. Please get that message to him this morning. It's important. And could you give Jack a call? I need to see him as soon as possible."

"Trixie, I don't know what you're up to, but promise me you're going to be careful."

Trixie crossed her heart and held up three fingers. "Scout's honor."

Chapter Forty-Four

Doc poked his head out of the bathroom. "Ms. Tanner, are you sure this is going to work?"

"No, I'm not sure of anything, but we have to try something, right? Now, be quiet and get back in the bathroom. If someone hears you, it'll ruin everything. And I'd like to point out I didn't ask you to participate in this sting. You inserted yourself."

"No. I volunteered. Lord knows you require a lot of looking after."

Nelson's voice came over the radio tucked inside the drawer of the bedside table. "Could you two stop your yapping? This is a stake-out, not a gripe session. Trixie, don't do anything stupid. If this plan of yours works, play it safe. Doc and I can handle those two. Do you remember the safe word?"

Trixie rolled her eyes. "You're like an old woman. Of course, I remember it: coffee."

"Good. We're going to radio silence," said Nelson.

* * *

In her past, Trixie had participated in stakeouts in a variety of places; cars, vans smelling of greasy takeout and body odor, disgusting abandoned buildings, and there was the occasional time or two she'd laid in weeds and underbrush for hours in a ghillie suit but never in a bed.

She was struggling to keep her eyes open when she heard movement outside her door. Trixie glanced at the clock on the wall: three thirty. Over the past several days, she'd learned the routine of the nurses, and normally, at this hour, there was very little movement in the halls.

The door latch clicked. Instantly, Trixie was alert. She tightened her grip on the revolver and lay still. Was it possible this crazy plan had worked? The door slowly opened, and a silhouette quietly slipped inside.

"Who's there? I asked not to be disturbed," said Trixie. A tall, slender figure stepped into the light. "Sandi? What are you doing here at this hour?"

"I heard you were leaving later today, and I didn't want to miss the opportunity to say goodbye."

"This is an odd hour for a visit, don't you think?"

Sandi stood at the foot of the bed. "This kind of visit needs to be done at an odd hour. It's a shame. You and I might have been great friends, but you couldn't keep your nose out of business that didn't concern you."

"And what business would that be? The murder business? Camille's death? The attack on me and my friends; on Brittney? Which business, Sandi?"

Sandi moved to the side of Trixie's bed. "You really are very clever. I saw the boards in the Command Center. You figured it all out, didn't you?"

"It wasn't hard once I started really looking at the facts. And I've got to give Martha a large amount of credit. She's the one who always included your name whenever we were making lists or notes on the boards. Sandi is a nickname for Alexandra, right?"

Sandi sat on the edge of the bed and pointed the knife at Trixie. "You women are clever; I'll give you that."

The steel of the blade caught the light, and Trixie felt a tingle of fear run up her spine. "Does Dan know who you really are?"

Sandi let out a humorless bark of laughter. "Please, he's too busy looking for his next conquest."

"So why did you stay with him? Why didn't you kill his other lovers?"

"Oddly enough, Dan and I are very much alike. He never loved the others; it was more about the chase. However, in his own dysfunctional way, Dan cares about me."

"And do you care about him?"

"I guess as much as I care about anyone."

"Why did you kill Camille? What made her different from the others?"

"Camille was an annoying fly that wouldn't go away, constantly buzzing around. When the affair between her and Dan ended, I thought I'd gotten rid of her, and then Dan brought her back. The two of them were always thick as thieves and had this freaky connection. Then, one day, when I was planning a little surprise for the child bride, I saw Camille. She was in the right place at the right time. One should never squander an opportunity, don't you agree?" A ghoulish smile spread across Sandi's face.

"What was your beef with Brittney? Why did you try to murder her?"

"She gave Dan a kid. That was something he always wanted, and it was something that would link them forever. Even if Dan divorced her, she would always be in the picture. I had to get her out of the way."

Trixie pushed the boundaries. "Why didn't you and Dan have children?"

"Me, have a child? That wasn't going to happen. That would've gotten in the way of my little hobby. Beings like me are aberrations of nature. We're feral creatures who are gifted at concealing who we really are. We walk among you, and you think we are just like you, but we're not."

"If you're not like the rest of us, what are you?"

Sandi stood. "We're apex predators."

Trixie's eyes followed the knife. She tightened her grip on the revolver. "I believe I know how this is going to end, but I would greatly appreciate you answering a few more questions. Indulge me?"

"Your questions are getting tedious. Make it fast. I'm on a schedule. Daddy will expect me to meet him soon." The ghoulish smile returned. "Once he's finished with your friends."

"Your father is in on this?"

"Of course, he is."

"What's his part in all of this?"

Daddy recognized what I was early on. He helped me learn to control the urges and how to hunt."

"The first skeleton that was discovered, I'm assuming that was Sara Adams?"

"Sara was my first. You never forget your first, anything, do you?"

"Why did you kill her?"

Sandi's expression took on a faraway look. "She took my boyfriend, and it made me mad. It wasn't planned. It just happened. Once Sara was dead, I didn't know what to do with her. I called Daddy, and he came and helped me."

"Did you kill Samuel, too?"

"Samuel came looking for Sara while daddy and I were cleaning up the mess. Daddy took care of him."

Trixie was stunned into silence. She watched amusement and pride dance across Sandi's face but no remorse. She knew she should give the safe word, but there were just a few more pieces of information she needed. "Who's your father?"

Sandi pointed the knife at Trixie. "Now you're just insulting me. You know who he is, you wrote it on the boards in your Command Center. Bernard Cooper is my biological father. He taught me everything I know."

"What about Richard Jeffries? Did you kill him?"

A slow smile slid across Sandi's face. "Obviously, I have underestimated you. How did you know?"

Trixie shrugged. "When we discovered you weren't in Richard's will, it was really the only answer. Why would you go to the trouble of burying bodies on land that would be bequeathed to someone else? I imagined that made you angry, maybe angry enough to kill Richard."

"There wasn't a choice. His mind was deteriorating. We couldn't risk him telling someone who I was." Sandi took a step closer. "I've been patient, but I'm tired of answering questions. If daddy was here, he'd say less talk, more action, and daddy is always right." Sandi lifted the knife and took another step toward Trixie.

Trixie pulled the revolver from beneath the sheet. "Sandi, stop."

Sandi hesitated for a beat and then lunged at Trixie. Trixie squeezed the trigger. The sound of the revolver was deafening in the small space. Sandi stumbled back and looked down at her abdomen and the bloom of blood seeping through her shirt and then up at Trixie. Surprise registered on her face, and then she crumpled to the floor as Doc burst from the bathroom and Nelson charged into the room.

CHAPTER FORTY-FOUR

"Jack, Kathleen, and Martha, they're in danger."

"Relax. I posted officers at both residences." He chuckled. "Unfortunately for Bernie, he went to Martha's house first. According to Officer Williams, Bernie was begging to be taken into custody. Did you know Martha has night vision goggles and a stun gun?"

"I'm not surprised. Is Kathleen okay?"

"You don't think I would've left my lady unprotected, do you? She's fine."

"Did you hear everything? Did you get it all?"

"I got it. Trixie, you are the damnedest woman. Why didn't you use the safe word? You could've been killed."

Trixie shrugged. "Somehow, I just couldn't work *coffee* into the conversation."

Chapter Forty-Five

Trixie sat on her back porch with Martha and Kathleen. Each with a glass of cold sweet tea and lemon. "So, what do we do now?" said Martha. "Going back to my usual life will seem so dull."

"Actually, I'm looking forward to a little dull," said Kathleen. "I've had enough excitement to last a lifetime. And with each of us nearly being killed...." Kathleen's hand fluttered to her throat. "I've never had such a...." She looked at Martha. "In a weird sort of way, it was fun, and the adrenaline rush was like nothing I've ever experienced."

"I know exactly what you mean. One might even say it was a bit addicting."

Trixie smiled at her friends. "I didn't realize how much I missed all the excitement of the chase. However, the nearly getting killed part is something I can live without." Trixie waved at Jack Nelson as he made his way to the porch. "What can we do for you, Deputy? Would you like an iced tea?"

"Nelson opened the screen door and took the chair beside Kathleen. "I'd love one. Spring is gone, and summer has officially started. The weatherman said it's going to be in the nineties today with high humidity."

Trixie sat a glass of tea in front of Nelson. He picked up the glass and downed half of it in one long gulp. "Now that hits the spot."

"What brings you out here on such a hot day?" asked Trixie.

"The jawbone that was tucked into the waistband of your slacks, forensics was able to match dental records and confirmed it was Sara Adams."

"Have you been able to get any information from Bernie?" asked Kathleen.

"He wants to make a deal. If we take the death penalty off the table, he'll tell us whatever we want to know."

"And what does the DA say about that?" asked Trixie.

"Let's just say Bernie's going to have to give him something big and fast."

"How did Bernie react when he learned Sandi was dead?" asked Kathleen.

Nelson finished his iced tea and sat the glass on the table. "There was nothing; zero emotion."

Trixie stood and moved to the screened door. She looked out at the wooded area and where the trails were. She felt the call of the run, and she wanted nothing more than to feel like she was flying. "I'm going for a run."

Kathleen frowned. "Trixie, honey, in this heat? Are you sure you should? Did the doctor say it was okay?"

"Kathleen, I haven't run in weeks. I need to get back out there. I'm running the Brookville trails, which are shaded. I promise I'll only run a mile or so. Stay here and enjoy the iced tea and shade. When I get back, let's cook out."

Trixie made her way along the sun-dappled trail at a slow jog. The air was thick with humidity and the sweet scent of honeysuckles. Sweat trickled down her neck and back. A few minutes into the run, her shirt was soaked. Her bangs collected the sweat and dripped into her eyes. She shoved the hair away from her face.

Even though she was running at a much slower pace, her body began to relax, and the euphoria eased in and settled over her like an old friend. She embraced it and welcomed its return. Her pace picked up, and her legs lengthened. The burn in her quadriceps and calves reminded her she was alive and healthy and more than a little grateful.

From behind her, she was aware of footsteps rapidly approaching. Another runner, or something else? For a moment, she tensed, ready to fight, and then relaxed; the monsters were gone. They were never going to hurt anyone again. She eased to the left to let the runner pass, but they didn't. She glanced to the side and stumbled as she saw Doc running next to her. He grabbed her arm to steady her.

"What are you doing here?"

"Ms. Tanner, you are always asking me that question. I can't help that we frequent some of the same places. Statistically, our paths are destined to cross."

"After all we've been through, don't you think you could call me by my first name?"

Doc looked up at the sky and then met her eyes. "I guess I could manage that, I mean, we are friends, right?"

Trixie looked up at him. She was aware of her wet bangs and sweat-soaked shirt. And she was acutely aware he had not let go of her arm. She cocked her head. "I don't know your first name. Do you have a first name, or is it just Doc?"

Doc moved closer. "Why do you need to know?"

Doc's woodsy cologne mixed with the scent of fresh laundry and the outdoors smelled like safety and comfort. She looked up into his dark eyes. There was no fury or fight in them, only emotion and longing. "Because when a girl kisses a guy, she should know his first name."

Doc pulled her into his arms. "Eli. My name is Eli."

Acknowledgements

A big thank you to my amazing critique partners, Lynn Chandler Willis and Lawrence Kelter. I couldn't ask for better! And I can't leave out my wonderful Birch Literary agent, Cindy Bullard. It truly takes a village!

About the Author

Karen Fritz lives in North Carolina with her husband, two daughters, one maniacal Doberman, and a bougie cat.

SOCIAL MEDIA HANDLES:
  Facebook: Karen Fritz

AUTHOR WEBSITE:
  karenfritzbooks.com

Also by Karen Fritz

Crossroads - originally published by Wings Press

www.ingramcontent.com/pod-product-compliance
Lightning Source LLC
Chambersburg PA
CBHW050158120726
47903CB00002B/675